By Maureen Duffy

THE PARADOX PLAYERS
THE MICROCOSM

The Paradox Players

a novel by

MAUREEN DUFFY

SIMON AND SCHUSTER · NEW YORK

PUBLISHED BY SIMON AND SCHUSTER
ROCKEFELLER CENTER, 630 FIFTH AVENUE
NEW YORK, NEW YORK 10020
FIRST PRINTING

LIBRARY OF CONGRESS CATALOG CARD NUMBER: 68-25745
MANUFACTURED IN THE UNITED STATES OF AMERICA

For Joan

'Existential anxiety has an ontological character and cannot be removed but must be taken into the courage to be.'

PAUL TILLICH *The Courage To Be*

October

. . . all ripes and rots that rose upon first

PICKING up the pen he began to write, the ink characters stalking away from him irrevocably across the paper wastes, burdens of intention laid across their slanting backs, and suddenly he wanted to call them back, to cry stop, that wasn't what I meant, how it was at all; remembering. He pushed the pen aside, screwed the sheet into a crackling ball and dropped it onto the floor, where it began to uncurl, whispering, slyly offering the black scrawl like a mess of tea-leaves slopped in a white sink which might have meaning or be nothing but dregs. He thrust out a foot and booted it into a corner under the single armchair, then he got up from the bunk and went over to the stove, swinging open the little mullioned doors to poke a blaze from the cinders, more for something to do than because it was cold yet, as he'd lit the fire in the first place for company not warmth. An ember scuttled glowing from between the bars and fell to the hearth, rolling on til it lodged itself against the fender and died. Watching it anxiously he became aware of himself shut up with this live thing burning sullenly inside a wooden shell. Suppose it had fallen on the floor, he thought, or deck, as I'll have to learn to call it now. The idea of change swept through him, giving him back his purpose, reminding him of the stack of paper on the folding table. Smoke stung his eyes and shrivelled his tongue to ash from a gusty down-draught. He put out a finger and touched the stove-pipe where it had bubbled in places with papery layers of orange rust, bursting them open in little crescent mouths with his nail and scalding his finger. He drew it back into the comfort of pursed, moist lips and licked down the taste of metal with the smart. Probably worse out on top. One of the things I'll have to fix before the winter sets in. Clanging the doors to with the side of his boot he went back to the table and selected a new pencil to sharpen, picked a used razor blade from the cloth with cringing fingers, and began to whittle it into a full soft point, the shavings flicking neatly into the hearth. Then he restored the deliberate arrangement of the table, drew a clean sheet from the pack towards him, paused, straightened the pen which lay a little off-centre so that nothing present should impinge on his mind, that there should be remembering, pure recollection, and wrote the month, October, and this year's date, and paused again, hearing the unfamiliar sucking of the water against the hull as he began his voyage from here to nowhere, and the words drew him out into the night, back through the hours he had already travelled since the morning.

'So you fancy to buy her?' the little man questioned.

Sym nodded, leaning forward in what he recognised was a pose that had become habit with him, legs wide apart, elbows resting on the knees, his hands clasped over the void between. He was tempted to stare around, to swing his head in time with the dozen pendulums swaying at the corners of his eyes, his brain stuttering with the nervous erratic ticking of a half-hundred clocks. On the table at the little man's elbow four gold baubles gyrated at the end of gleaming rods under a glass case. He had been working on it when Sym pushed the door open and had put it aside reluctantly to talk.

'You haven't seen her yet. Maybe you'll change your mind.'

'It isn't necessary,' he heard himself saying, and in imitation of the little man, to humour him, forced himself to go on with the unfamiliar pronoun, 'she fits.'

'Fits what?'

'My pocket, my needs.'

'Needs?'

'I'm starting a new job locally and I need somewhere to

come home to, somewhere that's quiet.' He heard himself again, speaking like a man lost a long time away from civilisation in a desert or among mountains, his faculty for conversation grown stubborn with disuse. No one had asked him why for a long time. The exchange struck him as too full of significance though he wasn't sure what it might mean. No one asked why or when among the men he had been with, knowing that information that wasn't volunteered or spilt out over a ringed bar table on Friday night, forgotten by Saturday morning, was likely to be taboo; the man who asked it suspect.

'Wanting to know far and away too much that one is. More than's good for himself or us. No names, no packdrill, as the sergeant used to say.' Sym felt a flicker of resentment as he waited for more, but the little man only nodded.

'How do you want to pay?'

'Will you take a cheque? I could go to the bank but . . .' His words trailed away as the resentment rose again and he thought how ridiculous it was this feeling, and that he had been on the move too long.

'No need. That'll do. I trust you.' He laughed. 'I was prepared for less, for spreading it over a bit in fact.'

'I'd rather get it done with. You never know.'

'That's true. I'd better take it while it's there. Anyway I know where to find you if it bounces on me.' He laughed again and rubbed his hands. 'She won't go anywhere under her own steam and the river'll be rising any day now. The name's Collins, A. J.'

He took the thin buff oblong out of his pocket and began making out the cheque, thinking that it was the first time in his life that he'd ever written three figures, and there was a kind of satisfaction in it, mixed with incredulity, like playing hookey from school. It was money he'd earned and saved but it had meant nothing to him before, even when he'd stretched out his hand with the rest, shuffling in a shackled line through the hut door and shouldering their way out again, all tall men with greenbacks to burn and no place to go but the first pub the beer-wagon could make with its singing dusty load under the tattered canvas, throats parched from a week of sun and squall, caked clay soling their boots, overalls bleached with cement, hair a mat of coarse sandpaper and eyes rimmed from staring into the sunset where the road would wind.

He hadn't burned all his, converted it into the molten spirit that crackled and hissed along their shrunken veins, expanding the heart and the voice til it was punch-ups all round and the dead, out cold, loaded into the truck by the merely dying when the doors were slammed behind them and the bolts slid to. No, though he'd stood his round, of course, all his instincts for self-preservation jogging his elbow, knowing no kind of luck worth having follows a mean man, a lesson he'd learned when they'd been building high and every floor that raised the honeycomb of glass and steel and concrete nearer the sun demanded its blood price and the man without friends was marked for destruction, a falling load, a slippery girder, a tool that splintered in the hands like ice, sending cold fangs of steel deep into the flesh, still, as he paid and drank it was as if his self stood outside the lighted windows peering through the letters on the glass so that the scene inside was refracted and alien. There'd always been plenty left to put away although he'd often wondered why, what it was for. His mates when they caught him at it one day thought it was for a paternity order and were full of solicitous advice on how to dodge any such legal efforts to tie a young man down, spoil his fun, and didn't he work hard enough for it then. He let them go on thinking they had the answer. It gave him an extra prestige among them as if he'd passed his initiation and become a man.

Now that money would mean something, something he could see and touch, that he could make what he liked because it was his, paid for in pints he hadn't drunk, women he'd never had. He signed the cheque and turned it over.

'There's not much point in putting the address on the back. You know it better than I do.'

'That's true, very true of course. Though I never actually lived on her myself; bad for the clocks all that damp and up and down. No, my mother lived there. She was eighty-four when she died. Marvellous old lady. I don't know how she stuck it. I had a terrible time getting her off. Wanted to bring her out in a stretcher they did, but I said it wasn't decent and she was coming away in a proper box like anyone else or not at all. That got them. Couldn't leave her there, you see. Had to do something about her, so I won in the end of course. I think she'd have been pleased. You may find a few things still lying about. Do what you like with them. I've taken all I want. This is the key to the padlock on the hatch. There's a dinghy too that goes with her. Look after the oars; they're a thieving lot the river people. Wouldn't trust them an inch. But then most human beings are unreliable. Not you or me of course, present company and all that, but you watch them, you'll see.' His eyes strayed back to the clocks again. '*Mimosa* she's called. Ask anyone; they'll tell you, once you get over the lock.'

'Came to the lock gates in the early morning or at least that was how it seemed with an October milk spilt over the water and the trees letting fall their leaves very gently as I passed under but when I say gates I mean gates into, or onto perhaps for the lock isn't just a barrier across the river it's the people who work it and the land that encloses it, the banks flowered and shrubbed with plants I don't even know the name of but thick enough and individuals in the noon light, and as I opened the gates on a latch a thick-set man with a pug face was winding the thick portcullis into position to hold back the invading, swarming waters so a tiny launch, almost the last of the season it must be, could swell up the tide and chug its way through onto the upper reaches. Then I thought for the first time that they were just tourists and that I lived here, was part of the river. It was a shock to hear him ask, "Yes, sir?" and I said, "*Mimosa*," smiling nervously I expect if I could have seen myself, and he nodded and walked on. Not everyone's allowed in then. If you haven't the right password you're out. I tried to look big and confident and walked up the path in the only possible direction and there was the weir. Across the other side I could see what looked like an island with trees and that was probably where I should find *Mimosa* but first there was the boil of the water-race to cross, a concrete catwalk about three feet wide with only one side railed. The naked side dropped six feet into dark water that slid like poured oil over the lip of the weir another fifteen feet into the cauldron below. I shall have to cross this twice a day at least and in time I suppose become as agile as the lock-keeper but this morning I felt a sickness in the guts and a curious prickling up the backs of the legs as they stiffened against the impulse to drop me over the side. Kept on as best I could trying not to look down and my wrist aching with hanging on to that rail. Halfway across there's a kind of trellised arch with a high wicket gate where the weir makes an oblique turn towards the island and from here to the next bend the ledge seems even narrower though I suppose its only an illusion, and the water boils like scalded cream. There's a lay-by in the middle of this bit and I leant on the rail and looked downstream towards the brick red flight of the bridge with clouds of misty sunlight floating on the crown of the river and drifting between the piers so the underside of the arches was dappled with marshfire and my eyes began to ache with the thin white radiance. I thought I hadn't seen anything like it since I was a child and that I'd lost the power of seeing things in that way, and too that this was the right place to come, that I'd made the right choice if it gives me back that kind of seeing. Just beyond the catwalk bends again and there's a series of metal gates controlled by great cogwheels about four feet in diameter that regulate the volume of water. I thought it was running fast as Collins had said with all the rain we've had lately. This part of the weir has rails on both sides and a pointed roof. Between the uprights and the crosspieces hang huge symmetrical webs with fat common-cross spiders motionless at the centre, black bull's eyes against the light. At the end of this section is another gate onto the island with a sagging notice saying *Clack's Island Private*. There was a smell of moist earth and grass and a gloom of spreading trees. A row of boats of all sizes and conditions was moored along the bank to the right but there didn't seem to be anyone about to ask for *Mimosa*. Then I heard a hammering somewhere through the trees so walked out of the sunlight towards it along a beaten earth path that brought me to a slipway with a couple of sheds.'

A cabin cruiser was propped up on blocks beside the slipway, stripped of paint; a big man in sandjeans and tattered blue ropesoles chiselling out squares of corky wood from the hull.

'Could you tell me where I find *Mimosa*?'

The man turned to look at Sym then back to his work, the steel wedge biting chunks out of the soft wood with every blow. 'Bought her have you or is old Collins just letting her? Don't let that mean bugger overcharge you. Wouldn't pay for a decent burial for his own mother so he'll be even worse with strangers. If you're buying have her surveyed first and then offer him half what he's asking. If you're renting keep him waiting for it and then give him something on account. She's over the other side by the upper weir. You'll see her. Lies by herself. The old lady liked it like that. Been a good little boat in her day but neglected. Never saw him with a pot of paint in his hand when he was down here, not that that was often. Boats you know, you've got to be at them all the time. Ever lived on the river before?'

'No. This is my first time.'

'You'll learn, learn fast; got to. I have mine out this time every year and make her all watertight for the winter. Usually send the wife and kids home to her mother for a fortnight while I do her up. Then I know the job's done properly at quarter the cost. Still she's just a bit of deal. *Mimosa*'s different; double-diagonal teak, lovely bit of wood. Follow that path through past the heap; that's where you tip your rubbish for Clack's boys to burn. See you around. Don't forget; she's the one by herself.'

Sym shifted the duffle bag on his shoulder so that the cord no longer cut so deeply into the muscle and followed the path into the trees again. It was very quiet. The hammering fell muffled on the air like conkers dropping into a bed of leaf-mould. The path came out into a clearing and wound on past a mound of half-calcinated rubbish where blue- and green-bottles flashed iridescent in the sunlight in their ceaseless droning quest for somewhere to drop their load of eggs. On the summit lay the blackened skeleton of a child's pushchair and a sofa stuck its bulbous ankles in the air, springs and stuffing spilling from the charred holes in its hide where the flames had licked but not taken hold. The path took him on into the trees again where a thrush poised in its wormhunt to cock its brown head and snake-eye at him. He had never felt his senses so vulnerable to their surroundings. At last the trees drew back leaving him alone again on the bank of the river. To his right was another jumble of craft and then to his left a black peeling hull with blue superstructure and tarred deck that must be *Mimosa.* Disappointment ran through him at her dilapidated state though he pushed it down with the thought that he had no right to expect any more for that money. The man in the sandjeans had shaken him and the river and the island seemed flat and leaden in the slanting sun. Must be hungry, he thought, just get on board and shot of this bag then I'll see if I can find my way back and something to eat.

She lay low in the water; a gangplank lodged on the deck reached steeply up to the concrete jetty. He went down crab-wise, and ducked under a rotten mushgreen tarpaulin stretched on a wooden framework, covering what he supposed must be the wheelhouse since the wheel was there in front of him, just the sort he'd seen decorating pub walls, inlaid with dark oxidised brass and still attached by a chain to the heavy rudder that had been hacked out of a single tree trunk. He dropped the bag on the unvarnished planking. It was dark and a little chilly under the awning and he suddenly wondered what he was doing there, whether it was the right boat. In his pre-occupation with getting down the gangplank he hadn't even checked the name on the bows. He felt in his pocket for the key, hoping that it would fit the padlock on the hatch leading down to the cabin. Perhaps it was all a hoax, some hideous situation out of Kafka where meaning and reality withdrew leaving the self naked and impotent. He fought back his panic.

He had made the choice to come here. Just across the water barrier there were people and cars that he could see and touch and would confirm him in his own existence. He fitted the key carefully in the lock and heard himself let out a little sigh when it fell open in his hand. Putting it carefully in his pocket, he eased off the hasp and lifted up the heavy hatchcover.

Peering down into the dark interior he half expected to see water swilling about below but there was only a smell of damp, the rising desolation of the unlived in. A steep flight of steps led down six feet into the well and turning his back he began to lower himself through the hatchway as if he were gingerly entering the cold waters of a swimming pool. At the bottom he turned. There was a door in front of him, another to his left and a galley on the right with light reflecting green from the surface of the river through two small oblong windows. He pushed open the door in front and stepped through. The sense of relief was so great he almost laughed. He could stand upright with no difficulty and the room was steeped in light from a row of round, brass-rimmed portholes on either side. A skylight running the whole length of the cabin left the roof open to pouring sunlight and the drift of clouds. This must be the saloon. It was about eight feet square, panelled in an umbrous wood with a couple of built-in cupboards and a divan bunk. A black stove squatted in a blue-tiled hearth, there was a table that let down against one wall and an old armchair. Through the open door in front of him he could see a built-in wardrobe with a full-length mirror flyblown with mildew and dust. Behind the door was another large bunk. He would be able to lie in bed and look straight up into the sky. Another doorway led to the small cabin in the bows. There was nothing in it but a pair of oars, a length of thick chain that disappeared through a tube in the roof and a solid baulk of timber at least four by four thick, going straight down through the floorboards. There was a hatch in the roof but no light came through it. Must be covered with something, he thought. It was dark in the little cabin and the river seemed very close. He could hear the knock and gurgle of it as it slipped past the bows. He was glad to turn back to the main cabin.

Now he tried the other door at the foot of the stairs. Inside was an Elsan lavatory in black plastic and a handbasin with a tap running into it from a piece of rubber tubing. He turned it on and dark brackish-looking water dribbled into the basin. He lifted up the lavatory seat cover and looked inside. It was quite clean but a smell of faded though once-powerful chemicals reached up to him. He dropped the lid. Inspecting the galley he found another small sink, a full-sized gas-stove and a rusty boiler that must be attached to the stove in the saloon. The taps gave more muddy water with an insinuating smell of the riverbed. He fetched his bag from the deck and placed it on the bunk. Then he sat down beside it and looked around. His head was muzzy with hunger and he found himself unable to focus his thoughts. He stood up and opened the portholes to let in some warm dry air. Then he took a wallet from the neck of the duffle bag and stowed it safely in an inside pocket. Taking out the padlock and key he climbed the steep steps again, closed and locked the hatch behind him and went up the gangplank to the bank. It seemed less steep now. Perhaps he was getting used to it already or maybe the tide was rising. *Mimosa* certainly looked higher on the water. She tugged a bit at her ropes as the race swirled past. He'd felt the slight swing several times down below but it hadn't bothered him absorbed in exploring his new possession.

He backtracked his earlier route through the island and out over the water again across the spun concrete thread drawn tight above the river. Beyond the lock lay the village and beyond that again, bound to it by the twin links of road and river, was the city. At the corner of the main street just before the bridge he found a convenient pub where there would be food and drink, and swung open the door.

Gradually as he sat in his corner taking down mouthfuls of hot pie with a long swallow of bitter and watched the coming and going of custom, he felt his sense of reality return. He had a lot to do before night. It would get dark early. He must buy lamps and paraffin, blankets for the bed. Then he must see about food. He would need a kettle and a saucepan, a frying pan too was an essential. He already had one each of knife, fork and spoon, an enamel plate and a blue-ringed mug which had been with him up and down the country. Many of his mates had had a plate, knife or mug which had become a kind of mascot, an element of stability in their shifting lives, a reminder of a way of life they wouldn't accept, at least not yet, but couldn't altogether root out of their consciousness. He must lay in tea, sugar, butter, bread and eggs too. Even a castaway needs some kind of provisions. He must begin to play out the Crusoe existence he had chosen for himself.

The door was pushed open and the man in the sandjeans came in. He got himself a flat vinegar brown pint of mild and stood with it to his open lips looking round the bar over the rim of the glass. Sym noted the strong yellow teeth in the open jaw distorted through the bottom of the mug. He came over to Sym's corner.

'Hallo then. How's it going? Let me get you another. Bitter is it?' He couldn't refuse. He nodded agreement. 'Do you think you'll stay?' The man eased himself into the seat beside him.

'Yes, I think so.'

'Well if there's anything you want or want to know. Clack'll put the rent up I expect. Always does with newcomers. Supposed to be tenpence a foot and she's about forty feet I reckon but he'll call it a shilling to make a round couple of quid.'

'What do you do for cooking? There's a stove but what about heat?'

'Calor, bound to be. You'll see a cylinder on the deck somewhere. Probably empty but you hump it round to the yard where you saw me today and Clack's boys'll swop it for a full one. Cost you thirty bob. Should last a good couple of months with just one of you. There is just one?'

'Oh yes. There's only me. At the moment anyway.' He felt driven to add this knowing that people find a man living alone at his age a perpetual curiosity, a subject for speculation. It was only the hypothetical paternity order which had saved him being dubbed queer before. Not that he cared but it was a possible source of distraction if you knew that people were wondering about you, thinking of you in a certain category, ticketed and filed whenever they looked at you, their response, preconditioned by their assumptions, to a thing not a person.

'My name's Walden by the way. My parents must have given me a Christian name I suppose but it's got lost somewhere along the line. Even my wife calls me Walden. We're all a bit mad. You must be too. Everyone's a bit mad who lives on the river. You'll see when you've met a few of them. Look at old Collins for instance. He's the only one you've met up til now. Nutty as a fruit cake; all those clocks. Harmless though like most of the rest of us. If we were sane, which means if we conformed to the pattern of our society, we'd do what everyone else does, get a house and car and all the modern gadgetry. But we don't. We try to make life as difficult as possible for ourselves by doing without all those things, even without mains water and sewage disposal.'

'That's another thing I've been wondering. How do you get rid of it?'

'Over the side on a dark night. Strictly against the rules of course but there aren't any other provisions so what else can you do? Water you get from the standing pipe on the bank. Most people fill their tanks up with a hose and then use that til they run out. There's a good little shop just up the road sells most of the specialities you're likely to need. You can borrow our hose til you get one of your own. You in a job?'

'Start a new one on Monday.'

'That helps of course to keep you from going too far over the edge I mean. I do a bit of this and that myself, whatever turns up. Just now, when I've finished the boat, I've a few thousand gross of plastic ballpoints to put names on with an engraver. Seems they sell better if they're called Sally or Robin. Kids I suppose and girls' names go better than boys. My two love it. Apparently they're the most popular kids in their classes because anyone who's a special friend gets a free named pen. They've learnt corruption young.'

Sym bought another round. Walden enjoyed talking and for once he felt himself caught up, not watching from outside. By the time he got up to go he was feeling more relaxed and cheerful than he had for months, years even. The street outside the saloon door seemed to vibrate with meaning which at any moment would become incarnate at his feet. He would know what it was all about at last, his life, all life would take on a new dimension, the simplest action would be significant. Drink had never taken him like this before. He had always been uninvolved, keeping himself apart. Perhaps it was drinking on an almost empty stomach or Walden's words which had set up such an echo in his own mind that his head seemed to reverberate with them.

An hour later he was crossing the island again, his arms full of loot, his stomach too demanding for him to notice anything except that his load grew heavier with every step. The boat had definitely risen on the tide, so much in fact that he walked straight across with no difficulty at all. Which is just as well, he thought, in my half-cut state. Outside the hatch he looked for the cylinder of gas and found it beside the stern rail. A thin copper tube led from it down into the galley. He turned the indicator on the top to the 'on' position, unlocked the hatch and went down below. Striking a match he tried to light one of the burners on the cooker. For a moment nothing happened and then there was a rank smell of cat's pee before the jet lit with a minor explosion.

Quickly he emptied the carrier bag holding the food, broke two eggs into the pan whipping them with a fork into a homogeneous yellow mass that was somewhere between an omelette and a scramble, spread two large square slices of a cut loaf with butter and slapped the egg between to make a hot greasy sandwich. Picking out his new plastic water container from the heap on the bunk he went up onto the bank and filled it from the standing tap. Now he could have tea and bread and jam. Later he would find permanent homes for the things he'd bought but it was sleep he wanted first. He dumped the rest of the stuff on the floor and stretched out on the bunk. As he receded into sleep he was aware of the gentle noise and movement of the boat against the current and the flow of clouds overhead.

It was almost dark when he woke. The cabin seemed dim and unfriendly and he was hungry again. The first thing was to have light. He took two thick white candles from their new box and lit them, tilting each one on its side til it had dropped a coin of grease to stand on. Then by his two-candle power he poured paraffin from a gallon container into the hurricane lamp and the blue oil lamp with the double burner he had bought at the boat-shop and lit them. They gave out a clear soft yellow light that filled the centre of his room but left out the corners so that he felt himself ringed with disconcerting shadows. 'Have to invest in one of those pressure lamps,' he muttered, and then he smiled because he was already beginning to talk to himself. He had wondered when that would start. Rummaging in the duffle bag he found a small transistor set, pulled out the fishing-rod aerial, clicked the knob forward a couple of notches and filled the space with pop music. Swinging the hurricane lamp he went out into the little galley and filled the kettle with what was left in the water container.

With the tea safely brewing he decided to fill the container again while there was still a dusky light left outside to see by. He climbed the steep steps and pushed back the flap thrusting his head out into the darkness under the tarpaulin and drew his body up after him. As he turned he was horrified to see dozens of fat spider bodies hanging round him in the twilight on invisible threads, head-high, within inches of his face. Ducking low and retching with fright he scrambled onto the gangplank and up its slope. He stood on the bank breathing thickly and looked down at *Mimosa*. From there there was no sign of the hideous curtain of living beads. He had always had a horror of them as long as he could remember and though he had schooled himself to look at them dispassionately from a distance, to treat them like any other insect, this was his worst nightmare given terrifying substance and even worse he had somehow to go back, to deliberately pass through them before he could get back into the boat. He ran a hand over his head feeling the scalp crawling and peered over his shoulder to see if there were any clinging to his back. They must live in that rotten canvas tarpaulin. Tomorrow he would strip it to the bare spars and kill every one he could find. If you wish to live and thrive but he couldn't knowing they were there. He had already made up his mind to sleep in the cabin with the hurricane turned low until he had had a chance to go through the boat inch by inch. Lying there below him with the lights shining through the portholes, oars of yellow light rowing gently through the shadowy water, the current slipping past as if she were moving upstream, he felt almost proud of her until he remembered and turned shivering to the tap, letting the can overflow as he filled blind and bracing himself. I must go back, I must.

Not daring to look up he ran, flung back the hatch, almost fell down the steps and drew the hatch down behind him. Gratefully he turned to the hoarse whistle of the kettle, music and warming mellow light. When he had eaten he explored the cupboards. The wardrobe was damp behind its mildewed glass. There must be a leak in the deck above. He decided against hanging his one suit in there till he had bought a plastic bag to put it in. Treasures were displayed as he went from one small brown door to another in the main cabin: a brass primus which would come in handy when the gas ran out, a small black Bible, its cover warped with damp, he would have trouble keeping his few books dry, an elderly pressure lamp that he would try as soon as he bought some methylated spirit, and in the recess by the stove a bucket nearly full of sizable lumps of coal gleaming like a raven's wing in the light and a bundle of sticks bound with a twist of wire. He would light the stove, that was the next thing. He was unused to the river silence, felt it like an animal outside the thin wooden walls moving its oiled liquid muscles gently around him. A fire would keep it at bay. He thought of the brightness, the easy cheer he would find in the *Yacht* so close across the water. Probably Walden would be there already, warming his backside and conning the bar over the top of his glass, but between lay the wheelhouse where his horror dangled like the hairy shrunken trophies in a headhunter's hut. He set a match to the heap of paper and sticks crushed behind the bars, heaped on pieces of coal as the flames were sucked upwards by the draught, poured himself more tea and sat down again at the table. The announcer's bloodless voice had reached the shipping forecast. Sym had never been aware of it before but now it increased his isolation while at the same time bringing a kind of comfort, a feeling of kinship as if he were really riding the humpback of the night sea somewhere beyond Dogger.

Should he begin now? What should he say? What was there for him to say any more? Was he even capable of getting anything down. He would begin easily like an exercise in writing, a child's shaky hand stumbling over the trivia of the day. It should be very clear and simple with no attempt at fine writing since no one would ever see it; he wasn't writing for anyone, hardly even for himself. Then why do it, why bother? But he put that thought away. That wasn't the way to begin. That could come later if at all and only then if it grew out of the context. First he must put the facts down with a kind of humility. He cleared his throat and felt his palms break into a skin of sweat that he stroked away with cold dry finger tips. The old excitement was rising in him making him draw in his breath and hold it. He must clear the table and get the pack of paper, pen and pencil out of his duffle bag, careful not to let the controlled force gush out in worthless action. He moved carefully but surely, taking the mug and plate and food remains out to the galley. He brushed the crumbs from the table into his palm and threw them into the grate. The pack stood waiting. He drew a sheet towards him.

The whisper of the pencil ceased. It was all there. Now came the difficult part. He paused. A bubble of tar spurted blue and green flame into the heart of the fire. A duck muttered in its sleep where they roosted along the bank. He had seen them earlier in the day, mallard, the iridescent necks of the handsome drakes burning with the same sharp colours as the sizzling tar. He wrote on.

'But why am I here, what am I looking for prodding at old scars, not even wounds anymore, long since healed though never quite erased? And this idea of keeping a diary, posturing in front of your self so that there are two selves, the one who speaks and the one who listens and they both know where that can lead; this whole idea belongs to adolescence and the terrible struggle for integration. I should be beyond that. I remember beginning a diary once addressed to God but whether it was the father-god or the god-in-us, the true self as the Eastern mystics would say or some of them anyway, the ones who are willing to say anything, that I don't remember or never decided. I remember it didn't get beyond a few spasmodic entries and maybe this one will go the same way. I see it may be a kind of compensation, the devilish need to write forcing itself out under a guise of fact and that perhaps all writing that isn't simple communication must be schizoid in its manifestation if not in origin; the creation of false selves, false worlds for them to act in. Looked at this way I suppose a diary is no worse, no more of an indulgence than any other form of scribbling. One way would be to write poetry of course but then that isn't up to me. You don't simply stop writing poetry, it gives you up. Suddenly it doesn't happen any more and that's that. Like Wordsworth's clouds of glory, the visionary power of seeing which I began to guess at again today, the mystic's intimations of his god, in the dark night where the perceptions thicken these things cease. Perhaps that's why I'm here: a concealed hope that if I retreat into myself, into the dark, suddenly there will be a voice saying, "Sing me something," and it'll all come back. A delusion I suppose looked at honestly but no worse than any of the others I've suffered from.'

He let the words trickle slowly through his head. They had an air of self-consciousness and pretension but he let them stand. They are like that because that's how I am, he thought, and that bit about the Eastern mystics that's the kid whose candy's been taken away howling and lashing out at the cat for spite. You think you've got over it, reasoned the smart away but you haven't. Rejection, that's what you can't stand. You should be used to it by now, it's happened often enough one way or another, but it's always there, the cry, just waiting for you to open your mouth and out it sobs: she didn't love me, he didn't understand, they don't want me.

His eyes ached from staring at the yellow page in the poor light. He drew his finger tips across the closed lids and down his cheeks rubbing them comfortingly over the sandpaper of his chin. Weariness throbbed in his legs and lay leaden in his stomach. Tomorrow was Sunday and he had a lot to do. Carefully he untied the knotted string from the parcel that held his new blankets. The hurricane lamp could burn low all night in case the boat decided to sink under its new owner. He had a feeling boats were temperamental and might object to a change of ownership or was it only their own names they grew attached to? The thought of trying to escape in the pitch dark, water swirling round his ankles and the rest of the livestock scurrying from every cranny in the old timbers, chilled him. He raked the embers together into a dying blaze, doused the other lights and crawled under the blankets heaped narrowly on the bunk, dropping his shoes over the side but keeping the rest of his clothes on for safety. From there in the firelight and lampglow the cabin was comforting, rather than hostile and filled with unseen menace as he had begun to feel it. He turned his head to look up at the sky. Wrack of clouds drifted palely overhead. There must be a moon. The distant backdrop was an inkwash with a scattering of stars. He might have been the only man left on earth lying there holding them in his mind. *Mimosa* shifted gently on her moorings as if making herself comfortable for the night. A tomcat wailed its yearning into the dark; the ducks squabbled sleepily and were silent. Was there anyone up there, out there, inhabited worlds? Supposing we are the only ones after all with all the loneliness of unique responsibility. We've comforted ourselves with little green men on Mars, tall pale Venusians, wise and gentle who'll take some of it off us, this burden of existence, of being alive and comprehending in an inanimate universe but suppose there isn't anyone, we go on from galaxy to galaxy like an exploding seedpod scattering ourselves through space as we expanded across our own little planet, long Viking ships of discovery, and then? His mind drew back, homing on the tired body in the bunk, folding in upon itself, withdrawing into memory and dreams.

He dreamt of Anna and remembered it on waking, the pain of it sharp and obsessive. He couldn't remember what they had been doing but he had seen her quite plainly, saw her now behind his closed eyes, and he knew from the pain that she had rejected him again as she always did. He had pushed it out of his conscious mind so successfully that he could think of her and what they had done, of their life together without any emotion, could speculate on it, even wonder what she was doing now but in dreams it was different. He couldn't deceive his mind or his body in dreams. It hurt and it went on hurting even when he woke, as if he had cried in his sleep like a child and found his eyes wet and swollen when he tried to open them. They betrayed him, kicked him in the groin when he was flat on his back with his eyes closed, made him sixteen again nursing his imaginings against the cold sheets and then at the last moment she turned her head away from him, thrusting him out into consciousness, hung up on her withdrawal.

It was very cold in the cabin, the roof above him embossed with polished studs of condensation and the top blanket sown with minute droplets given off by the warm breathing animal beneath. He passed his hand across it and brought it away wet with little dark fibres sticking to the palm. It would be cold outside the warm byre of the bedclothes. From where he lay the room was light and anonymous with no remembrance of the horror he had felt the night before. He would have to buy a stove on Monday. The fire was alright but it took too long before it made any impression on the chill air. The sky above promised a good day. It was early yet, not quite eight by the tin alarm clock on the cupboard. It would warm up as the sun got stronger and he was going to be busy. He rolled the clothes away from him briskly and put his feet to the floor. Beginning to shiver he groped for his shoes and stood up. Hot tea and breakfast would make all the difference. He could wash later.

While the kettle boiled he faced another problem. Constant use of the plastic Elsan bucket would fill it in a few days. There must be some other answer if he wasn't to be emptying and repriming every week. The little washbasin with its outflow to the river gave him the answer. He would fetch more water from the tap to flush it through.

As he stood beside the tap and lifted his head from the clear cold flow splashing into the polythene carrier he thought about the night before, his eyes blurring as he stared at the flickering surface of the river, separating the reflections of boats and trees into impressionistic dabs of colour that faded and deepened with the pulsing current. The island was quite silent, nothing moved among the trees. The tenement sprawl of boats in every stage of disrepair, though there were one or two he noticed better maintained than the rest, seemed deserted, abandoned to the rocking stream. A small fleet of mallard picked and dabbled their way against the tide, at home among the taut anchor chains, rubbing their smooth painted sides familiarly along the quiet wedge shapes of the hulls. It already struck warmer up on the bank. The first thing to do when he had eaten was to tear down the framework that held the rotting tarpaulin and its obscene inhabitants. He would buy paint and tar, fix the chimney, polish the wheel until *Mimosa* regained her self-respect.

It had looked so easy from up on the bank, just tear it down, but it wasn't. He took out a crumpled silver packet of tobacco from the duffle bag and the little cardboard envelope of papers. Considering, he laid an even trail of moist amber shreds along the white gully, rolled it between the soft pads of his fingertips and flickered his tongue along the thin gummed track like a dried snailpath. He lit up and drew down. Rolling his own wasn't merely affectation, something the virile Western heroes of his childhood Saturday mornings at the pictures had done, a playing for time before the decision exploded in action. Often it had been economy, first a habit he had taken from his father as part of how to be a man and now it had become part of the savour, a tactile pleasure almost as great as the smoke itself. Even Anna had liked it, taking the packet from him to sniff at with delicate nostrils. She had wanted him to try a pipe but the social implications were too wrong and the idea of holding the bowl in his hand while he sucked at the sizzling dottle had made him feel sick.

He felt the same sickness now as he visualised pulling the swathes of old canvas down about his head. There must be another way. He climbed the weathered rungs of the rickety ladder that hung down the side of the wheelhouse over the water and stood on the tarred curving coachroof that was the deck. He had only two tools, a hammer and chisel that had also been his father's and that had been almost the only things he had taken away with him from the home that he and Anna had shared. He poked the cutting edge of the chisel under the canvas flap and levered up. The tarpaulin was the colour of dried lichen and as brittle but a large slice came free before it caught on the nail holding it to the framework and tore jaggedly. In the sunlight he saw them squatting along the frame, paralysed by the white day, the jointed legs drawn up under the soft vulnerable bodies. They made no attempt to move, to get away. They might have been blobs of jelly or inanimate fungoid incrustations. But he sweated with the knowledge that every one was alive. He would have to kill them, there was nothing else he could do but even as he lifted up the chisel and smashed it down, disintegrating the blob into a broken mess like a dropped egg, he felt horror at himself and pity for them. The others didn't move and he went on smashing methodically down the line until he reached the nail. He tore again at the canvas and killed again, on and on to the end of the spar. Now he had to force himself to stretch out a hand and try to tear back along the side pieces. It ripped away in small panels, the spars crossed and double-crossed for greater strength, and each one with its line of squatting victims waiting for him.

The frame was nine feet wide and ten feet long. As the sun mounted its elliptical autumn arc he tore and smashed, sometimes hanging over the river as he worked his way round the sides and across the stern in the fear that one might move at last, scuttle obscenely over his clinging hands and drop him into the water. Their bodies dried on the spars behind him leaving small circular stains fringed with the broken and twisted wires of their shattered legs. When the last mouldering piece had fallen to the deck of the wheelhouse he stood up straight on the coachroof and looked trembling downstream. Water and sky were pale luminous reaches, all other objects without meaning or relation. He was conscious of himself only as a thing, a stick or pole devoid of feeling or reason, a dried teazle whispering huskily in the little wind along a bank. A cold runlet of sweat down his back made his flesh shiver. It was done, there had been no other way. Yet he regretted it and when he swung himself down into the wheelhouse the spars above him reeled like a gallows.

Gingerly he gathered up the torn panels, turning each piece with the chisel to make sure that nothing remained alive. Here and there were traces of web, empty nests, papery remnants of those who had died a natural death, pitiful insect ghosts. He carried them all to the heap in the middle of the island. Someone had set light to it during the morning and it smouldered resentfully under a reeking, eye-stinging layer of smoke. The flies had temporarily deserted. Pulling back his arm he slung the lot into the very centre where he could no longer see it.

Up on deck he had noticed an old deckscrubber, the bristles gapped and worn but it would suit his purpose. Plunging it into the river he sluiced away the yellowish stains and snapped twig legs as if he could wash away memory with them. Then he scoured his own hands and frothed soap bubbles over his face, lathering away the sweated salt. He would go out for a couple of hours and come back when his raw emotions no longer winced at every thought. Looking down on *Mimosa* she would no longer seem so shameful. Jiggling the coins in his pocket for comfort he went up the gangplank, through the trees but not looking as he passed the heap and over the weir-path.

Outside the lock gate he turned right along the towpath. At once he became part of the Sunday morning stroll in the sun. Drawn out by the warmth and gentle light a scattered promenade flowed along beside the water. A child in bright blue coat and hat ran down to the edge where tame waves rippled and spent themselves in a flurry of scum. A swan and two cygnets, their white still singed with brown, drew noiselessly towards her, their snake eyes fixed unblinking on her paper bag of crumbs. She screamed thinly, half in fear, half in delight, and threw the bag a couple of feet into the water. The swans thrust at it with their beaks, pushing it under the surface in their frustration until the soggy paper tore and let the crusts bob up and drift aimlessly like homemade boats before the orange bills snapped them up. The child's father whirred his cine camera at them while the mother made anxious hiccoughing sounds.

Dogs sniffed and cocked their legs along the bushes, fishermen cast ostentatious lines, a weary eight pulled raggedly towards the clubhouse. It was a conscious effort to enjoy the last of the sun before it sank into its grey underworld for the next four months.

As he walked the promenade lapped around him. A handsome dark-haired woman in a hot red coat hung on her young husband's arm as he pushed the high gleaming baby carriage proudly in front of him. Their clothes were Sunday best, the baby cocooned in pink and white fleece, its woolly helmeted head on a flounced satin pillow. Sym saw the shiny new pride and felt them betrayed into conformity by the 'honey of generation'. Nothing had altered. His reactions were still the same as they had always been.

He remembered how Anna had changed, and expected him to, when the baby was born, as if they had been children playing all this time and now they must put their toys away and grow up. But it hadn't been a game for him. Suddenly she wanted carpets on the floor, bills paid, meters that gobbled up his beer money in exchange for the heat and light that had always been included in the price of a night out, special foods at very special prices, doll's clothes, insurance, and finally a house, a mortgage. The word had made him laugh.

'But they don't give mortgages to writers, you know that.'

'Well we can't go on living like this.'

'It's not a bad flat.'

'She shouldn't have to sleep with us. It isn't good for a child. Besides there's no garden.'

'We're no worse off than anyone else. Look at Nick and Barbara stuck in that mudfarm in Somerset, woodworm in the floorboards and an old sock for sewage. And Harry and Elizabeth; a perforated ulcer from trying to run two jobs at once and hardly a thing written in two years. Do you want me to do that? Is that what you want?'

'I just want to live like other people, have a few of the things they have. Not hand to mouth like this all the time.'

'It's not my fault if they don't pay me enough to keep a family on.'

'You could try television. That's how Nick bought the farm after all.'

'Two television plays and isolation for the rest of your life. You know you'd never stand it. Besides it's not my line. I've tried but the telly-welly boyos just don't like my stuff. You can't force them to take it. And I can't get reviewing because I'm not on the old boys' network.'

'How did writers manage in the past? Most of them had wives and children.'

'And most of them had private incomes too. What was it old Quiller-Couch said about a poor boy having as much chance in our society of becoming a poet as an Athenian slave of the sixth century.'

'That's off the point. You have to face conditions as they are.'

She began to lay the table and there was a new obstinacy about her movements, a deliberate placing of knife, fork and spoon just so with the side plates neatly aligned, that had never been there before. This wasn't an ordinary row that could be solved with a few drinks and early to bed. He knew she would turn her back on him using sex or rather its withdrawal as a whip to bring him to heel. Hot words poured through his head but at the same time he held them back realising that she couldn't help herself. Now she had a new toy to play with. Up til then she had been content to play his game but the games men and women play are different, complementary but quite different and because of her essentially feminine nature she could no longer take his seriously. It was his fault for letting it happen. She always left those things to him with a kind of fatalism that if it happened it happened and they would deal with it then. He had done his best to prevent it but when this time something had gone astray he hadn't been very worried, even a little proud as he watched her moving about until he saw that it wasn't just the shape of her body that was changing but the contours of her mind with it.

He laughed now, looking down through the blue reflection that lay like a skin on the top of the water to the pebbles and mud at the bottom. A piece of bright orange peel rolled in the swell lazily to and fro in the shallows of the riverbed. They had been defeated by something as simple and material as money. That was all there was to it. No subtleties of emotion, no psychological conflict tearing each other apart, nothing worthy of high drama, only the old disease poverty. They had clothes on their backs and food in their stomachs but it wasn't enough.

Isn't enough, Sym thought, kicking a pebble into the water where it sank beside the drifting peel. The more our society has, the more complex the life it offers, the more we need. We can't go back to bread and jam and tea anymore than the hunger marchers of the thirties could have dressed in skins and made themselves mud huts to cut the cost of living. It creates the need in us and then won't let us satisfy it unless we conform. When we don't, we feel guilty and insecure.

He had compromised. Got himself a teaching job, become an amateur writer producing less and less, the creative energy drained out of him by a day's hard graft; killing the goose that laid the golden egg he called it wryly to himself as the months passed and there was no comforting stack of papers growing daily thicker under his hand. But he was eligible as a mortgagee, as a teacher. He was caught like everyone else til death did them part. The very word made him shudder as he felt himself die a little each day.

He looked up. The three swans had reached him, the child's bread all gone, and were eyeing him hopefully, their beaks dipping and mouthing over pieces of slimy weed dredged up from the mud. One thrust its bill at the piece of peel, attracted by the splash of colour, but dropped it back disdainfully. 'Even something as beautiful as you is on the make but I've nothing for you,' Sym muttered.

'There are worse things to talk to than swans, particularly mute ones.' Walden stood beside him, a little girl holding each of his large hands. 'Go along now,' he let go of them and pushed each gently from behind in the direction of the lock gates. 'The products of my lust or folly,' he explained. 'They're just open, if my built-in timepiece is working this morning. It's time for communion. Like all good Catholics I take it in one kind only.'

They turned back towards the pub. The little girls were running across the weir. Sym noticed that they were very clean but wore only thin cotton frocks faded with washing and shrunk too, and scuffed sandals. They had the self-contained serious faces of children who are treated as equals.

'I see you're a Protestant,' Walden said as Sym ordered a bag of crisps.

'I'm hungry. Not used to the open-air life yet I suppose.' He helped himself to free biscuits and cheese from the bar, topping them with a crisp vinegary onion.

'And what's your problem?' said Walden, tipping his glass. 'Wine, women or song?'

'All three,' Sym tilted his own carelessly so that rivulets of beer flowed over each corner of the glass and he had to pretend to laugh and choke a little so he could wipe them away.

'You don't want to let them get you down; keep them all well under control. They like a firm hand. Show who's master.'

'But which one do you mean?'

'All of them, all the bloody lot,' he laughed and slapped his hand on the bar. 'Man must be master of his fate.'

'That doesn't sound like orthodox Catholicism to me,' Sym said, looking across the heads that were beginning to fill the bar out through the plate glass that gave on a stretch of hazy sunlit river and the three pink brick arches of the bridge.

'Oh I had my adolescent attack of Roman fever like most kids and then I found out about girls and that you wouldn't really go blind if you didn't jump out of a warm bed into a cold bath as soon as you woke every morning, and before I knew where I was my temperature was back to normal and I've never had a relapse.'

'There are some things you can't help admiring them for of course: Their positivism and a kind of vigour.'

Walden laughed. 'You don't have to be a Catholic to have that, though for some people it seems to be the only way. Drink up. The hours are shorter on Sunday. Two pints of ordinary please, Alec. I can't stand the keg stuff, full of gas and fills you up with wind. They jazz it up for the little boys after they come off lemonade. Hardly a wholesome pint to be found anywhere these days until you get a hundred miles from London. Alec does his best with this, don't you, Alec? Knows it's more than his life's worth to serve me up the bottom of the barrel.'

The barman grinned and put the two full jugs carefully in front of them with a proper respect for the contents or Walden's custom. Sym wasn't sure which.

'How are you getting on with *Mimosa*? Pretty name for a boat though I doubt if it's the original.'

'Not too badly. I ripped all that rotten canvas off her this morning as a start. Now I'll have to get some paint and start doing her up a bit.'

'You want to make sure the deck's sound before the rain starts. Particularly over the bunk. If there's a leak ten to one it'll come through there. She's tarred on top, isn't she?'

Sym nodded.

'Can't do anything about altering that then. Anway a good old standby tar, keep anything out. Get a couple of bags of sawdust from the woodyard and brush that in on top. Make sure you work it well in round the hatches; that's where the rot starts. Have you had a look at the bilges yet?'

'I've thought about it but I'm not sure where the boards come up.'

'I should find out p.d.q. or you won't know where to start pumping when you come home and find the furniture afloat. She must have a bit of water in her by now though that doesn't hurt a wooden hull. Seams open if they're too dry. But you'll find a lot more gets in from the wheelhouse now you've taken that tarpaulin down so I should get some P.V.C. sheeting to cover it or you'll spend every Sunday morning pumping out. I wonder how you'll stick it.' He looked at Sym over the top of his glass.

Sym felt his head singing a bit under the bitter and sudden onslaught of technicalities but he tried to look intelligent and forceful. 'I reckon I'll make out. Anyway it's all part of life's rich pattern as they say.'

'What are you trying to prove to yourself? Or maybe you're on the run from something.'

'Do I have to be?'

'I told you we're all mad on the river. Last home of the English eccentric. You don't come here unless you can't accept what they call civilisation on its own terms. At least you don't stay. That's why I say, "What are you running from?" Are you queer?'

'My wife left me, or I left her. I can't remember which now but that wasn't the reason.'

'What was?'

'She wanted a home and all the things that go with it.'

'And you didn't want to provide them? Get caught up in the rat-race. Why should you? But you shouldn't have let her walk out. Should have been firm. Make them so they can't do without you and then you say what goes.' He turned to study the other customers. 'You see those two over there?' He waved his half-empty glass towards a pair in stained working clothes who were drinking pints of dark mild beside the mock inglenook. 'Clack's boys. Tom's the older one with the wall eye. He's the carpenter. The other one's Dick, half gypsy, lives in an old beached pontoon with a tribe of kids and a thin little wife. Clack leaves most of the business to him. Too busy boozing with his yacht-club cronies to bother much with us. I sometimes wonder what they'd say if they cruised by in one of their gleaming model toys and saw our inelegant huddle, and if they know that's where a lot of his money comes from.'

'Does he ever come in here?'

'Oh no. His stamping ground is further up in the village. If he came in here one of us might ask him for something. Spoil his drink. His wife's another of your homebodies. That's why he spends so much time away. They've got a boy at Oxford. His mother made sure of one conformist in the family.'

'They have their point though, women I mean,' Sym said. And then as Walden laughed, 'Apart from that. It's harder for them with their instinct for nestmaking, maternity and all that. That's the trouble. You can't really blame them.'

'It's like that old music-hall song of Gus Elan's. "It's a great big shame and if she belonged to me." That's how I feel having seen many a good man tamed. "I'd let her know who's who." And so I do or before you know it you're knackered. Selfish I suppose but you have to be if you're to survive at all. Besides I'm not convinced it is instinct. A lot of it's what they've been taught by their mothers and the advertising people.'

'The trouble with me,' Sym said, 'is that I can always see at least two points of view at once. All my instincts are to agree with you and if you hadn't said it first I should probably have said it myself. But as soon as I hear you say it I can see all the flaws, pick all the holes in the argument.'

'Well, if all you need is a bit of opposition to make you swing back my way I've got just the one for you.'

A woman had come in through the glass bar door, stepping quickly in and out of the smoke haze through the puddles of sunlight on the soiled portwine carpet. Her dark hair seemed still a little tousled and the face pale from sleep.

'Sassie,' Walden bellowed. She smiled a little and turned towards them, opening the gold twist at the top of a large handbag and burrowing for a purse. 'What do you want? I'll get it,' Walden said putting an arm round her. From the matt liquorice softness of the bag Sym realised it was real leather.

'Gin please.'

'Gin, Alec. This is Sym. Bought *Mimosa*. Straight?'

'Tonic please.' She turned to Sym. 'Hallo.'

'Hallo.'

'We were talking about conformity; male and female attitudes to,' Walden handed her the clear liquor in the stemmed glass and poised the fizzing bottle of tonic. 'Say when.'

'All of it. And what did you decide?' The two men watched her as she sipped lingeringly, tasting, then sighed a little. 'That's nice. What did you decide?' she asked again.

'That women are much more conformist than men.'

'Oh you would of course, wouldn't you!' She laughed.

'You don't agree?' Sym questioned looking at her directly.

She dropped her eyes and said with a practised demureness that would have been actressy if it hadn't been so accomplished, 'But you don't expect me to, surely?'

'No I suppose not.'

'Let's say we have our own ways. Women are such ingrained individualists that conformity doesn't really affect them. Not deep in themselves I mean. Even when they seem to be conforming they're only suiting their own purposes.'

'Whatever they may be,' Walden said. They all laughed.

'You don't seem to like women very much,' Sym said.

'There's an obvious answer to that one, and it's true too.'

'My round. Same again?' The others nodded and Sym pushed a ten-shilling note and the two mugs across the bar at Alec. The room was full now. Loud conversations were carried up to the ceiling on clouds of smoke and bounced back again. As he waited for the drinks the voices seemed to swell and burst into chorus, reminding him of Wednesday mornings in the college chapel; the strong young tones like a monastery choir giving the same sense of communion. 'Who in the same night that he was betrayed, took bread . . .' He shoved the thought away impatiently and reached for the glasses. 'Where were we?' He handed them each a drink.

'I was going to ask what you're running away from,' Sassie said.

'Must I be?'

'The world would say you are.'

'Perhaps I'm like the Indians, retreating in order to advance.'

' "He who fights and runs away," ' she looked at him over the top of her glass.

'When you come to live on the river,' Walden said, 'you opt out. Sassie fights a continual guerilla war with "the world". She makes a sudden sally, picks off a couple of the enemy, puts a stink bomb under a convention or two and retreats in good order. I prefer to stand and hold them all off like Horatius keeping the bridge. She wants to know what your angle is.'

'Oh passive resistance, non-co-operation, that's me. You can't win but at least you don't let them get away with thinking you agree, that you accept their lousy terms for living.'

'No, I can't have that,' Walden thrust his glass at Sym aggressively. 'You make it sound as if none of it's your own fault or your own choice. There's too much of that Welfare State way of thinking. "I couldn't help it." That's how they all whine as if they had no self-determination, and expect to be spoon-fed, National Assistance, free teeth and glasses.'

'You can't help the family or the conditions you were born

into. I thought everyone admitted the need for the basic social services.'

'Well I don't. Of course you can help the circumstances you're born into. If you're weak and passive you'll choose this kind of family. Whatever we are we make ourselves.'

'Then you must believe in a soul.'

'I don't use those kinds of words,' Walden said fiercely.

'Alright a pre-existent self or whatever you like to call it.'

'What do you know about time and how it works? What does anyone know about it, even your Jodrell Bank lot with their great lunar dish, what do they know about what it really is or how it acts?' He leant forward aggressively, 'Damn all, clever as they'd have us believe they are.'

'You mean choice may be able to work backwards so that at any given point what you are you've chosen?'

Walden didn't answer but turned towards the barman again. 'Do you believe all that too?' Sym asked Sassie.

'The important thing is that he does surely. What you believe is right for you.'

'Even if you believe in Fascism or Nihilism?'

'There's nothing you can do about it, is there? You can't not believe what you believe or change what's rooted in your own personality.'

'You don't think there's any abstract truth then?'

'No, I suppose I don't. It may exist but it doesn't mean anything until it's been assimilated and then it's subjective. What do you think?'

Sym took the pint Walden held out to him. 'Me? I'm like most people; don't know what the hell to think.'

'Nimbly put,' said Walden. 'That way you get the worst of both worlds. A statement that doesn't commit you to anything except the listener's sympathy, sheltering in the crowd while casting a backward glance at traditional Christianity.'

'I think I'm hoping that science and the future will provide some sort of viable answer.'

'Space monkeys,' Walden spat. 'And what are we supposed to do in the meantime while the sages are fiddling with their knobs hoping to come up with an answer? Sit about like a lot of blue-arsed baboons picking each other's fleas and waiting to be shot up in a rocket whenever they say so? They won't find you an answer and if they do it'll only be the one we know already that every man is responsible for his own destiny.'

'What about being responsible for other people's? You know: Love thy neighbour.'

'Residual Christianity again, conveniently made official by the State. An excuse for poking your nose into other people's business and feeling virtuous while you do it and for feeling superior to the poor buggers on the receiving end, like the lady of the manor with her basket of titbits and castoffs for poor old Giles the gardener with the toe-ache. You don't fall for that kind of stuff?'

'That wasn't how I meant it. Involvement was what I meant, in the human condition.'

'There's no such thing. We're all responsible for ourselves I tell you.'

'I still think most ordinary people haven't a chance. They live their little lives according to the circumstances imposed on them by society and then they snuff out like the proverbial light.'

'Morons and rogues, yes. What else do you expect?'

'Humanity, I suppose.'

'Gentle Jesus meek and mild, that slop. It's for kids. Those two over there,' Walden jerked his head towards the two standing by the fireplace, 'what's the good of saving them? We should concentrate on the important things like E.S.P. and the people who are capable of really getting somewhere but our society is dedicated to cosseting the feeble. In the natural world they'd have been torn to pieces long ago.'

'I still think you're very hard on them. They're probably just confused and unhappy like so many others.'

'Because they haven't the guts to be anything else and there's no one to tell them any different. They go and fill up the doctor's waiting rooms with their psycho-somatic aches and pains and all he can do is give them a bottle of coloured water and grumble about malingerers. In the old days there was a priest or vicar or God to take your troubles to but they've robbed them of that and left them with nothing.'

'So you do care about them a bit,' Sym said triumphantly.

'I see what's going on. That's not the same thing. They've lost the crutch they leant on but if they stood upright they wouldn't need it.'

'We'll never agree,' Sym laughed.

'No, but it makes a good argument.'

'My round and then I must go,' Sassie said. The bar was half-empty now. 'All gone home to their Sunday dinners like good little boys. Same again, Alec, please.'

'Two pints and a gin and tonic, seven shillings exactly, Mrs. Parks.' The barman winked at her across the glasses and then at Walden. Sym thought he caught him winking back but couldn't be sure. He seemed to be looking in on an old conspiracy almost as if he wasn't there at all. For a moment he felt himself outside again beyond the bevelled window wistful as a kid with a bag of crisps and a bottle of lemonade waiting for the crack in the door loosing a flood of light and voices and a head in silhouette saying, 'Want anything else? We shan't be long.' Then Sassie handed him a drink. He noticed that she had grown more awake as the rounds progressed but even so it was a banked down, slow-burning vitality contrasting with Walden's roaring bonfire. It must be the drink that was making him see things this way he decided. But he welcomed it as he had before. It might be spurious but it was life of a sort.

'Where have you gone?' she asked. He realised they were both looking at him.

'Sorry, I was miles away.'

'You'll do,' said Walden, and turning to the woman, 'Don't you think he'll do? Anyone who can resist both of us and go off on his own like that shows promise I think.'

'It's not fair to tease him, Walden. He's younger than either of us.'

'How do you know? I just look young.'

'She didn't mean in years,' Walden said.

Sassie drained her glass and picked up the leather bag from the counter. 'I must go. I'll see you around, both of you.' Suddenly she was gone. For a moment Sym wondered whether she had simply dissolved into the smoke and then he saw her already pushing open the door and walking quickly past the window.

'She's taken to you. You're in, lad,' Walden said.

'How do you know?'

'I know Sassie. You'll be alright now. Needn't be lonely when you feel like a bit of company.'

'She's easy then?'

'No, not easy. She has her favourites. She can pick and choose.'

'Supposing I don't?'

'Then you'd be a bloody fool. You're young. You have to get it out of your system.'

Alec rang the bell and flashed the lights on and off.

'Is there anywhere in the village I can get a cheap meal?' Sym asked.

'Plenty of places. Most of them alright if you're not looking for the diners' club.' Walden finished his drink in one long swallow. 'Good, that's given me an appetite. See you around.' He tapped Sym lightly on the shoulder and walked confidently out into the sun. The beer didn't seem to have affected him at all.

Sym finished his own drink more slowly. He thought of leaving it then realised that Alec would notice and his reputation was at stake. Last out, he wandered along the high street dazzled by the white pavement until he found a café that looked clean and cheap and had a juke-box playing in the corner.

As he ate his roast beef, Yorkshire and two veg, steamed jam roll and custard he considered Walden and Sassie. He wondered if they did. The idea of her, of them together, repelled and yet attracted him. Promiscuity had always fascnated him because it was something he had never sampled for himself. He had always had sex with people he was involved with and there hadn't been many of those. He had brought himself up on a concept of romantic love, a true post-Lawrentian, so that anything else had seemed distasteful to him. He couldn't imagine making love to someone and not saying, 'I love you,' but sometimes he wondered if this was just a new kind of puritanism that had straightened his experience and understanding.

Mimosa when he got back was huddled low in the water as if ashamed but he went quickly and cheerfully down the gang-plank and fell asleep with the alarm set to wake him an hour later so that there were still a few hours of daylight left to carry on with the cleansing he had begun in the morning. He was determined to sleep in the cabin that night and he would need the fire lit for when cold fell with the dark. The smoke from the little chimney cheered him as he went up and down for water and scrubbed and swabbed the decks and paintwork. The real work of painting and repairing would have to wait until he could get to the ironmonger's but he made a list of the first things he would need and a thorough inspection of every part of her except the bilges. Those he decided to leave until he felt more capable of dealing with whatever he might find. He had no idea what to expect and he wanted to face it in full daylight with a whole day ahead of him.

As light flowed out of the saloon to lie in opaque oil-smooth pools on the surface of the river he lit the lamps and set out his table top with papers and pencil, reclaiming the day's happenings for himself. When he came to Walden and Sassie he sat back on the bunk and puzzled, his sharp front teeth nipping horny half-moons of skin from the edges of his finger nails. They both had the same trick of looking over the top of the glass, the bottom of the face masked, only the eyes quizzical, mocking, and they had both asked him the same question: what was he running from? Yet even though the formula was identical he wasn't sure that it was the same question.

'What do words mean then?' he wrote. 'Only what you make them? That's what she would say, and he would too but with a different emphasis on "make". Is it emphasis then, and did I put mine in the wrong place? Or perhaps I never knew where to put it and so what came out wasn't strong enough, unique enough and in the end didn't even convice me that I had something worth saying. No one else is going to be convinced if you're not yourself. Perhaps I was too young to begin playing at husband and father, even writer, and Anna couldn't give me time because she had to get on with living through the child and that won't wait. But time is like any other commodity, it has to be bought and if you haven't the money . . .' He had written himself round in the same circle.

'That is not what I meant at all.' He got up and went past the galley and up the ladder, pushing up the heavy hatch until he saw the sky overhead. He shivered a bit as he looked up and round. He had done his work well. The spars that had held the roof were clean black bars against the lighter sky as his eyes accustomed themselves. A few sparks flew over from the chimney, reminding him of the warmth down below. He had meant to put down only the facts but speculation kept creeping in. He must be firmer with himself and only tell what happened. But what about memory? he thought, and even what happened is what I saw happen. He shivered again in the chill rising from the dark water which he could hear whispering past just out of sight. The trees screening the bank cut off the island completely. He would have one more try. He would answer the question they had both asked him for his own satisfaction and then he would put it away. He went below.

'Why am I here? I am here to find a point to work from, something that isn't as shifting as subjective impulse. I am here because there is no authority I can accept: no one can tell me anything because I can't accept that they know. But there's nothing Kafkaesque about me. I am a real person in a real physical situation which I have chosen myself and which I can alter at any moment. But I can't keep on as I have been, withdrawing further and further into myself and finding only silence or contradictions.' He paused remembering Sean's words one evening when he had refused again to join the rest of the gang on the run into town. 'You're going deeper and deeper and no man can throw out a hand to help you. This way you'll end up in the bin, God help you, or swinging by your own necktie.' He had jumped up into the lorry, the tailboard swung up and bolted behind him and it had gone off down their road with Sean hanging on to the roof, looking back at him where he stood in the dust of the unlaid track, swaying as the lorry gathered speed, his wild moustaches and long fierce curls under the old green felt making him look like a stage Irishman.

The new job suited him; digging holes for the gas board. They were an easy-going lot. When it rained they sheltered in the green canvas hut while heavy drops spattered on the roof, smoking, swapping tales, boiling successive mugs of thick tea; when it was fine they ripped up paving stones and dug into the sour city earth. Alf the ganger knew them all through and handled them like a team of thoroughbreds, coaxing, curbing gently but firmly, never driving a man so far he had no way back. Because they went home in the evenings the job was only part of their lives not the whole as it had been on the roads. Sym found them sharp after Sean and the others. All grave thoughts were laquered over with a smart answer so that a casual listener would have thought it all a laugh, birth and death and sickness, crime and courting together. But Sym, trained in words, in undertone and nuance, knew better. He learnt to add his quip to the pile, his card to the delicately balanced structures they built and destroyed with a word and then built again, Alf guiding their tongues so that when it fell no one was broken underneath.

'I come round your place last night, Charlie, but you wasn't in.'

'Oh no, what was you after then?'

'Mate of mine was gonna measure you up for a suit.'

'If he was a mate of yours it'd have holes in the pockets.'

'When we found you wasn't in I left him outside and measured your missus up instead.'

'Yeah, I know. She said the trouble was you only had a three-inch rule on you.'

'I'm sorry you wasn't in. You'd have looked lovely in this suit.'

'What's your mate then, Stan?'

'He's the undertaker.'

'They give you a whole suit now then. In my day it was just a wooden overcoat.'

'They have to. Need mahogany trousers to get some of them to the boneyard what's walking about today. You don't want the poor old bearers overcome before they've got 'em sited over the hole.'

'Tom's old woman had the dropsy and burst in the box. Running all over the road she was before they could stop her. First time she ever run anywhere in her life.'

'What's the good of running if no one's chasing you?'

'You married, Sym?'

'I was but she took off.'

'Ah maybe you're like Stan, only got a three-inch rule in your pocket.'

'It might look like that when I'm not using it but it's one of the folding ones, opens out to four times the size.'

'Look at that old rain, stopped again just when the conversation was getting a bit interesting.'

He knew that with Alf he was doing the same as he had with Sean, making a symbol more and less than the flesh-and-blood man. Harking back again, he thought but he hankered for the feeling of warmth and security the symbol gave him. At work he knew the language, could move and speak freely, almost become involved, identified in a familiar childhood country.

Sometimes it seemed as if he had always lived on the river and as if October would never end. On Saturdays and Sundays he scraped and tarred and painted. He borrowed a hose and cleaned and refilled the water tank so that clean cold water flowed when the taps were turned on. The tank had been furry with brown weed, the bottom bedded with a black squelching layer of mulched leaves from the trees overhead. In the six inches of liquid mud covering it he thought he had seen a twitch, a flash. It was a fish. He couldn't imagine how it had got there except that there was some rumour that the old lady had used river water for washing. He caught it carefully in a jam jar. It was plump, about four inches long and very healthy. Sym emptied it over the side into the stream, hoping it would have enough instinct for survival left after its enclosed life in the tank. He wondered what it had fed on and how it had managed to avoid being sucked down the pipe when the water flowed out. Perhaps the old lady had kept it as a kind of pet.

One Saturday morning the gas cylinder ran out. He had realised for some days that it was going because the rank smell seemed to become stronger every time he lit it. He was obviously scraping the bottom of the barrel. Undoing the coupling he hauled it up the gangplank and across the island to the slipway. Walden's boat had gone and a handsome launch had taken its place. The shrivelled figure with the wall eye who had been pointed out to him as Tom was varnishing the hull with plodding strokes of the brush. Sym lowered the metal cylinder with a clang.

' 'Morning.'

' 'Morning. Want a new one do yer? Good job you come now. We'd have all been gone home soon and you'd have been without all weekend. Dick does all that. In there.' He waved his arm towards the big derelict hut beyond the slipway. 'Go on in. He'll see you alright.' He watched as Sym picked up the cylinder then turned back to his deliberate movements spreading the syrupy varnish over the planes of smooth wood.

Inside was half-light. Bats might have hung high up among the dusty beams but the only sound was a thin music from behind a door at the far end. He put down his burden again outside it and knocked.

'It's run out,' Sym said when the door opened and Dick's dark face under the tumble of greasy curls looked out at him questioningly.

'You're lucky. There's only one left. Waiting for them to come in.' He swung the big grey canister inside. 'Twenty-seven and six that'll cost you.'

Sym took the money from his pocket.

'Have you carried one of these before?' Sym shook his head. The gypsy swung it up onto his shoulder. 'I'll bring it round for you. It's a matter of knack like most things but you could do yourself an injury carrying it the wrong way.' His thin fine bones looked hardly strong enough as he walked ahead across the island. He ran across the gangplank like a cat and lowered it gently to the deck. 'Don't want to drop it. Might go straight through the bottom then we're all in trouble. Can you fix it up alright?'

'I think so.'

'Make sure it's nice and tight or you'll blow yourself up. Alright now?' He laughed and ran back, up the bank and into the trees before Sym could answer. He shook his head as if dazed. He felt as if he had been through some experience he couldn't quite grasp and had seen someone vanish, dissolve in front of him. It was as if simple happenings had a meaning that was more than their aggregate of facts and he wondered whether everyday life was meant to be lived at this degree of intensity or whether it was more than the human mind could cope with and it would stagger and crumple under it as he had expected to see Dick's thin bones snap. 'Human kind cannot bear very much reality,' he heard the words echoing in his head in warning.

But then, he thought, he didn't make it did he? That was the whole point. And maybe he was looking in the wrong place like me. All the wrong places.

> 'Down the passage which we did not take
> Towards the door we never opened
> Into the rose garden.'

Now at last summer seemed to be running out, to be down to the last cloudy lees. Overnight the wind rose, rocking the boats on their moorings that suddenly seemed cobweb slight to hold them. The trees bent and lashed at each other and in the morning the river swirled with leaves torn from their sockets while the survivors clung pale and bloodied for a few days more. Walden advised him about extra ropes, a new springer to stop *Mimosa* bouncing about too much. Sym imagined her breaking loose in the night and flung spinning down the weir race like the lemon boats of the willow leaves. His new blue P.V.C. cover had to be weighted with bricks to stop it ripping from its lashings under a swollen belly of wind and hurling away in a shining blue cloud. At night he sat in his cabin listening to wind and water roaring past or handhauled himself across the catwalk to the *Yacht*, to the comfort of Alec and Walden. The pile of papers grew under his hand as he recorded the speculations, the happenings of this new life and winter walked steadily towards them.

November

The leaves laucen from the linde and lighten on the ground

NOVEMBER. Fog. He thought of *The Ancient Mariner*, of the dim red sun like God's own head and the dew that dripped from the shrouds. 'Shrouds'—the word tormented him with its ambivalence yet delighted him at the same time; not to be pinned down, circumscribed. But when he took the book from the shelf and turned the limp damp pages he couldn't find the bit he wanted and realised that his memory had tricked him. He had misremembered out of the childhood impression the poem had left on his mind unless the mist was seeping in through his nose and mouth and swirling about in his head behind the eyes. He thought of a game they had played as children, 'Watch the smoke come out of my eyes,' and while you were watching they burned your unguarded hand with the cigarette they had drawn on. Sym was always caught because he always felt it was possible and worth looking for. 'The fog hangs from the trees, grave clothes above the water,' he wrote. 'Every stay and spar is beaded, wooden surfaces, rails and deck, sweat, clammy under the touch.'

The river isolation he had felt before had been nothing to this as the air thickened around him cutting him off completely. He heard the water drops falling mournful on every side but his senses were blanketed so that he couldn't tell on which hand the sound of water fell. As he stood on deck and tried to part the grey curtains he could see only the planks under his feet, the white rail and a slow leaden swell of river a foot beyond. The invisible trees that overhung his diminished world shed slow tears on his head as he stood looking up, their leafless twigs downdrooping like the falling notes of a dirge.

Somewhere beyond, the world was going about its business. Every day he joined it for a few hours and then the mist would thin, even a little sun come through but as it came time for him to go home it drew closer, shutting off the bank and the other boats, making the catwalk a tightrope crossing over a void that he must set his foot on and travel in the confidence that an end existed that he couldn't see. Once halfway over he met an old man, a dank drab bundle of rags that swayed and swore as it stumbled towards him. Sym drew into the nearest passing place, sensing that the bundle wouldn't pause or step aside and frightened of contact with it. He caught a thin sour smell as it passed and thought how easy it would be to topple the tattered ragbag into the river except that he couldn't bring himself to touch it. 'Or he might topple me,' he said to himself as the figure shuffled fiercely into the mist still muttering. 'Who would know?' Both ideas intrigued and horrified him.

The new stove was a compact comfort. The fire he knew would have drawn sullenly, its vitality dampened, the new zinc chimney fog-dulled to gunmetal like dark underarm sweat patches. Every evening he brought home a gallon of paraffin, lit the lamps and cooked his supper. As he pushed his plate away the problem would stare back at him like a bit of undigested gristle. What should he do with the next few hours? Sym felt a kind of torpor begin to invade him as if his body was sinking into the half-life of hibernation. Now that the evenings drew in so early, work on the boat was impossible. There seemed only two possibilities: his stack of paper and the *Yacht*. When the fog thinned, leaving the air dank and raw, he found himself going there more and more, his feet taking him automatically towards the talk and sedating warmth. After, he would return briskly, nimble across the catwalk full of Dutch courage, often with Walden's bulky shape in front of him stopping to pee ceremonially into the river.

'Every little helps as the old lady said,' he would laugh, his voice booming across the surface of the water like skipped gunshot, and in the following silence the ducks would protest sleepily under the trailing wicker of willow branches.

Sometimes Sym crossed the island alone coming out of the dark trees to find *Mimosa* glowing quietly below but when the night seemed impenetrable he skirted the rim of the bank passing the other boats, lifting his feet high to avoid the trip wires of mooring ropes and chains. On this tack one night he thought he heard a duck up late skittering its wings and leathery paddles below the concrete parapet beside a steeply slanting gangplank. Then he saw the hands.

For a moment he couldn't understand them. That there should be two white hands clinging, slipping, scrabbling on the roughened surface seemed so incongruous that he heard himself laughing and wondered if he was getting the D.T.s. He hadn't had much. Walden had been missing that evening. Only Dick had been there drinking two careful pints of mild, his bright black eyes shifting continually towards the door and then mocking back to Sym as if he knew a joke he wasn't sharing; meeting someone he had said but the someone hadn't showed up.

The hand scrabbled again and this time there was a whimper. Peering over the edge Sym saw the human shape half in, half out of the water, the clothes and hair draggled, the face smudged white against the black water. It was Sassie.

'Hello. What are you doing down there?'

'I slipped.' She sucked in her breath and the hands scrabbled again.

Sym reached down. 'If you don't pull me in too I'll pull you out.' He caught her hand and heaved. She was lighter than he had expected. 'Come on up then.' There was a squelch as he hauled her on to the parapet beside him.

'I've lost my shoes. They're stuck down there in the mud.'

'You'll fall in again if you lean over like that.'

'But I can't leave them. They're my best.' Together they stared down into the dense water, churned muddy and pitch under a moonless sky.

'You'll never find them in this. Better leave it till the morning. If they're bedded in well they might still be there.'

She still seemed unwilling to leave them. 'Perhaps if I got a stick and poked about?'

Sym shook his head. 'There's all sorts down there. You'd more likely fish up an old bike or a set of tin cans.' He saw her shiver. 'You're soaked. You can't sit here: you'll die. You'd better go in. Have you got a stove; one that'll warm up quickly I mean?' He helped her to her feet, the brackish water running off the hem of her dress and down her legs.

She looked down. 'Hell, what a mess! I should have taken that offer then this wouldn't have happened.'

Sym put his jacket round her shoulders and an arm under her elbow. 'Now what about it?' She seemed not to be listening and he shook her a little.

She focussed her attention on him but as if it was an effort and as if she was considering something quite different. 'About what?'

'The stove, to dry you out.'

'Oh I'll manage. Go straight to bed. Soon be warm in bed.' She was still looking up at him, searching his face for something now but he had no idea what it was.

'You'd better come back with me. It's warm, I left the fire on. I'll make you a hot drink. Do you want to get some clothes? I could lend you some things.'

Suddenly she seemed to make up her mind. 'Yes, let's go now, I'm cold.' She shivered again as if she had just remembered the clinging wetness in the chill air and turned along the bank.

'You'd better take those things off,' Sym said when they were below with the hatch closed. 'I'll put the kettle on.'

Sassie looked about her. 'I like it. It's comfortable and right.'

'Right?' He came through from the galley and threw her a towel. She laughed a bit. He went into the cabin and rummaged in the long drawer under the bunk, taking out a shirt and jeans. 'I've put you some clothes on the bunk.'

She laughed again and went into the cabin with the towel, pulling the door to behind her. For a moment he stood staring at the blank door face, knowing what would happen and sweating because all at once after the long months of denial on the roads he wanted it with an intensity he had thought faded, gone with adolescence. He rubbed his finger tips down across his eyeballs and went to make coffee.

'Do you have a comb?' She sat in front of the stove chafing the damp from her hair and when she took it from him she laughed again and began to tug and smooth the dark tangles. It was deliberate and he knew it but he played the game.

'Sirens usually sit on rocks to do that.'

'Luring brave but ordinary men to their doom.'

'Unless they block their ears of course.'

'Oh yes, you could always do that.'

'Ulysses, he was the only one who didn't and he got away with it.' He knew they were playing games.

'They had to tie him down though and he was brave and wise, a great leader and fighter.'

'And I'm not?'

'I don't think you know what you are yet.'

She was laughing at him again as he passed her a cup of coffee, the cup jingling unsteadily in the saucer. 'What did you mean before, something about accepting an offer?'

She looked at him with the familiar lift of the eyes only this time it was the rim of the cup as she sipped that hid the rest of the face. 'I'm not sure if you're old enough.'

Sym was irritated. Games were all very well but the rapid fluctuations in tension were making him feel almost sea-sick. 'Oh come off it.'

'Someone wanted to provide me with a bed for the night, that's all. Nothing very unusual.'

'Do you usually take the offer?' He hit hard this time, determined to have some of his own back.

For a moment the face shadowed and then cleared and she shrugged. 'Surely Walden told you, I'm choosy. They get what they pay for—my company.'

'Isn't that rather dangerous?'

'Little girls end up at the bottom of the river with their

throats cut you mean? There are one or two guiding rules. Never bring them home or go home with them. Always drink where you know the landlord and make it quite clear what the limit is. If they choose not to hear or think they can change your mind then they don't deserve any more anyway.'

'You sound like Walden in a strange way.'

'We are alike in many ways.'

'What's Mrs. Walden like? I've never met her.'

'Joyce? Oh she's fine. He'd go to pieces without her.'

They had come to a full stop and for a moment there seemed no way of beginning again. Sym moved restlessly but Sassie stared at the glowing mesh of the oil stove, swilling a few dregs at the bottom of her cup. Sym felt himself extraneous, *Mimosa* no longer his. She possessed it as a cat would have done and like a cat he found himself wanting to stroke her.

She lifted her head sleepily and looked at him, the face feline under the warm touch of the fire. 'Have you forgotten how?'

'How did you know?'

'Oh I just knew.'

Sym moved towards her. 'How much will it cost me?'

'It's a free gift. Maybe your soul but no one values that much these days anyway.' He covered her laughter with his mouth.

When he woke in the morning she was gone. He wondered for a moment if it was all fantasy and if so he must be in a pretty bad way. Then he saw the damp patch on the floor where she had dropped her wet clothes when she changed. The clothes were gone but she had dressed herself in his jeans and shirt again. He wondered when he would get them back. He had realised last night that she was probably older than he had thought: a slight puckering of the flesh between the breasts, belly muscles that had lost their first tautness, upper arms too soft; about forty, he thought, but the thought only gave him a strange surge of pleasure.

It was Saturday. He got up hungry and fried eggs to put between bread and butter. As he ate he considered what to do with the day. Was it just a flash and then they would go on as before? Should he go and look for her? Did he even want to, want it to be anything more? The meshes wrapped closer round him. He was caught and he knew he was caught. He took a sheet of paper and worried at it.

> 'Sins in a nett I seke to hold the wynde.'

He drew the line through his mind in the warm saloon trying to pin his reactions to the paper.

> 'Yet may I by no meanes my wearied mynde
> Draw from the Diere: but as she fleeth afore,
> Faynting I folowe.'

Caught that was it. Sometimes it was the hunter who was caught by the hunted. The roles were reversible, turn a corner and there she would be laughing and backing you up against the wall. He took down the book to be sure and flipped the pages into a blur in his haste to follow it to the end, to catch the half-remembered words. And there it was.

> '. . . for Cesar's I ame;
> And wylde for to hold, though I seme tame.'

Sym put the book back and stared out of the porthole at the grey water hurrying past. Walden? But then would she have spoken of his wife like that if she had been having an affair with him? There was no answer. And did it matter anyway? He looked at his stack of paper and decided to wait until he knew more. This was perhaps a case where he couldn't simply put down the facts without reflection like a child. They weren't things a child could play with.

He pushed back the hatch and went out into the morning. The fog of the last weeks had rolled back in the night under a crisp cold hand of frost and the leafless branches were drawn clear on the white sky. He blinked and started along the bank.

He would just look to see if there was any sign of life and then he would go on to the shops. With the change in the weather he could get back to his painting. Walden had shown him how to caulk the seams with cotton and tar to stop the rain pouring through the open deck into the bilges and now he wanted to finish it off with a coat of blue deck paint.

As he neared her boat he saw her sitting on the wall. At first he thought she must be fishing until he remembered the shoes. She was still wearing his shirt and jeans and was raking the riverbed with a boathook.

'Have you found them?'

She smiled up at him. 'I've got one.' It stood muddily beside her. 'It'll probably brush up alright. I'm still looking for the other. They were a present; I'd hate to lose them.' She prodded hopefully, clouding the water with mud and slime and waiting for the current to carry it away before she plunged again, this time hooking up with the crumbling spokes of an old umbrella wreathed in tendrils of lush weed.

'If it turns up downstream,' Sym said, 'they'll be looking for the body.' Half his mind remembered how she had gasped and twisted under him, not calling out as Anna had done but contained, the climax turning inwards. He wondered if she had had some dry underwear to put on and tried to guess from the fall of her breasts as she leant over the water.

She turned her head and looked at him over her shoulder. 'Leave me something.'

Sym forced a randy grin to cover his embarrassment at being caught with his thoughts showing. Sassie flicked the end of the boathook and sent her find out into midstream. Then she thrust down again, pushed the pole cautiously towards the gangplank and came up with the other shoe. 'There, now I can clean them both and put them to dry.' She scrambled up.

Immediately Sym made up his mind. 'What about a drink? I was just going shopping.'

She considered. It was a game again. 'Perhaps I'll join you.'

'I'll wait for you to do those.'

'No, you go on. I might change my mind. It's supposed to

be my privilege isn't it?' She turned up the gangplank and was gone, leaving him standing.

He looked at the boat. It didn't seem to have a name and was badly in need of painting if not more drastic attention. It was very small too. There could only be room for one cabin inside. He wondered if he would ever see the inside and then he walked away towards the weir. Perhaps she would stand him up. He would do all the things he had set his mind on before he saw her in case she intended to make him sweat it out. Perhaps she had had all she wanted and this was a polite brush-off. Had he been good enough? What was a woman like that used to? He wondered where the shoes had come from. She had said a present and, like the handbag, they were expensive. He could only think of one way a woman would get that kind of present. 'I've got a dirty mind,' he said to himself as he pushed open the door of the ironmonger's with its jangling old-fashioned bell.

The bar when he got to it was crowded with characters he had come to drinking acquaintance with over the last weeks. The totter was there dressed in the best of his weekly haul of cast-offs; a pair of white plimsolls with 'Taffy Davies 1944' printed in marking ink across the toes, blue pin-striped jacket over a collarless shirt and jeans and a lady's chiffon scarf in green and gold round his throat against draughts. His gums mumbled on his words and spat them out moistly but Sym always found them worth picking up. The local bookie in immaculate business suit, neat Alpine hat tipped back on his head like a thirties newshawk, flitted between betting shop and flat pint taking half-dollars and bringing back tips from the horse's mouth.

'Your nag, Alec, she went round the other way. Nothing for hard luck.'

Alec pulled Sym a pint and sighed. 'Aren't you lucky you're not a betting man.'

'You can't have all the vices.'

'That's the trouble with women,' said the totter, 'they let you down.'

The boatman leaning on the end of the bar leant towards them and sang in a deep clear voice.

'And she left me with a basket of oysters.'

Sym peered about. There was no sign of Sassie. He spotted Clack's boys in their usual corner by the fireplace talking to a stranger. Dick was doing the talking as usual. He raised his glass to Sym and gave him his little secret smile as if he knew it all but wouldn't say. When at last he saw her through the glass door it was nearly closing time and Walden's great shape bulked behind her.

'You nearly didn't make it,' Sym threw his remark over her head at Walden. He found himself between relief that she had come and disappointment that they were both there.

'We're all going for a walk,' Walden said, nodding to Alec for their usual round.

'I was going to finish the deck,' Sym tried to assert a show of independence.

'Nonsense,' Walden thrust a pint at him. 'You can do that tomorrow. What else are Sundays for? Six days shalt thou labour and the seventh shall thou do more than on the other six put together. Besides today's too good to waste.'

'It might be raining tomorrow.'

'There is nothing so offensive as the sight of the righteous man bent on self-flagellation. I leave it to you.' Walden turned to Sassie. Sym nearly smiled. He was beginning to learn the rules and how the game was played and he knew he had won this hand if he could keep his face straight. She would have to ask him.

'We can't go without you,' she said. 'That's the whole point.'

'Oh well. If you assure me tomorrow will be fine.'

'Of course it will be fine.'

Outside the door Walden's two children were waiting for them with a serious patience and a little white terrier bitch on a lead.

'This is Jane and this is Sophy.' They smiled at Sym briefly out of their grave faces and shook his hand. They wore the same clothes he had seen them in before with the addition of two felted cardigans darned at the elbows. Jane, the elder, spoke to her father in beautifully articulated syllables, clear as flowing water, asking if they could let the dog run free once they were off the main road. It was called Trudy. They were so unlike the children of Sym's own childhood that he wondered if they were acting too, but if they were there was no lapse into spontaneity as they passed over the bridge and down onto the north towpath where ordinary children would have erupted into a run, race you to that tree and back. Only Jane bent down and freed Trudy and the little bitch set down her moist black liquorice nose and laid their trail into the park.

'It isn't right to keep them on the lead when they can run free, is it, Daddy?' the youngest turned her small brown pointed face up to Walden.

'That's it,' he said. 'We keep animals in a state of subjection and so we have a responsibility towards them and that means giving them as much freedom as we can.'

'I sometimes think you would have made a good schoolmaster,' Sassie said, 'at Lowood Institute.'

'Children don't like being talked down to so I try not to talk down to mine at home. God knows they get enough of it from some half educated pedagogue all day.'

'Most of the ones I taught talked down to me,' Sym said.

'They recognise when people aren't sure of their ground, or themselves, straightaway of course. Many of them are already more intelligent than their teachers will ever be so why should they accept an authority that's based on externals?'

'I thought this was a walk,' Sassie said. 'I shall go home if you're going to wrangle about education.'

Walden laughed and put his arm round her. 'Isn't she splendid? What shall we talk about then? The lady commands.'

'You could try just looking at things for a change, absorbing.'

'Like a sponge,' Walden pulled a face.

They had come to a large wrought-iron gate in the high wall bordering the path. 'Through here,' Sassie said.
'Come back, Trudy, here,' the children called.
Sym stared at the gate as he held it open. Ivy still twined its intense green between the bars and from the middle a face looked out curling into metal fronds where the hair and neck should be. It reminded him of Walden. They passed through, closing the gate behind them.
'This is a part the tourists don't know,' Sassie said. It was very still. Sym heard the dog panting as it lolled its tongue across the brown turf questing rabbits perhaps or the sheep grazing in the distance who lifted their long incurious faces to stare a moment and then dropped their snouts to rasp away the torpid grass. Farther still the tall brick chimneys of the palace peered above a woven screen of dry branches through the smoky afternoon. Sym would not have been surprised if time had been suspended. The animals were heraldic on the dun green ground and voices when they came fell flat, rejected like whispers in a cathedral.
A long thick branch lay across their path. Walden stirred it with his foot. 'It's quite dry. It would make splendid firewood.'
'What a waste to leave it there,' Sassie said.
Sym lifted it onto his shoulder. 'Then we'll take it with us.' He felt strong and as if he were taking part in some ritual with the ridged bark chafing his neck. For a second he wondered whether he had caught a quick glance pass between Sassie and Walden and then forgot it watching the children running ahead of them behind the little white bitch soundlessly like figures in a dream, their skimpy washed-out clothing and thin brown legs flying. Even Walden seemed subdued while Sassie turned her head to take it all in, a half-smile on her face, as if in some way she had created it or owned it.
'Well, what do you think?' Walden asked him restlessly.
'Why do you always have to try and impose yourself on everything?' Sassie spoke almost angrily. 'Why can't you let things go their own way, people make up their own minds for a change?'

For the first time he looked apologetic. 'You know I can't so it's no good asking me. We all have to be what we are and try to make things the way we are. Anyway he hasn't answered.'

They stood still and looked at him. 'I feel like a ghost,' Sym said slowly, 'as if I'm not here at all. Is that what you want me to say?'

'We want you to say whatever you think,' Sassie said. 'That's all anyone can say.' She looked defiantly up at Walden.

He gave a great shout of laughter that stopped the children in their flight and lifted the sheep faces towards them. Sym felt the afternoon lying under his feet like a pale golden sponge that sucked the life out of him into its own quiescence. They were coming to the far wall now and another gate with Walden's face looking in. It would be there on the other side too. The bitch was called and put on the lead again and they passed through to stand immediately under the high walls and perilous chimneys of the palace and then by what must have been a postern gate into a flagged courtyard.

'Through that arch,' Walden said, pointing, and the little procession wound towards it, Trudy straining in front.

Sym was last, the long thickness of the branch self-consciously weighing on his shoulder. As he came out of the light he saw they were in a kind of vaulted stone hall where a guide was directing the upturned faces of a few late autumn visitors. They turned to stare at the little group, particularly, Sym thought, at himself and his burden and he wondered if he could be arrested for stealing wood from a royal park or whether he could plead a commoner's right to gather kindling. Walden had engineered it all and was probably roaring his head off outside. There must have been some other way they could have come. Well, he couldn't drop it and run. They'd think he'd stolen the silver too. Besides he'd carried it all this way and he wasn't going to ditch it now.

Walden was grinning out in the sunlight. 'Fancy them still being about, the tourists. That gave them something to think about.'

'We shall probably go down as the palace ghosts. They'll go home to Milwaukee or Memphis and tell how they saw the real thing in little old world England.' He thought as he looked at them that in a sense they were just that as far as the rest of the world was concerned; fugitives from another time making no contact with the nuclear age, glimpsed briefly through the haze, wondered at and then forgotten, and he questioned for a moment who was right until he saw again the blank faces following the guide's finger as it led them through the pre-digested facts without even the labour of reading the guide-book. He felt proud of his branch again and shifted it onto the other shoulder. The brown fey children, the little white pointed dog, Walden's vigorous bulk, Sassie's dark mesh of hair and pale face and himself, young man with a log, could have hung in portrait on those walls and been completely in place.

A cream and silver coach was parked beyond the main gate, Kulturtours, that had brought the guide's little flock, and the main road was aswirl with city-going traffic but on the other side they went down the steps to the water's edge out of reach of the roar from the racing engines and stood watching *Whale*, the little tug, chuff its blunt brown shape into the lock while the dog snapped at the ripples from the wash as they broke on the pebbly strand.

Once over the weir Walden and the children left them. 'Come in and I'll find us something to eat,' Sassie said. So he would see the inside after all. 'There's not much room. You'll have to make yourself small.' He sat down on the bunk.

It was surprisingly cheerful. There was a Chinese print on the wall, bright cushions and curtains. He noticed a strange pungent smell that was explained when she lit a stick of in-cense, nipped it between the wooden prongs of a peg and stood it on a narrow ledge where the slow trickle of aromatic smoke curled itself about the cabin like the quiet drift of music. Behind his head he noticed three plant pots with thin pale green shoots under glass where they caught the full sun through the little window.

'What's this?' Sym asked. 'Mustard and cress?'

Sassie laughed, pouring hot water onto the powdered coffee in two brown pottery mugs. 'Mary-jane, common hemp,' she said. 'But I don't think it'll come to much. It's amusing to try though.'

'Don't they take a dim view of people growing their own?' he stared at the innocuous-looking shoots in amazement.

'Who are "they" and how do they find out? Besides I'm only growing myself a new mooring rope. There,' she put a plate of sandwiches on the low table before him, 'I'm breaking a rule for you.'

'Which is?'

'I told you before I never let anyone come home with me.'

He wanted to say that he was different but he saw it was another hand in the game and he was afraid of making the mistake that would put him out altogether, so he reached out for a sandwich to hide behind.

'And now I shall turn you out,' she announced when the plate and mugs were empty. He knew it would be a mistake to argue. He got up smiling. 'Don't you want to know why?'

'I want to know but I'm learning not to ask.'

'Good. Then I'll tell you. I'm going out this evening and I have to get some sleep in first.'

'I'll look out for you on my way home,' Sym said as he ducked his head through the hatch.

'That was clever but I never make the same mistake twice.'

He looked down and saw her face framed in the wooden square of the hatch, a portrait again and took himself up the gangplank and along to *Mimosa* with a depressed jauntiness, trailing the dead branch that had waited disconsolately for him propped against the mooring post. *Mimosa* lay almost reproachfully low in the water, chill and disordered with a litter of unsatisfactory memories. The thin sunlight had drained out of the sky, leaving a brief twilight streaked with yellow ochre that faded into the grey shiver of a winter dawn. There would be a frost again tonight. He would light the fire for comfort and company and tomorrow he would saw up the branch.

When he had filled the cabin with warmth and light and tidied away the dirty breakfast leavings he fell asleep on the bunk, his knees drawn up tight on his misery like a child that cries itself into the dark, and when he woke it was quite dark and late, too late to turn out across the weir, and he was hungry. He cooked the pair of polished brown kippers he had bought that morning, dissected and ate them, dipping unbuttered bread into the thick tangy grease and heaping a neat pile of hair-fine bones on the side of his plate beside the long herring-bone of the vertebrae. Then he ate three slices of bread and pippy raspberry jam to damp down the flavour of smoked fish and sat back with his fourth mug of tea.

It was no good going to bed again just because the hour said so. He was wide awake and fidgety. He cleared the table and sat down to his paper. He was pleased with himself. The used pile was growing while the clean diminished. There might even come a point where he would have to buy some more. He had broken through his own self-imposed barrier of silence. The rule of simplicity he had laid down for himself seemed to be a magic key. Sym wondered if it would vanish if he tried something more difficult, the analysis of his own feelings in the new situation.

'Am I already in love with her and what does that mean anyway in this context?' he wrote. 'Where could this relationship go and do I want it to go anywhere? I can't imagine marriage or her ever considering it. Perhaps the husband is still around somewhere. Was she trying to make me jealous today or was it a statement of fact? I suppose she was going up to town for an evening of someone's company but if she doesn't sleep with them why do I feel as if I'm being deprived? She still has the clothes I lent her which she'll probably give back at some time unless she regards them as fair exchange, payment in kind. Like the bag and the shoes? But then she said . . .' The pencil stopped. He realised he had come round in full circle and the point was blunt anyway. He took a razor blade and sent little white flakes of wood curling into the fire where they spurted into sudden fierce flame and died. He would go back to the beginning, to last night and stick to his own rule. It seemed to be the only way that would work for him.

He had reached the end of the walk for the second time when he found that his biggest lamp was burning low. In his concentration he hadn't noticed it, straining to see the writing until he was aware of near blindness. It was a messy job re-filling. It might be simpler to call it off for the night. He snuffed the last glow to preserve the wick and put his papers away by the faint radiance of the fire. As he moved into the cabin his mouth suddenly turned dry and sour with fear. He stood still, holding on to the door frame, his heart thudding in response to a muffled knocking along the hull of the boat. Sym steadied himself. It sounded as if a large animal was trying to get in but it must be a big piece of driftwood caught between the hull and the bank wall. He wondered whether he should go up and move it along with the boathook. A big enough piece caught awkwardly could poke a hole in the bottom. But it had sounded from the river side. He listened again and thought he heard soft voices.

Pulling the door to to shut out all light from the fire he climbed on a stool and cautiously raised the skylight. He had heard voices then. There were dark shapes moving on the surface of the river. Two strange craft, rafts he thought they might be, were being paddled quietly up-stream, a course that would take them round to the other side of the island. They were unwieldy, inclined to swing off course; just planks lashed together he thought. The second man in particular found steering difficult and swore softly. He must have bumped against *Mimosa* in passing. A sudden patch of light calm water showed up the first figure in silhouette and instinctively Sym knew it was Dick, the slight body and curly hair. He imagined him smiling in the dark as the other man swore and struggled with the current and he felt his flesh cringe a little though it might have been the cold knife edge of dank air that slid over the rim of the skylight and through the open neck of his shirt.

They were almost out of sight now. He closed the heavy

frame and stepped down. Lying in his bunk he asked himself if the other man could have been Walden and if so what it meant though he had no reason to think that it should be. He carried the idea with him down into sleep and a sense of apprehension ran confusedly through all his dreams so that even though he slept late he woke bleary and dull with a taste of bile on his tongue.

Now there was the same problem: after a morning of painting the deck, standing up to shade his eyes against the soft haze from the surface of the river as he waited hopefully for her to come along the bank and bending down again to the parallel lines of the planking, he felt giddy and depressed. Should he go and look for her in the *Yacht* at communion with Walden? He would wait. Why should he strip his dependence bare for them both to smile over? It was her move. Suppose she didn't come? His feet were on the gangplank but he turned back again, his mouth aching for the long pull that would go straight down and flood his gut with soothing liquid. Instead he made himself coffee and sat in the sun drinking it. A small noisy launch roared past setting up a wash that rocked *Mimosa* and slopped the coffee in the mug. The man at the wheel yelled sorry but didn't drop his speed. Sym heard Walden's voice, 'Cut your bloody wash! Think they own the river in their fancy dress and fibre-glass bottoms. Bloody hearty-beasts!' But the words were only in his own head.

It was just gone two when he saw her coming along the bank, not hurrying, as if she was out for a stroll, a brown paper bag in her hand.

'We waited for you. When you didn't come I remembered the painting.'

'What did Walden say?'

'I think your virtuous application to duty upset him rather.'

Sym laughed, delighted. 'So you came to find me?'

'Well I didn't really want to take these back again. I thought you might need them.' She gave him the bag of clothing.

'You'll stay now you've come?' Sym asked.

'Yes, I'll stay.' He let her lead him down into the boat.

It was lucky he had done that bit of painting he thought later. They had watched the bonfire that Dick had made of the rubbish tip for his own and Walden's children on Guy Fawkes' night and Sym had remembered it as an attempt to warm the dying sun as the flames leapt against the backcloth of trees and the children skipped like marsh fire patterning the shadows with their sparklers. But the sun sulked and wouldn't be drawn. He had never known a year when the days drew down so soon, shuttered into perpetual twilight. Work grew slack as rain and wind railed on them day after day. Often he didn't bother to go at all. They lay together in the cabin watching the firelight until it was time for her to go he no longer asked where and he would seek out Walden or spend himself worrying his unasked questions into words.

Once as they lay there he had queried, 'What do they do at night on the river?' He had heard the voices again two or three times, loading an engine into a dinghy, even towing against the current which was running high and fast now.

'"Watch the wall, my darling, while the gentlemen go by."' Sassie touched his bare shoulder lightly with her finger.

'Meaning?'

'Ask Walden, he might tell you.'

'You know damn well he won't.'

'Why do you think I know?'

'You all know except me. Dick's in it, I know that.'

'Then ask him.'

Sym moved restlessly. 'Sometimes I get tired of playing games. You're all like a lot of kids.'

'It's all a game, can't you see that?' Sassie drew him round to face her. 'It just depends what kind of game you like, what you're best at.'

'The rest of the world isn't playing.'

'Oh they pretend they're not with their long faces, going to work in the morning as if it were something important or real but they're all only pretending. Haven't you watched children playing? How serious they are being doctors and fathers and mothers?'

'And is this all pretence then?' he looked down at her.

'You have to decide that for yourself. I can't tell you.'

He kissed her hard and long to block out the doubt that spread like a fungus in his own mind and then she laughed a little, seeing through it, he realised, and pulled him down to her, making him forget. But after he knew what she had done and the question came back at him unresolved. Sometimes he wondered if she couldn't help pushing him so far and then grew frightened and called him back. Perhaps he wasn't the only one who could make mistakes. It comforted him a bit.

One bleak afternoon he had gone along the bank from *Mimosa*, away from the other boats and the weir to the far end of the island where he turned up into the undergrowth looking for wood for the insatiable blackleaded belly of the stove. He had never been here before, never walked the whole circumference of the island. Sym wasn't conscious of treading quietly but the silence among the trees imposed itself on him until he was almost tip-toeing. No birds sang or stirred on the leafless branches. Soon he came at right angles to a path that led deeper into the stillness and he followed it until he found a beached pontoon with flaking wooden walls but a neat watertight cap of tarry roofing felt. Smoke rose straight into the air from the pointing finger of chimney but there was no other sound or sign of life. Was this where Gypsy Dick kept his family or perhaps it belonged to the old man Sym had passed on the weir in the fog though he couldn't imagine him sober enough to light a fire or repair a roof?

The path led him on again, more concerned now with tracking it than with the wood he had come to find. And then it ceased as a path, only an indentation in the line of trees showed where it might have been like the shadowy tracings on an aerial photograph. He pushed in among the trees and the way closed behind him. He felt a childish thrill at the thought that he might get lost but his adult mind spoiled it with the correction that he had only to keep on in a straight line and he would come to the river again. It was all around, comfortingly encompassing the island. The thrill subsided; he remembered why he was here.

Underfoot the soil was rich with leafmeal spilled from the trees, sometimes gravelled with beachmast that Sym crunched with a satisfaction he couldn't pin down but lay somewhere, he thought, between sensual and aggressive or perhaps they were the same thing anyway, his mind led on. He paused to roll and light a cigarette, carefully blowing out the match before he flicked it away. The twig kindling scattered everywhere like rooks' droppings was pretty damp but the risk of setting the whole island ablaze wasn't one he cared to take on. Sym imagined them all formed into a bucket chain vainly trying to damp down the licking flames and being driven back to the water's edge into the shallows while the trees above them burst into fiery bud, put on their orange and crimson leaf again and crumpled self-consuming in a flurry of ash and sparks. It would be like the end of the world or an M.G.M. epic. He smiled to himself and moved on again.

He was changing and he knew it but he couldn't decide the quality of the change or whether it was for better or worse, richer or poorer, sickness or health. Walking in the silent wood he tried to examine this change. Did he love Sassie? If so it was quite different from his love for Anna but then had he really loved Anna or were these all questions he should have grown out of into a kind of acceptance? He thought, felt and saw more than he had done before coming to the island but he was sometimes aware that it had a feverish quality about it hallucinatory perhaps. At other times he wondered if he was mad, if they all were. If it was something in the river air. The Elizabethans had believed in the ability of the dank night air to bring sickness; if you slept with the moon shining on you it would send you mad. Perhaps they had all slept in the moonlight or were too far from urban reality adrift in little cockleshells.

His arms were nearly full now, enough wood to last them a few weeks but he couldn't decide whether to turn back or to keep on to the bank. It was difficult going with the ungainly lengths of wood, ducking under branches that reached out to take them back again, fighting his way backwards against twisted ropes of dried bramble that tore at his clothes. Suddenly the going was easier. He stood up, straightened his aching back. It seemed to be a small clearing and on the other side dense scrub again. He moved forward looking for an easier way through. Then he noticed that the branches in front of him were dead, not just dormant in a winter death but dry, skeletal. They had been stuck upright in the earth as if they were growing but Sym lifted them out quite easily.

There was a flicker of movement that made him start and then he was looking into four pairs of eyes.

'It's no good,' said Jane. 'He's found us.'

'I'm sorry,' Sym said. 'I didn't know.'

'Nobody knows, do they, Jane?' said Sophy. The other two children, whom he just recognised from the bonfire night as Dick's, stared at him with dark unmoving eyes.

'Now we shall have to move,' said Jane.

'I won't tell anyone,' Sym tried to reassure them.

'Daddy says you can't trust people, doesn't he?' Sophy asked again.

'She talks too much,' Jane explained. 'She's only six; she gets things mixed up.'

'Suppose I promised?'

The small brown boy spoke for the first time. 'What's a promise?'

'It's saying you'll do something when you don't mean to,' Jane supplied.

'Promises are like pie-crust, made to be broken,' Sophy chanted.

Sym wondered why they were so hostile. 'Then you'll have to move,' he said.

'It took us ages to find this place,' Jane seemed to relent a little. They had hollowed out a natural dip, roofing it with a piece of canvas beneath a screen of bushes.

'Why aren't you at school anyway?' even as he asked he knew it was the wrong thing to say.

'Daddy says it's a . . .'

'It's a holiday,' Jane cut in smoothly but he felt it was a lie. He couldn't remember any possible holidays at that time of the year.

They all stared at him and he began to feel uncomfortable. How could he extract himself with his adult dignity intact? 'I was looking for wood when I found you. Is it better to go on or to go back the way I came?'

'We go both ways,' said Sophy.

'But we're small; we can get through. Adults find it difficult. We heard you coming miles away,' Jane said. Her sense of superiority overwhelmed him. He was glad he didn't have to teach her. She'll give some poor devil a hell of a time later on, Sym thought.

'I'd better go back then,' he turned away from them. 'And if I meet anyone I won't say I've seen you.'

'Thank you very much,' he heard the small grave voices chorus politely behind him.

He was tired when he got back to *Mimosa*; the children had deflated him. Half past three and it would soon be dark. The clouds hung low and impenetrable. The surface of the river was a sheet of dull aluminium; the air between water and sky struck rawly into his flesh. Sym broke some of the wood for the fire, made himself tea and sat warming his hands on the blue-ringed mug and prodding the fire with the poker for a semblance of life.

'. . . dead and interr'd
Yet all these seem to laugh
Compared with me
Who am their epitaph.'

When it was fully dark he left the warm cabin and went through into the small washroom. He had a job to do that he had been putting off in spite of Walden's assurances that that was how everyone did it. He took the seat and cover from the top of the plastic bucket and carried it flinching up the ladder onto the deck. The mingled smells of chemicals and ordure slopped a little in their passage into the air turned his stomach. Stepping to the side, Sym braced himself against the rail and tipped the lot overboard, steadying himself as he imagined himself slipping and pitching in after. Kneeling down and leaning over the catwalk he was just able to dip the bucket into the current and swill it vigorously twice. Gingerly he put his nose to it. The smell had gone. He felt quite pleased with himself. He had successfully polluted the river. He stood up; there wasn't a soul about. No one shouted at him from the bank. It was easy really. He wondered whether the fishes minded. He thought of the summer swimmers and the weekend sailors who toppled out of their dinghies. It was always said that the plumpest bream lurked in the shadow of the houseboats. No wonder their flesh was so murky and unappetising.

Reprimed he returned the bucket to its place, the Aegean blue chemical making his eyes smart until he dropped the lid on it. Perhaps civilisation makes us too squeamish. Why is it we can all stomach our own corruption, excretion, but not someone else's. He had read somewhere that it was very difficult to make astronauts accept urine reprocessed into the drinking water system. Every man wanted his own back and threw up at the thought of someone else's. It was the knowing that made the difference. After all we accepted sewage farms and filter beds without a blink simply because most of us never gave it a thought. The small boys ducking each other in the oily lower reaches by the docks didn't seem to take any harm. Sym wondered what Sassie would think of her philosophy reduced to these terms. It was Hamlet and the nitrogen cycle bundled up in a job lot together and a lot more too he suspected if he sat down and thought about it.

Living on the river certainly made you less fastidious. It must be very like the centuries before hygiene and hot water. Even Sassie had a slightly tousled look—he had noticed it the first time he saw her. Ironing was difficult; clothes were drip or rough dried. Washing itself was a problem both for the body and its coverings. Sym was conscious of the smell of his skin, tangyer between the thighs and underarm; he snuffed at it as he remembered doing as a child. He was aware of his underwear slept-in because of the shock of stepping naked into the morning and the fear of a sudden catastrophe in the night that wouldn't wait while you put your clothes on. Once a week he went to the public baths and soaked beside the coalman and the dustman. How did the wives manage with babies and small children? Sym couldn't even begin to imagine.

At first he had hung his clothes in the wardrobe after he had sealed the deck above until he had gone one day to put on his suit and found it spotted with mildew and smelling of toadstools. It had been cleaned and never removed from the polythene bag the cleaners had put it in. Now he wore the river uniform: jeans, crumpled shirt and heavy sweater with a blue donkey jacket to top it all.

Curiously though he had never been so well in his life. Mentioning it one day to Walden he had decided that along with squeamishness in urban life went a proneness to minor ills.

'That's right,' Walden had said. 'The children never have colds, don't even bring them home from school.'

'What makes a cold then?' Sym had asked.

'The desire or the need to have one. Breaks the monotony, gives the poor buggers a day or two off when they can't stand it any longer.'

'What about germs—those little wiggly things they see under a microscope?'

'Germs come in when the resistance is lowered; any crackpot scientist'll tell you that. Nothing lowers the resistance quicker than boredom and misery. Simple. Here there's always something to do or not to do. Less pernickerting concern with the material trappings.'

As usual he had taken it too far Sym had thought but all the same there was something there. He would like to know whether Walden put down the whole of twentieth-century progress on the debit side: infant mortality rates, greater life expectancy, better social conditions, the lot. In fact he would go and ask him. He would eat first and then go and seek him out. They would have a good evening going at it hammer and tongs together and he wouldn't think what Sassie was doing or where she was. Outside the wind rose from the whipped skin of the water and drove the clouds scurrying leaving the sky with a bitter clarity.

December

. . . all grays the grass that green was ere

'TONIGHT,' she said, 'I want something different.'

'You're not going out?' he tried to keep the eagerness out of his voice.

'We'll both go out.' She sat up. They had gone to bed in the half-light of the afternoon leaving the oil stove burning in the saloon for warmth and the door open. Sym kept it on at nights too now.

He had wanted her to take her clothes off but she had complained that it was too cold and they had made love, 'Like Eskimos,' he said. 'Suppose we had six months of night with nothing else to do? How long before we'd melted the walls of our snowhouse?'

'Imagine the blocks of snow shrinking away like ice-cream on a hot day until there was just a double bed standing in the middle of a great plain of ice.' Sassie had laughed and kissed him and he had wondered whether she was changing a little too. 'We'll take my dinghy and row up the river,' she said now.

'Won't you be cold?'

'I'll get another sweater before we go.'

'I don't know how good I'll be at rowing. I haven't done any for years and then it was only once or twice when I was a student.'

'It's easy really and we're not in a hurry. If we go now you'll have the tide with you coming back when you're tired.'

'I'm tired now. I've been working hard.' He drew a finger down her back to the base of the spine so that she shivered a little. How was it she always knew the tides and the weathers, he wondered, almost in advance as an animal knows them.

'Perhaps we'll meet the smugglers or pirates you're always hearing.'

'Oh it's too early for them.' Realising she was determined to go Sym zipped up his heavy-duty levis and felt around for his boots. He had bought them second-hand from a tot shop and they reminded him of his father. When he looked down it was almost as if he was walking with his father's feet. They were a size too large to take the thick seamen's socks he wore now and he dubbined them religiously to keep out the wet.

'You haven't taken my advice.'

'They shouldn't make so much noise, then I wouldn't know they were there.'

'Isn't it a kind of voyeurism?'

'Yes, I suppose it is. But then girls who undress in front of open curtains with the light on have a responsibility too. Weren't you taught at school not to leave money lying about as a temptation to the weaker brethren?'

He thought a shadow crossed her face for a moment then she said, 'Oh but ours was a church school. We were always having religion sold to us in some shape or form. In the end you didn't take any notice. It was just something the priests had to say as part of their job.'

'It doesn't make it untrue.'

'It does to a child. If you don't like the person who tells you something then you can't accept what they say, and if you don't accept it it isn't true.'

Sym wanted to say that she wasn't a child any more but he was afraid she would change her mind about staying with him and decide to go out after all so he picked up his coat, turned the fire low and went up onto the bank. He was hungry but he had noticed that she rarely felt hunger. He hoped he would be able to row on an empty stomach.

As if she had heard his thoughts she said, 'Are you hungry?' He pulled a face. 'I thought you would be. Wait a minute; I'll get us something when I fetch my sweater.

She disappeared up the gangway into the little boat. Sym stared at the dinghy bobbing on a painter over the stern. His eyes were half shut against the cold wind. A faint radiance of starshine spread over the water giving an illusion of light now that his eyes were used to it. He thought they must be mad to trust themselves out on the icy water but supposed that the exercise would warm him up. The dinghy was in better condition than the boat as far as he could make out. It seemed to have been recently painted.

She had only been gone a few minutes but he was chilled through.

'I was beginning to think you'd find a solid block standing here like Lot's wife if you were much longer.' He looked hopefully for any indication of food. She held out her hand opening it gently over his palm. Something small, round and hard lay there like a dry pea. 'What is it?' he asked.

'Your supper.' He heard her laughing in the dark but couldn't see her face.

'Hell!'

'It's a slimming pill. It'll stop you feeling hungry.'

He was cheated like the sea anemone in the story whose mouth closed on a pebble. 'Games again.'

'They work though. Try it.'

He rolled it between his fingers. 'I think I can manage without it.' He held it up so that she would see and with a sudden pressure of finger and thumb spurted it over the side.

'You shouldn't do that. They're costly,' Sassie said. 'Now you'll be hungry

He pulled the dinghy towards them by the painter. 'Let's get on with this crazy idea.' He helped her down into the boat and they moved out towards the middle of the river using their hands to fend off the tall shapes of the other hulls. Setting the oars in the rowlocks he asked, 'Which way?'

'Turn her round and we'll head upstream.'

'You'll have to guide me.' He drew heavily on the left-hand blade dipping it deep in the water and the boat swung round. He corrected with the right until they were pointing straight and then began to pull against the stream. It took him a few hundred yards and all his concentration to settle himself into a ragged rhythm. His right arm was much stronger than the left and the dinghy moved crabwise through the water but they were progressing faster than the current drove them back. Sym had been afraid that he would fail completely. It was like a test, an examination that he had to pass although he wasn't sure what it would admit him for if he did. Sassie leant back in the boat and he could see her quite clearly, the features softened by shadow like a dream woman. He thought she was smiling again but couldn't be sure. He pulled away from her and it was as if he was pulling towards her although the distance between them remained the same, and he forgot his hunger and cold. The flash of water from the blades drew his eyes, bright drops sewn on the dark stuff of the water. Could she see him as clearly or was it an illusion worked with the refracting mirror of the polished surface of the river?

'The dinghy's in pretty good condition,' he said now that he could rest a little. 'Did you do it up yourself?'

'It was done for me. I came up one morning and found it had been cleaned and painted inside. Then it disappeared completely for a couple of days and when it came back the bottom had been done. Very well too.'

'Weren't you worried, when it wasn't there I mean?'

'I knew it would come back.'

'And you didn't ask of course.'

'Who'd done it? No, that would be silly. People who ask don't get things done for them again.'

'Someone must be using it and want it in good condition.' She shifted a little to one side, upsetting the balance of the boat and making Sym pull hard on the left-hand oar to even the course. Pointing to a groove in the stern she said, 'Sometimes they fit an outboard on here.'

'Where's the nearest timber yard?' Sym asked suddenly but he wasn't quick enough.

'You're learning.' She trailed one hand through the water so that it gleamed wetly under the breaking skin of water. 'It's like running your hand through glass; it's so cold.' He expected to see her lift it back into the boat running red, the fingers sheared away, but it was quite whole of course though without substance in the starshine. 'The moon will be up soon. It rises early tonight. Pull towards the right, your right or we shall run into Swan's Island. They nest there.'

He looked towards the small dark mass fringed with untidy trailing hair of willow and matted scrub. 'Does anyone live there?'

'Only the swans.'

They were moored under the branches he could see. One or two of them unfolded their long necks and made stately towards them like intercepting coastguards. Sym had never been on a level with them before, beak level. There were stories that they could break a man's arm with a blow from one wing. Sassie made chirruping noises at them as if they were domestic fowl and they followed the dinghy in a kind of dignified homage.

'They won't hurt unless they're teased except in the breeding season,' his thoughts were answered. It was like looking at a negative, the white forms moving against the dark background as if by daylight they should be black, on pale water.

A little shiver went through him and he was conscious of the lurking cold that ran its hands over his body as soon as he slackened his effort on the oars, and he pulled strongly, thrusting away from the sensations of cold and hunger that threatened him. Through the lighted windows of riverside bungalows as they drew past he could see other people's lives, the quality of light giving a clue to the activity inside even before he could make out distinct figures: fireglow for lovers, the dinner-party candle-lit, a bedside lamp for solitary reading, the fantasy blue of television. They passed other boats too, swinging quietly with the tide on their mooring chains, sometimes quite dark and silent, others dropping chequers of light and music into the night.

'Are you cold yet?'

'No not yet.' He had worked up a sweat again under his thick wrappers that seemed to oil his muscles and keep them swinging and dipping the blades without his thinking about it. Occasionally he grew overconfident and one oar would dig deep or skitter on the icy surface to remind him that he was still a novice. 'Are you?'

'We'll come to a drink soon. No sign of your smugglers.'

'You probably warned them. Besides we've got their boat.' He heard her laugh but couldn't see her face anymore. The moon had risen behind her and she was leaning slightly forward, whether to see better or shrugging off the bitter air he wasn't sure, but he could see her breath rising whitely and thought he must be cocooned in a froth of steam like a carthorse. He felt that somewhere over his shoulder there were lights and warmth but he couldn't turn his head to look. He might upset the boat with any sudden movement and the picture of them floundering in the cut-glass embrace of the river, the icy slivers probing his gasping lungs made him almost sick with fear. It was the lack of food of course. People drifted for days in open boats in the North Sea or the Atlantic and were found alive. He watched his body swept under the bridges, towards the open sea under a cloud of scavenging gulls, carrion, and fetching up on an oily shore rocked gently by the waves and very dead. 'Can you swim?' Sym asked.

'We won't have to, we're nearly there.'

'There's always going back.'

'Pull over to the right bank, that jetty, see?' she pointed. Carefully he eased the dinghy across the current until it bumped against stone steps. Sassie stood up with the painter in her hand, was over the side with a practised movement and holding the bobbing coracle steady for him as he stepped out. His leg muscles seemed to be atrophied, the palms of his hands had blistered at the base of the thumbs. The stone stairs were unreal, inclined to slip sideways or melt away under his feet. She drew the boat along the wall and knotted the rope through a ring. Then she led him up through the stark trees of a bare winter garden to a complex of large buildings bulked against the sky. They passed round the side and he was just conscious of light raining onto empty flower beds before he followed her into a hall where warmth fell over his head like the cosseting folds of a blanket.

Sym was afraid for a moment that the contrast might be too much for him and he would curl up on the spot and sleep but as if she knew this too there was a touch on his arm and he was guided into a high bar decorated in traditional Spanish hacienda style with arches and alcoves and bullfight posters on the walls. Sassie led him to a corner under a trellis twined with dusty plastic vines and settled herself where the subdued lighting fell most kindly on her face.

'I think two whisky-macs after that.'

Sym went over to the bar and ordered from the barman in white monkey jacket and red cummerbund, wondering if he wore Spanish heels below the black silk trousers. 'The usual for Mrs. Parks?' the waiter asked.

'Two whisky-macs.' The price stunned him and he brought them back reverently lest he should spill a drop of the liquid gold. But they were good, ran molten down the thoat into the taut body and lay innocent as amber or rich honey in the bottom of the glass.

'In a little while, when we've had another couple of these, we'll have some dinner,' she leaned back on the silk quilted bench.

'Here?'

'There's a dining room through there.'

'You might have warned me. I'm not really dressed for it and I've only got a couple of pounds on me.'

'No, this is my idea. I'm paying for it.' The liquorice bag was on the seat beside her. Her coat had fallen open and he saw that she was wearing soft black wool with a gleam of something at the throat.

'Well, you're dressed for both of us, so that will have to do.'

A tall greying man stood over them swaying slightly. 'Sassie my dear!'

'Hallo, Lance. This is Sym.'

'Let me get you both a drink.' They sat silent while he went to the bar and came back again. 'How nice this is,' he continued. 'You haven't honoured us lately and now I see why of course. Charming, delightful.'

'But not for you, dear.' She said it almost gently, Sym thought.

He made a face. 'I love you all, you know that. Still I mustn't interrupt. You'll be in again.' He smiled through his gapped teeth and bowed away.

'An old flame of yours?'

'Of anyone's. Poor Lance.' She was letting him see down the passages of her life, a door opening suddenly just a crack, voices, figures in cameo, and then shut again. 'Shall we eat now?'

They were beyond soup and hors-d'œuvres and all introductions to their main course when she set down her knife and fork and said, 'You're very young,' as if this was the real substance of the occasion.

This time he should protest, defend himself. 'Old enough to have a wife and child.'

'That's what I mean. "Have"—how can you have a person? Things, possessions, images, symbols: if you reduce people to those you can have them. "He had her." You might as well say he used her. Masculine arrogance; little boys boasting.' She said it all lightly, smiling at him and rolling the wine she had ordered caressingly round the glass but he felt the words bite and remembered Anna. He had never talked to anyone about it, feeling it a kind of betrayal, a thrust she couldn't defend herself against by absence. So he had said simply, 'Writers shouldn't marry. I'm a bastard to live with,' and that had been enough. Curiously he felt no disloyalty this time. The sore was healing now he was forgetting to give it a private lick.

'Don't we play at being what we're expected to be instead of what we are, is that what you mean?' She nodded. 'But can we help it? Where men are men and women are women for want of a better arrangement as somebody said.'

'We're all frightened.' She leaned back now letting the light fall full on her face so that it was older and harsher than he had seen it before backed by the grotesque make-believe of the décor.

'You're not frightened?' It was half question, half pleading.

'All of us, if we've any sense, and if we haven't diverted it all into tiny material fears we think we can cope with. That's why we can be exploited so easily, made to do and be what ever's required of us.'

'They crack the whip and we jump because we're full of fears and inadequacy.'

'And we don't love ourselves, we despise ourselves.'

Sym looked round at the two or three dining couples and wondered what their conversations were. 'Why do people live on the river?' he asked.

'Sometimes because they've half glimpsed the real anxiety and they can't blind themselves with the getting and spending anymore.'

'Can't it be just as big a delusion?'

'Not quite,' she said slowly. 'You can't disguise it so well. It breaks through.'

'So I must have seen a bit, a corner of something to be here at all?'

'When I said you're very young still I also meant you still have a chance.'

'And what about you?' Sym said. 'You see it all.'

'Look,' she said, 'people are going to dance.'

A three-piece band had been playing while they ate but he had thought it was only a background like tea-time music. Now as she spoke one or two couples had begun to circle slowly. 'Can you dance?'

'What, in these?' He looked down at his jeans.

'Why not?' Sassie stood up, the coat falling back. They danced very close as if they were alone on the floor, the other couples their own shadows. He felt the softness of her belly through her dress and once he rested his mouth against her neck. Some of her years had rubbed off on him, leaving her younger, while he would be her age as long as their relationship lasted.

Going back the tide pulled with him at the oars and he was caught up in the ease of it. Once she said, 'It'll be a hard winter,' as they slid from the black ice of thick shadow into the cold clarity of the moonlight. The air stung his throat as he sucked it in. It reminded him of his childhood, his boot flawing and shattering the glass puddles in the gutter on his way to school and sliding downhill on the rimed pavements. Children knew so much more about the weather and then as you got older it receded behind grimy windows, you became indoor creatures, only surprised suddenly by a clash of sunlight as you opened the street door before you could shelter from it down a subway or behind the curtaining reek of the top of a bus.

'You're like a cat,' he said. 'You always seem to know what weather it'll be. Don't you ever get caught out?'

'Sometimes, but you'll see I'm right this time. There are certain signs you can't miss.'

'I'll look out for them.'

But he didn't have to look; they sought him out, dredged him up from the deep sleep he had fallen into after he had brought the dinghy, wearily by now, to the stern of her little boat and seen her inside, then back along the bank to *Mimosa*, feet numb, arms dangling brokenly from their sockets. He turned over protesting. What had wakened him? Switching on the torch he kept always beside the bunk he looked at his watch. It was three o'clock. Late for the smugglers, damn cold too. He didn't envy them, not tonight. Then he heard the wailing, demonic, echoing through the wooden skin of the hull like a buzz-saw.

It was a cat of course; he knew that at once. There were several on the island, some belonging to the boats, some gone wild in the undergrowth and hardly ever seen, except that sometimes you were conscious of fierce yellow eyes following you out of danger. The yowling rose to a swearing scream. Claws scrabbled on the planks over his head. It couldn't be a mating couple or even the toms fighting at this time of the year. Sym lay still. Two bodies struggled and pounded up on the deck. For a moment there was silence. A shape leapt across the skylight, another, and the fight began again. It was a fight to the death. Up there two furry bodies bit and clawed, tore at each other's flesh. The cold had driven a rat onto the boats and there one of the cats had cornered it and pounced. It was an uneven conflict, with size and two heavily armoured claws on the cat's side and the sharp-fanged snarl of the rat on the other, but his sympathies were all with the cat. They were very self-contained all the island cats but he had made friends with a little she who lived on the converted M.T.B. that lay like a great grey whale just before the weir. At first she had looked at his outstretched hand with disdain but gradually she had come to accept him and he had even found her sunning herself on *Mimosa*'s deck and beguiled her with cream from the top of the bottle until she would let him lift her up. Under the long tabby fur she had the light fine bones of a bird. 'They're the worst,' Walden had said once, 'the little girl cats. They fight like wild things. The toms are too lazy. You wouldn't think half a dozen kittens could hide in their bodies, would you?'

Perhaps it was Suki up there now. She had produced a litter a few weeks ago, five of whom had bubbled their way out of life as soon as they had entered in a bucket of water. The other, a black tom, was already growing fat in neutered serenity. She no longer had any time for him and had taken more and more to *Mimosa*. Should he get up and help her or let her fight her own battles? Even if he settled this one there would be others. Abruptly the thumping and swearing stopped. It was answered for him now one way or the other. Usually the cat won if the rat didn't jump overboard. It was safe in the water. Sym imagined her now if it had got away crouched staring into the dark, the striped brush twitching with frustration and then the burred tongue teazling the coat to rights.

That was the first time; night after night the conflict was renewed until it no longer even woke him. But he was half-conscious of it through his dreams and knew in the morning that the struggle went on. Once he thought the little cat limped and he wondered if she had been bitten but when he saw her again she seemed whole and he forgot about it in his new distraction.

'Have you emptied those bilges yet?' Walden nagged him. 'One day you'll find them lapping round your ears and you won't even know where to start.' Sym had noticed the river smell, 'unforgettable, unforgotten', they joked, had grown stronger in the last week. Was it the cold, the winter damps? Or was it the rising water level in the bottom of the boat? He knew where to look; had found it when he was painting the deck, a square cut in the planking: a hatch that must lead down. For a moment he had even been tempted to caulk it straight across, seal it off completely but he resisted. Now he couldn't put it off any longer.

'Chose a Sunday morning after Sassie had gone when I knew I had all the hours til opening time and wouldn't be disturbed. No one could wander along and tell me I was doing it the wrong way and why didn't I do this, that or the other. Took the old inch chisel and got it under the edge of the hatch and finally managed to lever one side up. Pretty heavy and it nearly bit my fingers off getting them under for a good heave. And there it was: a great gaping hole in the deck with the light falling into it and catching on the water swilling about at the bottom. Yes, there was water there alright but then I'd always known in my truthful moments there would be and it was almost a relief to see it. There was no way down and a five-foot drop to what I supposed must be the bottom of the boat and nearly a foot of murky water. I lowered myself over the edge and felt about with my feet. There was a loose baulk of timber that looked as if it had been used for standing on or I could try to straddle the pool of tears without coming apart in the middle. I got my feet on the beam and wriggled it until it was firm and I could stand up on it still holding on to the hatchway. Then came the nasty part of crouching down and steadying myself against the side of the hull or anything else I could find to hang on to.

What was I afraid of? What was there to be afraid of? I ducked down and held my breath, peering about til my eyes got used to the gloom. It had been cold up on deck with a rare grey light. Down here it was dank bone-gnawing cold with a foul raw stink of oil and rotten water. I was afraid of the dust and the dark corners, that something might fall on me, run over me while I was trapped down there with no quick way up. The hands and head are the most vulnerable; seaboots and tight tucked-in trousers and a highnecked jersey keep the body and legs armoured. I made myself crouch there til I could see clearly and the panic went out of my mouth.

In front of me there was an engine mounted on two heavy blocks with crosspieces. It gleamed still like dull brass and seemed in pretty good condition. So *Mimosa* must have moved once. I imagined the ghost of her chugging away under the bridge down under her own steam. She was no converted lifeboat. She had a history. I remembered Walden saying once that she was a naval pinnace. She might have been anywhere, any seas, in her time. The engine accounted for the oil in the bilge water.

A shelf ran round the stern on a level with my head and there were old pots of paint on it, a stirrup pump, a bucket on a fraying rope, a torn yellow plastic baler. That was the answer to the water problem. You filled the bucket with the baler, climbed out and tipped the bucket over the side. I reached up and took them down. No good putting it off. I might as well get started.'

It took him about five minutes to fill the bucket. Then he scrambled up with the rope, hauled it up, slopping some back into the bottom to be baled out again, emptied it over the side in a brown stream where it broke into tell-tale rainbows on the surface of the river. Pollution again. Then back down into the bilge for another. After half an hour and six buckets he sat back on the beam and unfolded his painfully bent legs. There seemed no visible difference in the level of the water. He thought of the great drinking horn Thor was given to drain whose tip stood in the sea. Was it coming in as fast as he took it out? If so the boat would have sunk over the past months. He bent forward trying to see beyond the engine, beyond the struts that supported it. He caught the roll and dull shine of water and suddenly he knew the answer. The bilges ran the whole length of the boat in interconnecting sections. It wasn't just the water he could see; there was water under the saloon and the cabin, even up in the little sharp fore-cabin, draining down towards him as he baled. Well, now he had started he would go on. He would get it all out until the bottom was absolutely dry even if it took him all day. He bent down again and took hold of the torn baler.

He was adrift in the open sea where every wave slapped an angry fist of water over the side and there was only the torn baler that dropped half back in again if he wasn't careful and the swinging slopping bucket. He bent and scooped, the bitter cold water staining and numbing his hands as he dipped into it. The muscles of his back and legs were drawn and stiff, his shoulders cracked with pain. His only respite was the moment when he straightened up with the empty bucket. Even the taste for a smoke had gone, driven away by the oily reek, His head swung on the frayed rope, his stomach filled with the rank brown liquid. Somehow he kept on, driving himself into an hour, an hour and a half, when for the first time he noticed a difference in the level, a beam began to show on either side that he could brace his feet on. Up ahead under the engine he saw the hair line of water advancing towards him leaving a wake of sludge and black-wet wood. As the level dropped it became more difficult to fill the baler crushed into the V-shape on either side of the keel. Now he saw why it was torn. Instead of half a dozen to the bucket he was spooning it in in driblets so that the last five took twice as long. But he wouldn't give up. The urgency of the sinking boat still possessed him. He tried the stirrup pump with its length of rubber tubing poked through a round hole in the hull that had obviously been made for the purpose but it was faulty and sent gushes of dirty water down his boot. He put it back until the last few puddles where the baler wouldn't reach and drove the handle furiously so that even the gouts that fell back were sucked away in the end and trickled into the river after the rest.

It was done. The last drains had been the worst and his bones felt petrified into their contorted positions but it was worth it. He shifted a bit on his haunches. He would have given anything for a smoke now but he remembered the river-bank warnings that any leak in the calor-gas system sank immediately into the bilges and would blow up if you struck a match. He wondered how he had learned so much without really being aware that he was absorbing it and if he would have the strength to climb out. He looked at his watch. It was half past twelve. He had been down there over two hours. The next time bilges were mentioned he would be able to say they were quite dry.

Behind him light crept through a slit under the decking and he could see the outline of the rudder. Once he had turned the brass-rimmed wheel in the wheelhouse, playing at ships, and the rough oak trunk of the rudder had turned in unison. As he stared at it and his eyes became accustomed to the penetration of grey light he saw the old chain that worked it and then high up in the stern a curious incrustation of the wood. He prodded it with his finger. The finger thrust through and was withdrawn leaving a round hole and traces of yellow powder on the tip. Further along, the plank had broken into small cubes like pieces of dried sponge. Bending his head he examined the underside of the shelf where two of the main beams ran. Only one was left. Big copper rivets stuck out like hatpegs to show where the other had been on the right while the left-hand one was crumbled in places to a broken honeycomb.

In his exhaustion he felt anger and fear; anger against *Mimosa* for a kind of betrayal. She had tricked him. He had been painting a rotting cadaver. And he was frightened. What should he do about it? What did it mean? It was beyond his experience, a responsibility that he couldn't cope with. He swung himself up onto the deck, put back the hatch and went up onto the bank. He took deep breaths of cold clean air to flush away the smell of corruption. As he looked down on her lying forlornly, a little higher now because of the weight of water he had drawn out of her, his anger died. He could have cried; she was old and somehow shameful and he was unequal to the demands she made on him. He set off for the *Yacht* remembering how he had first met Walden chisel in hand like a surgeon cutting the infected parts from his own boat but realising at the same time that *Mimosa* was probably beyond anything less than major surgery.

'So you're in a panic over a little bit of dry rot?' Walden said cheerfully, lifting a half-empty glass. 'Ignorance, that's your trouble. Know nothing about it.'

'It looks like a lot to me.'

'And it's been there a long time if they've taken one of the stringers out. Who do you think did that? The old lady of eighty?'

'What does that mean?'

'Well, if it's been there a long time why should you suddenly start to shout about it? The bottom isn't going to drop out just because you've found a bit of rot. It's a teak hull and teak isn't affected by dry rot. It's not as if you were going to sea in it. The only thing you've got to watch for is that she doesn't get stove in with some damn great chunk of driftwood. Don't let it build up too much. But then that'd be true of any kind of boat. She's a bloody sight stouter even with a bit of rot than these fibre-glass and tin jobs.'

'Is he right?' Sym turned to Sassie who had been listening, her head turned away as if she was watching for someone to come in but he knew she had heard it all.

'Yes, he's quite right. Walden knows about boats. It's the feeling of being cheated you don't like. You keep looking for abstract worth. You don't learn. You think now you'll never feel the same about her.'

Sym looked down into the dregs at the bottom of his glass. She had seen right through him. If they had been alone he would have been able to answer but Walden was there grinning at his defeat. There was no comfort for him here. Sassie drained her glass and picked up her bag. She was going and he had hoped she would come back and make it all better. But at the same moment he realised what it was that he was asking, that he should be able to run crying to her like a kid with a broken toy, saying it was all spoilt and would she mend it, kiss it, make it better. He still hadn't learned not to make that kind of demand, not to ask for a relationship of dependence rather than one of equals face to face. Not grown up; that was it. And she was removing herself from him.

'You're off then.' Walden said, and she nodded without speaking and was gone. Sym saw her shadow for an instant caught, stilled, on the frosted glass of the door. Walden emptied his glass too. 'Alright, let's have one more and then I'll come back with you and give it a look over.'

The verdict was the one Sym had suspected. 'She's been neglected. You could have her out and do her all up. That's a splendid old engine. I can remember when she used to chug up and down on Sunday mornings.' He ducked his head and swung his long body down the steps into the saloon. Sym put the kettle on. 'On the other hand since you probably can't afford it you can leave it. She's got years of life in her yet, far longer than you'll want. My God, I wish I had her. I'd do her up and sell her for a thousand. Lovely wood teak; tough as a walnut shell. Keep the rain out and plenty of air circulating and it won't spread. She'll go one day of course but then so will we all.' He accepted the mug of coffee and drew on it like another pint. ' "Christmas is coming, the geese are getting fat," and what are you doing about it?'

'I hadn't thought yet.'

'Come to Christmas dinner; Sassie always does. Only we don't call it Christmas.' He put the mug back on the table, 'You'll see.'

Sym was reassured: he no longer expected *Mimosa* to sink under him but at the same time, as Sassie had said, something had gone though he realised that it was in himself that the difference lurked. *Mimosa* hadn't changed, only his way of seeing her.

Flotsam became his obsession. There came a spell of clear

cold weather when he went to work every day, axing up the earth that had the iron set of frost in it now to reinforce it. He went out in the dark and joined the rest of the gang in Harry's, arms bent, elbows clamped to the table, hands stiff as mechanical grabs round the thick white mugs, blowing and huffing and supping at hot syrupy tea and dripping toast while they waited for Alf with the job sheets.

'Reckon we'll have to jack this lot in soon 'less they issue us with pom-poms. Ground's that hard.'

'You don't want one of them, you got five kids already.'

'That's all the short time we been on, mate; nothing to do but lie abed all day.'

'You heard about that new block of flats in Hertford Gardens where we dug that main up the other week? My brother works for the water board and he had to go round there to inspect. He says they put them up so bad they had to plaster two inches thick one end of the wall and taper it off to a quarter up the other to get it anywhere near the true. He says they're cracking already.'

'That's private enterprise for you. You wait, there'll be a time when they'll be scrambling over each other to buy a council job 'cos they'll be the only ones been put up a bit near the mark.'

'And they're asking six thousand for them. Makes you glad you haven't got that kind of money for the bleeders to do you out of, don't it? Most of them are newly-weds too, my old woman says, you can tell from the curtains. Poor young sods who don't know their arse from their elbow when it comes to a bit of bricks and mortar.'

'Don't you waste your sympathy on them, Stan. They got more to throw away than you ever earned in your whole life. Them silly young sods is earning thirty, forty pound a week.'

'Well, we got thirty in the summer, didn't we?'

'Yeah but we're not getting it now are we? More like twelve if we're lucky.'

'I hope you've got some well stowed away, Sym boy, against this hard old winter what's setting in. Not spent it all on that bit of stuff I see you with the other night. I don't know how a young lad like you can afford a woman like that.'

'Maybe he don't, mate; maybe she affords him. That's what a little bit of education does for you.'

'Now I know why my old mother said I was a fool when I wanted to leave at fourteen.'

'Young Mick's asked for an inside job, you hear that?'

'He knows what side his bread's buttered,' Alf said sitting down at the table. 'He'd rather have it regular than all up and down like you lot. Right now, we got a nice little one lined up here. Take it nice and steady and we'll be home for tea by lighting-up time.'

By Saturday morning when he looked over the side it was matted jungle thick, branches, boughs, split planks, half tree-trunks the thickness of a battering ram and, caught in the tangled mesh, bottles, tins, cabbage stalks, peelings: a floating midden. With the boathook, and a broken oar he had once salvaged as it drifted past, he began the sweating job of sorting the snarled lumber and sending it on its way. Some of the branches were five or six feet long and had formed a woven trellis from which each one had to be gently poked and prodded and, once free, guided along the length of the boat. He had been warned not to let them get caught under the waterline where they could do hidden damage. Sometimes he got a bonus and a whole tangled mass would break free under the push of the current and go drifting away like a floating island. Then the smaller objects which had been caught underneath would bob to the surface and spin away on their own. Sym wondered where it all came from. Some of it was big enough to hole a boat much bigger than *Mimosa*. The Thames was full of it, he had read, not only the stuff carried down from the upper reaches but big stuff lost overboard from sea-going ships. Under a pall of laced twigs covered with brown scum his oar struck the soft body of a dead swan.

A few feathers still embedded in skin broke away under the impact of the broken blade and were hurried away by the river, the buoyant needles twisting in the water race, but the rest remained, the head hanging heavy on the limp neck, dragging along the bottom where the fishes pecked at it with bony lips. Sym steered it gently, sweete Themmes run softelie, disintegrating under every touch until the current took it and the cortège moved away towards the weir. What were their natural enemies? Perhaps an otter upstream, a rat in the dark at its throat while the unsuspecting head was pillowed on the soft down of its wingpit or a poacher. A poacher would have taken it to feast royally or sold it for a regal price. Injured perhaps it had flapped away and drowned. Or died of grief? They were supposed to do that if for any reason their mate was taken away, though he suspected that that was just a legend against human inconstancy.

Trapped it had lingered outside his windows for a week, rocking a little with the changing tide, drifting from porthole to porthole and then back again, galley, saloon, cabin, like a sad ghost. When would it have begun to stink if he hadn't moved it, to call him with the unmistakable voice of corruption? He was glad he didn't have to see the head and thought of the stout bream he had seen lying in wait, only a flick of the muscular tail to show it wasn't a brown stone. He sent a procession of tin cans bobbing after it. Would it sink before it putrified completely or would the stained white pinions keep it afloat? Suppose it had been a human corpse, a drowned child or a woman drifting Ophelia-like, weed or floating hair? It did happen. Sometimes they were asked by the river police to keep an eye open at the locks. He didn't envy whoever found it, though some people of course would enjoy the nine days' fame. 'Yes I fished her out you know. Thanks I will have another. Nearly ran her down with the launch. Not a bad looker in her time. Some old pro wasn't it? Hazards of the profession I suppose. There's always some nutter longing to get his hands round their throats. Nasty business of course.'

He remembered all the swans he had met since coming to the river; the white sails making towards them from Swan Island, the daily converse with them as they foraged up and down the stream, greedy but beautiful with a kind of arrogance as if they knew they were protected, symbolic, heraldic against the unfurled banner of water and sky. Sym had never imagined them subject to this ignominious end knocking under his windows for release.

The sky hung a low belly of cloud overhead. 'Full of snow,' Alf said as they champed their way steadily through their Monday midday break. 'It'll be a white Christmas. What you doing for Christmas, Sym?'

The question seemed familiar. 'I'm going to some friends.' He hadn't given it any thought. Should he buy some presents, cards?

'The commercial feast is on us again,' Walden had said when they had found the bar of the *Yacht* gaudy with streamers on Sunday morning. The shops must be full of it but going to work in the dark and coming home in the dark he hadn't noticed. You usually bought something for the children but what would those grave faces find acceptable? And what should he buy Sassie? Should he try to compete with the real leather handbag and shoes? 'A present,' she had said. Walden was easy: some cigarettes and a half of Scotch. But what about his wife? How did you buy something for someone you hadn't even met? He took himself into the nearest local version of Selfridges, tasteful but expensive for the suburbs where the doctors' and business wives met for morning coffee in the Regency Room to commiserate their daily widowhood, and wandered between the exotic, hygienic pink and white fudge, sugared and scented counters, aware of the hard eyes of the immaculate, aloof assistants appraising his spending power. He grinned to himself as he bought their attention with an expensive bottle of skin perfume for Walden's wife. In the children's department he wandered lost. Boys were so much easier to buy for with the whole range of clockwork gadgetry to choose from. He couldn't imagine that those two would succumb to nurses' uniforms or dollies' teasets. In the end he settled on paints, brushes and good thick book of blank white paper. Even they must have to stay in sometimes when it was too wet. Then as an afterthought he added scarves. Now he was left with Sassie.

Outside the clouds had come lower. Specks of snow crunched underfoot on the pavements like cinders. 'In the bleak midwinter,' chorussed mechanically from a hidden speaker and the red-nosed elderly Rotarian in a muffler shook a collecting box at him as he passed the tree with its fairy lights and gaily wrapped imitation parcels brought out every year dusted and renewed. The butchers' windows were hung thick with corpses, plucked and blooded, each with its audience of bargaining faces. Sym saw it all with Walden's eyes.

Pushing his way through the market he was bombarded with colours and smells, gradations of orange, yellow and red and the ripe-rotten savour of crushed fruit. Nuts, young pine trees with their roots boiled, the leaves already falling, holly with plastic berries and lacquered paper-dry twigs drove him quickly into a side alley where no noise penetrated. His hands were clenched in his pockets against the cold and holding himself back from involvement with the shopping crowds. He passed a petshop with its tang of horsemeat and mousedroppings and stopped in front of a window his eye caught by a bowl overspilling with uncut stones like the precious fragments of glass, scoured and wetly polished by the sea, that children collect on the shore. There were antique clocks and watches and a tray of secondhand rings, some of them Victorian, clusters of opal and full moonstones, garnets and agates with strings of amber and jet beads. It was an incised seal ring that he thought might provide the answer to Sassie's Christmas present. He pushed open the door.

The man who appeared from behind a lighted glass door at the back of the shop was not the Quilpean figure Sym had imagined. He was perhaps only a couple of years older than himself though balding with a slight librarian's stoop, altogether like a junior lecturer. Sym explained his requirements. The man drew back the curtain at the back of the window and took out the tray. It lay on the counter, the stones catching the light with the dull gleam of unearthed treasure.

'We're rather low at the moment. So many people want jewelry at this time of year. But if there's anything there you fancy . . .' he waved his hand over the tray.

'That one,' said Sym.

He thought the man looked at him a little strangely as he drew it out of its place. 'The seal ring. Ah yes. Some people like them. They're rather unusual. The stone is original of course.'

'Original?'

'Roman, second century. The setting is later, much later.'

Sym picked it up between finger and thumb and held it towards the light. 'And the carving?'

The jeweller opened a drawer and brought out a piece of soft wax which he smoothed with his thin fingers before pressing the seal down. The imprint when he took it away showed a woman in long drapery holding a blazing torch and some other symbol which Sym couldn't quite make out. 'Quite perfect, you see.'

'And Roman you say?' He couldn't quite believe that anything so old could be so cheap and genuine.

'Oh yes, definitely Roman. Some of them are Greek.'

'You have others?'

'Not at the moment. Those you see on the wall.' He pointed to a hanging case. 'But not for sale I'm afraid.' The case held a treatise on incised stones and one or two examples. The name at the bottom of the treatise was the same as that over the door.

'I'll take this one then.'

There was a moment's hesitation. 'I think perhaps . . . Are you superstitious?'

Sym smiled. 'Not particularly. Why? Is it unlucky?'

The man didn't smile. He looked down quickly and then up at Sym with an intense stare. 'I feel I have to tell you. Some people find them unlucky.'

'Why should that be?' Sym looked at the ring trying to detect any malevolent influence.

'They are Gnostic stones.'

'Gnostic?'

'You know about the Gnostics?'

'A little.'

'They believed in the power of secret knowledge. All the figures carved on the stones have a symbolic meaning. Because the Gnostics were condemned as heretical the rings came to be used for magic.'

'Magic?' He wondered if he had wandered into a dream, yet the quiet figure and expression of the jeweller didn't suggest hysteria or hallucination.

'Black and white of course. The symbols are often of life and power and many of them are the same as those used in magic. Sometimes I have to take them back.'

'I don't quite understand.'

'One doesn't know how they've been used of course in all these hundreds of years. If people are susceptible strange things can happen. Sometimes it's the other way round. I get requests. It's none of my business what people do with them.'

'You mean modern witchcraft?'

'There's a lot of it about. You'd be surprised if I told you some of the things.' He might have been speaking of a seasonal epidemic of 'flu. 'Anyway I feel I should warn customers.'

'What about yourself? Aren't you affected?'

'No, fortunately I don't seem to be.' He smiled a gentle academic smile. 'Though there was one once but then one can never be sure.' His face was grave again.

'I'll take it,' Sym said. 'I don't think I'm particularly susceptible and anyway if it's a symbol of life . . .'

'And it might have been used for good,' the jeweller said eagerly as he fumbled in the drawer again and brought out a small velvet-lined box.

'White magic,' Sym said as he picked it up and counted out the notes.

Outside the snow had given up its attempt at falling and the raw wind gusted bitterly down the alley. Sym hunched his shoulders and hurried through the saffron-tinged twilight, past the town hall where the clerks were bent over their desks under the neon flare. A woman's face looked out at him for a moment and he could see the question in her stare, would she get home before the snow, and then the head bent back to the papers on the desk. The queue at the bus-stop was silent, each huddled into frozen solitude as if by speech they would lay themselves open and be robbed of their precious hoarded warmth. Witchcraft? He looked at each face in turn. He tried to imagine the round little man with rolled newspaper and briefcase dancing naked in the firelight. The little man stared back sharply. Sym grinned to himself and turned towards the headlit traffic. He had decided it would be better not to tell Sassie about the stone's possible malign history though he would have liked to know how she would react, perhaps by pitting the strength of her will against whatever force the ring embodied which could be dangerous. Even if there was no force? But if she thought there was? The bus drew up. The queue shuffled forward.

'If only it would snow,' someone said, 'it might get a bit warmer.'

As he crossed the bridge the homebound rush was on the move. Heaters whirred, faces appeared behind wiping hands as steam was cleared from windscreens. Hooters blared aggressively as they inched towards the beckoning warmth of home and supper. Men of goodwill fought each other for a two-foot lead in the crush. Sym ran down the steps towards the river. He preferred to walk along the foreshore. Already at the water's edge the longest waves had crinkled into ice that broke glassily underfoot. The mallard were close in and muttered at him quietly for bread. He would try to remember to put some out every day. It was fine in the summer when the visitors came with their stale buns and they could stuff their crops with fruitcake, grow fat and glossy as children's plastic playthings but it must be hard in the winter. He thought the drakes' tight curl feathers flaunting under their tails were less jaunty than usual, the white string ties no longer crisp. The flock seemed bigger than before. Perhaps they flew in from all the smaller strips of water, ponds and streams, to winter on the Thames.

At the lock the huge wooden gates were hung with ice. All day the lock-keepers worked to keep it free but at night the slow seep froze into a fantastic sculpted waterfall and the gates were immovable by morning. They had sanded the catwalk with ash from the boiler and the man on duty was just going home.

'Have you still got water over there?' he called to Sym.

'It was alright when I left.'

'We're leaving our tap running all night so if you're frozen up in the morning you know where to get some. I don't know how you stick it this weather.'

'Oh it's warm enough once you're inside.'

'Rather you than me. Well, I'm off. Good night. We'll have snow before the night's out.'

The lock-keeper was right. Sym woke in the night conscious of the soft drift of flakes blanketing the skylight and in the morning the cabin was filled with a cold white half-light until he went up and cleared the panes. It was a moderate fall and there was more to come from the look of the sky. He shovelled it away from the decks and gangplank and took the cover off the water tank. Last night when he had turned the tap in the galley nothing had happened. Now he saw why. The water had frozen into a solid ten-gallon block. There was no point in trying to unthaw it; he would just have to get all his water from the standing pipe while it stayed as cold as this. The standing pipe had run like an old man's nose in the night exuding an icicle like candle wax. He broke it away and poured a little boiled water that he had found at the bottom of his kettle over it. With a wheeze and a cough it began to flow. He left it running. He didn't fancy a trip across the catwalk everytime he wanted a cup of tea.

Later he walked across the island through the trees, his eyes marking the fantasy world of snow. It had smoothed away the eyesore of the dump, turning it into a white tumulus as if someone slept underneath. It had lodged in the rough northern faces of the trees leaving the other half blackly bare. Branches bowed under the snow masses. On the ground animal prints, the sharp herring bone of birds, dog-claw, soft cat-pad, were jumbled and criss-crossed where they had followed the same hunting track. As yet there were no other human trails except his own following him towards the boathouse.

Why had he come here? He looked at the rack that held the letters. There were one or two unmistakable cards, one that had Sassie's name on the envelope, two he recognised for Walden's children but none for him. No one knew where to find him even if there had been anyone who cared to write. His isolation was complete. This was all his world now. He picked up the one for Sassie wondering who it was from. He would take it to her. It provided a reason and suddenly he needed someone to send the cold away for him.

He called her by throwing snowballs at the door. 'The postman cometh!'

'I think I'm marooned,' she pointed to the gangplank deep in snow. The little boat sat low in the water under its white cap.

'I'll get a shovel and dig you out.' He almost ran back to *Mimosa.* While she watched him from the hatch he sliced away the packed snow until the metal blade jarred on the wood beneath. Then he scattered salt and ash, working his way towards the deck. Sym cut away the snowthatch from the roof and pitched the white deck-covering in shovelfuls over the side where it vanished into the stream like foam.

'You shall have some coffee for that.'

Hands and feet stretched tingling towards the stove he watched as she made the coffee.

'Don't watch me.'

'I'm sorry. It's a bit difficult to know where else to look in here.' She passed him an old copy of *Paris Match*. He turned its elegant pages wondering how she had come by it and why. When she handed him the mug he almost choked on the first swallow. 'This isn't coffee.'

'It's Irish coffee.'

'But you're not Irish.'

'How do you know? Anyway it's because it's cold and Christmas.'

Trying not to watch her while she opened it he gave her the envelope slightly crumpled and damp from his pocket. Would she use it to torment him with?

'It's from my husband.' She drew out a large reproduction, a timeless Nativity, looked briefly inside and propped it on the shelf where the abstract golden-haired angels let unheard music drop from their open lips into the cabin. The little boat rocked gently on the current. 'He always sends me one at Christmas; he knows I like them.'

'You've never bothered with a divorce?'

'Oh no. There's no point. We never thought it was worth it just to help them keep their files in order. Sometimes, often in fact, it suits me to have the status of a married woman.' She laughed, 'You'd be surprised how many people are impressed with the title "Mrs." And it helps him too to be able to say "my wife" from time to time. He has a very nice boyfriend with lots of money. Sometimes we all have an evening out together. It's rather a classic case.'

Sym listened greedily. She had never told him so much about herself before though even this was indirect. He wanted to ask her why she had married and if she had been in love with him and a dozen things that died as soon as he considered saying them, the rough sounds flung at the fragile ice-palace of the morning they had built between them.

'I like you doing things for me. I never have before.' It was a bonus, a pillow-case full of presents. He thought of the ring in its box and wished it were tomorrow now. Tomorrow the weather might change completely.

He noticed the pots on the shelf were empty. 'What happened to Mary-Jane?'

'I don't think she likes the cold much. You're coming to the Waldens' tomorrow aren't you? We usually start in the *Yacht* while Joyce cooks the dinner so you can knock me up at opening time if you like.' He felt his face droop. He was being turned out. 'I have to go shopping this afternoon.'

'You won't be in the *Yacht* this evening then? Alec's got an extension.'

Sassie put out a hand and touched him gently as if to soothe a hurt. 'Come and fetch me tomorrow.' It had to be enough.

The rest of the day he whiled away with buying food, clearing snow and wrapping presents. He went to the post office and sent Anna some extra money care of her mother's address for the child either to buy a present or just something she might need. He had wondered at first whether to do it this year since the legal tie had been broken. She hadn't asked for maintenance even but he had offered it. The child would be going to school soon and he had never even heard her speak.

Later he sat in *Mimosa*'s warm comfort reading. There had been no more snow during the day but it still lay everywhere like the traditional card tinselled with frost and children had been out all day building snowmen in the front gardens who now stared with coalblack eyes incuriously at the last-minute shoppers trudging burdened over the slippery icefields of the pavements. Snow-ploughs and lorries full of casuals with shovels and grit had gone about the streets all day and traffic was back to normal. Perhaps he would get a job with the council if it went on. The rates weren't bad. It was a cold wet stint but easier than trying to dig the frozen ground. He read on.

> 'And thus yernes the yere in yisterdayes mony,
> And winter windes ayain, as the worlde askes.'

Soon the drunks would be tottering home to sleep it off and the Christians trotting in their wake to service. Why did winter have to come again? He looked at the words again, trying to see what the unknown poet had meant, the implied attitudes behind them. The cycle of life and death he supposed. There must be death for rebirth. But why couldn't it just keep going in a kind of perpetual motion? Because things just don't work out that way. We're creatures of variety, up and down, contrasts, extremes. Nothing is ever still, even the cells in our body constantly changing and dying, and atoms and stardust drawn this way and that, colliding, swept up into new substances; nothing wasted. He felt the old dizzying vision of the world in flux seize him and whirl him out of the boat up among the stars where he spun and swung looking down on the turning earth. He closed the book. He was tired, snow-dazzled. He would go to bed and get up his strength for tomorrow. In the distance he heard the bells begin.

Something woke him quite early but he turned over and slept again, an instinct telling him there was nothing to get up for yet. When he did he washed and shaved with extra care and put on clean clothes even down to his socks. Yesterday's shopping had included a grand session at the launderette. He had hung up a drip-dry shirt overnight for the creases to drop out, most of them wouldn't show under his sweater, and even found a tie and slacks instead of the usual jeans. He coudn't imagine what dinner would be like at the Waldens' but he felt that Sassie would appreciate the attempt at festivity.

It was five to twelve when he crossed her gangplank and knocked on the hatch. She called him to come in. He was pleased. Now he could give her the ring in private. He saw at once that she too was dressed for the party and there was no trace of the slightly tousled look he knew so well. That meant she had spent extra time and care. Sym tried to think of something complimentary to say that didn't sound affected but gave it up. Instead he kissed her, holding her very close so that she seemed to flow into him.

'I suppose we do have to go?'

Sassie laughed and held back from him a moment. 'Merry Christmas. You'd better say it now or you won't get it in.'

'So I gathered though I didn't quite get why.'

'You will.'

'Merry Christmas then.' He felt in his pocket and brought out the little parcel.

She turned it over, feeling it for clues. 'What is it?'

'Look and see.'

As the wrappings fell away and she saw the box she paused for a moment and the cabin was very still so that Sym fancied he could hear the rush of water past the hull.

'Put it on for me.'

'Which finger?'

'That one. If it'll fit.' She held out her right hand, third finger. He slipped it over. A marriage which is not a marriage he understood and was pleased. 'It's got a little carving on it.'

'Yes. It's a portrait of you. I had it done specially.'

She laughed again. 'When have you ever seen me in a long négligé?'

'Wishful thinking. It's a seal ring. You don't need to sign anything anymore. Just leave your stamp. "Sassie was here." '

She held out her hand so that the snowlight fell on the amber stone. 'No one has ever given me a ring before.' Then she bent quickly and picked up a parcel from among others on the bed and thrust it at him. It was expensive. He knew that as he shook it out of its wrappings and laid it on the bed. 'Put it on.'

Sym pulled off his old sweater and drew the new one over his head. 'How do I look?'

She reached up and straightened his collar and he caught her hand and pulled her down on the bed among the parcels. 'Do we really have to go?'

'I suppose so.'

'I wanted you so much last night I couldn't even go out for a drink. I was afraid I'd get drunk and pick somebody up out of desperation.'

'Why didn't you?'

'The trouble is I can't fancy some old boiler who's only in it for the money and if I go and roll somebody else because I'm really wanting you I'm just using them and I'm left with the responsibility of them after and that just means misery all round. You'll have to look after me better or I shall be a menace to society. Now what am I going to do with this?'

'I was hoping you'd come before I got dressed.'

'Were you? It makes it easier if you were though I don't see why it should.'

She pulled him up. 'Come on. We'll have a few drinks.'

'It won't be long will it.' He held her, moving his body against her.

'No, I promise. Now we must go.'

'I don't know if it's safe for me to go out in that cold wind like this. I might do myself an injury.'

'Get me my coat. It'll take your mind off it.' He held it out to her not daring to put it on and she led the way up onto the gangway lowering the hatch behind. The air struck them with the sharpness of cold steel as they went over the catwalk in single file. Walden was already there, a glass with only a drain at the bottom to point out how long he had been waiting.

'Now we can start,' he said. 'And it's your round.' Sym paid up gladly. 'You look like Father Christmas with that lot.' Walden jerked his thumb towards the carrier bag Sassie had found to hold all their presents.

'That's us,' Sym said as he took the drinks from Alec.

'A splendid pagan figure,' Walden said. 'Cheers! As long as no one starts calling him St. Nicholas and trying to dress him up in sheep's clothing.'

'Only to keep out the cold,' Sym said. 'Cheers! I see you're in fine form. Full of the Christmas spirit.'

'It makes a Scrooge of me, the hypocrisy and sentimentality of it all.' His teeth gleamed, distortedly grimacing through the bevelled glass as he made a gully of his throat for the stream of beer.

'Let's leave all that for later,' Sassie said. 'Let's just enjoy ourselves. What time does Joyce want us back?'

'She knows it's no good expecting me til two o'clock no matter what some people choose to call the day.'

'I hope you've got plenty of booze laid on,' Sym said. 'Or do we have to take it back with us?'

'We shall probably be treated to some of Walden's special home made. It tastes of damp ditches and has a kick like a young bullock so go easy on it.'

Walden laughed. 'The only time I've ever seen Sassie out cold was after three glasses of that; pear it was and she drank it like lemonade. Folded up like a collapsed deckchair. We'll have to see what we can do for you.'

Like *Mimosa* Walden's boat *Grey Gull* lay apart from the others but round the other side of the island beyond the boathouse where the river was wide, a broad sheet of tinfoil that glittered as the wind shook it, between drifted banks of snow. The thin Christmas sun had pared away the top layer and wiped it from the branches as they passed between the trees and bushes but underfoot it had frozen hard in the night into a slippery path and once they had passed the boathouse there were only the soles of huge feet. Walden's, cut in glass.

'You can see how they came to believe in the Abominable Snowman,' Sym giggled pointing to the tracks. He was already a bit drunk and enjoying it. The little terrier barked inside as they went over the gangplank. He thought Walden's wife must need her for company on the nights Walden was out boozing, in this isolated part of the island alone with two small children. Walden opened the door and they followed him down the narrow companionway.

It was much darker than on *Mimosa* but it was the sparseness that struck him as soon as his eyes were used to the frail electric light. He had heard the knocking whirr of a small generator as they stepped on board. Many of the boats had them. They were temperamental things, liable to go wrong at the least excuse and their owners spent happy hours seriously tinkering with them. The cabin was quite big with a proper table set for six with an array of chipped plates, tumblers various and totshop cutlery bought in a job lot. There was a long bunk behind the table, one or two chairs, an armchair with torn upholstery, a plastic clock on the mantelshelf above the stove and that was all. Sym was glad of the open doors of the stove but even that seemed a festive touch, laid on for the occasion.

Trudy leapt up at them but the two children stood waiting silently. 'Cards for you kids,' Walden held out a couple of envelopes, one for each of them.

'What have you got, Sophy?' Jane asked looking over the younger child's shoulder. 'Oh that's alright; it's a funny one. Mine's a Jesus baby. That silly Jennie Stevens, I told her not to send me one of those.'

'You'll have to burn it, won't she?' Sophy turned her face

up to her father. 'Like we burned all the rest.' Walden didn't reply. Jane sighed loudly but with impatience rather than disappointment, tore the card straight across and threw the two halves into the hot coals. The sad smile of the woman curled, turned brown and broke into flame. From his angle Sym thought the first king, gold offering outstretched, looked a little surprised as his green robe fell away from him.

'We don't call it Christmas do we, kids?' Walden said.

'We call it Yule,' Jane supplied.

'A good pagan institution, Yule.' Walden flopped into the armchair and swung his legs over the arm. 'The human race has been celebrating at this time of the year since Paleolithic times. But don't let's get it mixed up with wishy-washy Christianity.'

A few attempts at home- or school-made paper chains were draped from beam to beam reminding Sym of his own childhood, of sticking the coloured strips into loops on a cold afternoon in front of the fire and stringing them with crayoned lanterns. Still there was a good smell coming from somewhere. 'You'll get a good dinner,' Walden said as if he could read his thoughts. 'Joyce is a good cook. That's why we keep her.'

'What did you get for presents, Sophy?' Sassie asked, dropping her coat over a chair and sitting close to the stove as if she were quite at home. Which she probably is, Sym thought. The children seemed to become more human in their catalogue of 'Daddy bought me this and Mummy bought me that.' 'And now you'd better see what we've got for you.' Sassie took the bag from Sym and began to distribute small brightly wrapped parcels and he thought looking at her that she made a warm picture against the stark background of the cabin. He was so busy watching that he didn't see that someone else had come in and was standing quietly inside the door. 'And this has your father's name on it so you'd better give it to him, Jane.' Sassie pulled the half-bottle of Scotch from deep in the bag. 'And this is for your mother I think. You can take this, Sophy. Joyce, you haven't met Sym, have you?'

As the child reached her with his present Sym turned to meet her. 'I hope it's alright. It's difficult buying for someone you've never met.' He said the words mechanically as she unwrapped it and was pleased with the little gasp of pleasure.

'You shouldn't have. It's lovely. Look, Sassie.' Sassie smiled at him approvingly.

'Mine's not bad either.' Walden held up the amber bottle so that the fire glowed redly through it.

'And what did you get?' Joyce asked the children. They took their presents for her inspection. Sassie had bought them a string of beads each and a red cardigan for Jane and a blue one for Sophy. Sym had noticed the ones they wore had been handknitted long ago in coarse grey wool and were darned even more than when he had last seen them. Joyce took them from their wrappings and helped each child to put hers on, drawing Sophy close to do up the buttons. She seemed so, he felt for the word, normal. He had expected someone to match Walden but she was any young married woman, quite pretty with fluffy fair hair damped a bit with the steam of cooking and a hurriedly applied dash of make-up. Sym had caught a quick glance of thanks to Sassie and she had been particularly pleased with the scarves, running their soft lengths through her hands as if gauging their power to keep out the cold.

'When do we eat?' Walden broke up the scene. Joyce pushed Sophy away and stood up, tucking up a strand of hair that fell across her eyes. Sym noticed that she had a faded look that was older than her years. For the first time he wondered about Walden's age. He had thought him about forty. Perhaps he had married someone a lot younger.

'It's ready now,' she said. 'Let's have a drink.'

'You hear that, kids? Your mother wants a drink before she'll feed us.'

She flared suddenly. 'Christ you've had enough, your share and mine while I've been stuck in here.'

He made a gesture of resignation, spreading his palms and shrugging. 'And you shall have yours. Fetch the flagon, kids.' The children disappeared towards the cooking smells and came back a moment later each holding a handle on the neck of a demi-john of pale orange liquid. 'This should be good. I've managed to hang on to it for a year. Siphoned it off last night so it should be absolutely clear.' He undid the screw top which gave a slight hiss and filled four tumblers, putting a little in two others for the children.

'What is it?' Sym sniffed suspiciously.

'Orange. I agree it looks more like a specimen of urine but the flavour's better. Cheers!'

It wasn't at all bad, a tang of bitter orange but otherwise a pretty strong white wine. Sym noticed Joyce drained hers and held out for more. Walden hesitated fractionally til she shook the glass at him and he felt her nerves begin to twitch, and then he filled it and she took it out into the galley. 'Take your places,' Walden waved towards the table. 'We are about to stuff ourselves.'

'I'll just see if Joyce wants any help,' Sassie followed her to the galley.

'Ganging up on us. You see how they always hang together. Even a woman as intelligent as Sassie can't resist the pull of the sisterhood. What do you think of this?' He re-filled the glasses.

'It's not bad. I only hope it mixes.'

It was a good dinner and there was plenty of it though the housekeeping obviously hadn't stretched to a bird. After plum-pudding, mentally rejecting Christmas pudding, and custard, the children took their new painting kits to a clear corner of the floor while the adults sat with full glasses and stomachs. Walden got up to bank up the fire then threw a week-old copy of the intellectual Sunday at Sym.

'Look at that. Just what I've always said: scientists know bugger all what they're doing or saying yet they set up to be god. Then all of a sudden one of them gets a fraction near a truth that other people have known for years and you'd think they'd discovered America.'

Sym read through the article outlined in heavy black biro. A physicist had suggested a new concept of time, a world in which time ran backwards to maintain the symmetry of the universe, where life began with death and ended with birth.

'It gives me the creeps,' Joyce said. 'Did you read it?' Sassie shook her head. 'He says that there might be people walking about among us that we couldn't see because they were on a different time plane.'

'It sounds like the two old dears at Versailles to me,' Sym said.

'What do we or they know about time? It's just as I've always said. Philosophically it's a perfectly tenable theory. People have claimed for years that they could cross the time barrier and now someone with a few letters after his name comes up and says it might be so and that merits a front page spread and serious attention.'

'You should be pleased,' Sassie said, 'that they're catching up with you at last.'

'What was it that man said about pearls and swine, one of the few occasions when what he said made sense? This kind of knowledge in the wrong hands is giving a kid dynamite to play with. Just as well none of the fools will believe him. They like things as they are: the nineteenth-century concept of science as verifiable fact.'

'Faustian time. It's a marvellous phrase.'

'And look what conventional morality did to him,' Walden sneered.

'I get so sick of all this speculation, pulling everything to pieces, seeing everyone as charlatans or rogues,' Joyce took a big gulp at her drink.

'That's a long word for you, my dear. You shouldn't bother your tiny mind about these things. You just accept what you're told like all the other morons and wait for the exploiters to lead you forward into saccharine sweetness and neon light.'

She didn't answer but Sym saw her duck her head as if to hide tears and then Sassie said, 'What about a little music,' and took a small transistor set from the carrier bag and twiddled with the knobs until a programme of light pops filled the cabin.

'Let's have some Scotch,' Walden said, unwrapping the gold seal and pulling the cork.

'Shall we dance?' Sassie stood up and she and Sym postured gracefully while the other two watched.

'Your turn,' Sym said when they sat down.

'Walden doesn't dance,' Joyce said. 'He thinks it's unnecessary. Beneath his dignity.'

'Then allow me,' Sym stood up again. Her dancing surprised him.

Her eyes closed, she pressed her body against him. He noticed as they danced on she was beginning to breathe pretty heavily. She must be a bit drunk but then so was he and it was Christmas so what the hell. He took her back to the table.

'That was nice for you. You enjoyed that,' Walden said. Joyce sat down and poured herself another drink.

'Our turn,' Sym moved away with Sassie. He was beginning to wish they could go home to the comfort of *Mimosa* and make love. Joyce's body so close had excited him but it was Sassie he wanted. He decided that in spite of the pallor and lines of strain Joyce was probably a couple of years younger than himself.

They missed the exact moment when it happened but suddenly Joyce picked up a glass and quite deliberately threw it on the floor where it smashed in a scatter of spilt wine. The children looked up from their corner and there was silence for a few seconds.

Then Jane said very clearly, 'Is she drunk?'

Joyce sank down, her head on her arms. 'No, not drunk,' Walden answered, 'just tired.'

'That's it,' Joyce laughed, 'just tired. Sick and tired. Sick and tired.' She got up and went towards the door into the galley.

Sassie crossed quickly to the children and bent over their painting books drawing their attention to herself. Puzzled what to do Sym stacked a few of the dirty dishes into a pile.

'Is she alright?'

'Of course she's bloody alright.'

Sym shifted uncertainly. 'Shouldn't you go and see?' Then as Walden made no move, 'I'll just take these through then.'

He picked up the pile of dishes and found his way through to the galley.

Joyce was leaning against the sink, drawing deep on a half-smoked end. He had been a bit scared what he would find and if he would know what to say and now he was relieved that there were no signs of tears.

'I thought I'd bring these through.'

'Thanks. Put them on the draining board; I'll do them later.' She nodded towards the top plate where he had scraped all the leavings together. 'They'll do for the dog. Poor little bitch, she should have some Christmas dinner too.' She picked up an enamel bowl from the floor and transferred the scraps to it. 'You're very neat. I like neatness in a man as long as it isn't finikin.' She bent down with the bowl and Sym tried to place the accent as he followed the line of her doubled figure. As she straightened up she pulled down the faded jumper and smoothed her skirt. 'Thanks for dressing up a bit, you and Sassie. It makes it more of a celebration and it's good for the kids. Makes them see there are other ways than this.' She looked round the cluttered galley. 'I'm not drunk, you know, only it's just that I don't think I can stand much more. You have to be superhuman and I'm not. Just ordinary. I thought I could take it, that it was fun not to live like everyone else and now I find all I want is a house with a garden and running water and shoes for the kids, and a bit of love every Friday night.' Her voice caught on the last syllable. 'Have you got another fag?'

Sym shook his head. 'Sorry. I'll roll you one if you like. No tailor-mades.'

'Thanks. That'll do fine.'

He held the gummed strip out for her to lick but she shook her head. 'You do it.' She watched as he ran his tongue along and passed the neat cylinder to her. He flicked a flame from his lighter and she bent her head towards it. 'That's my real trouble I suppose; I'm just bloody frustrated.' She laughed uncertainly. 'God, I could envy Sassie. You know he won't have it anymore? You didn't know that because all his talk you'd think he was after me every night, wouldn't you? Fourteen months now. Do you wonder I'm like this? Not pretty is it? That's what he tells me. It's not pretty. I ought to be able to think of other things, more important things: time going backwards. Christ if it wasn't for Sassie I wouldn't let you out of here and that's not pretty either. Anyway thanks for listening. I'm better now. You'd best go back or someone'll think the worst and I wouldn't hurt her, not that I could really. She's the only friend we've got. Sometimes I think she's a kind of saint. Most people wouldn't see it that way of course. Funny we both picked ourselves someone older, you and me. They must have something, something we need I suppose.'

'You're sure you're alright now? I'll leave you another roll.' He put it carefully on the draining board away from the patches of wet. 'There, you'll be in in a minute?'

'I'll be in.'

'Was she alright?' Walden asked.

'She's alright.'

'I know Joyce. I knew she was alright. Now where's the party? Let's have another drink. Time you kids were thinking of bed, monopolising Sassie like that. Go on, Jane. Tell Joyce I say it's time for bed.'

The children got up obediently but their mother had appeared at the door. Sym wondered if she had been listening, she was so prompt on her cue. 'Say good night to everyone.'

They turned gravely to say good night and then suddenly Sophy ran forward, dropping the adult poise, and threw her arms round Sassie's neck to whisper in her ear.

'What did she say?' Walden asked when they had gone.

'Never tell a child's secrets. Or anyone else's.'

'You should have had children of your own,' he said harshly.

'We should do a lot of things we don't do. I thought you were pouring us drinks.'

'It was the last of the Scotch.' Walden lumbered to his feet. 'I'm tired of drinking my own hogwash. Let's go along to

Alec's; see what the rest of the homeless are doing this merry Yuletide.'

'What about Joyce?' Sym said. 'It doesn't seem fair.'

'Fair? What is fair? I find that a curiously juvenile concept. Maybe he just wants to stay with Joyce. She'd like that. In the old days, when we first met you know, and all the world was young, she used to sleep around a lot. We both did. That was when we misguidedly thought we had a stake in things.'

'You're going out,' Joyce said from the galley door.

'Your friends think it isn't fair to go without you.'

'No, you go. I'd rather stay here. I can wash up quietly and listen to the wireless. Walden bought us one for . . .' she hesitated, 'a present. I haven't even tried it yet.' She went to fetch it. Sassie picked up her own and turned it off, replacing it in the carrier bag.

Joyce held out the new set for inspection. Taking it to admire, Sym wondered where he had found the money or if it had been paid for at all in the usual sense. It was an expensive little toy. He remembered the dark night figures on the river and the shape that might have been Walden's. He hoped for Joyce's sake he knew what he was doing.

A couple of pints later he had had enough. 'Let's go,' he said to Sassie when Walden had left them for a quick one.

'Alright. Wait til he comes back and I'll say I'm tired. He won't argue with that.' They left him in conversation with Alec.

As they pushed through the door a slight dark figure stood aside smiling to let them out.

'Good night, Mrs. Parks.'

'Good night, Dick.'

As Sym followed her through the bitter air the thought came to him that it had all been arranged. He felt his head begin to whirl. Walden was meeting Dick, Sassie was taking him away. That was why they had come and Walden hadn't protested. In the warmth of *Mimosa* he turned on her. 'What is it all about? What does it mean?'

'What do you think it means?'

'If I knew I wouldn't have to ask.'

'It's nothing. Just a game; all a game. It passes the time. What else is there.'

He shook his head unconvinced. 'And what about Joyce?'

'What about her?'

'He's destroying her.'

'Perhaps they're playing a game too.'

'Isn't there any reality then?'

'Why are you so concerned?'

'You can't do that to someone; just treat them like that.'

'Isn't there something in Joyce that asks for it? If it were really too much for her she would go. People have to make their own decisions.'

'I suppose I was really thinking of someone else.'

'Have you always tried to make other people's decisions for them?'

'I left my wife, if that's what you mean. She didn't leave me. I thought I was doing the best for them. We had a daughter.'

'Tell me about it.'

He felt the wound grow sore again as he talked and then the pain begin to die away until there was only a tenderness where it had been and even that would fade with time. 'So you see I was just like Walden in a way. When I saw their place today I remembered how ours used to be. I stuck the teaching for a couple of years but it was no good. I just couldn't do anything while I was working all day. When I'd got halfway through another book I couldn't stand it any longer so I packed it in. We lived on what I'd saved and the superannuation I drew out. I finished the book and there was another couple of hundred that took us up to publication day. When I saw the reviews I could have cut my throat. People say you shouldn't take any notice and I suppose it does get easier. Well I learnt from that. You see they're very kind to first novels for some mistaken reason but when the poor bastard follows it up with a second and they see he really means it they tear its guts out. If you can take that and still go on then you might make it.'

'What happened?'

He turned away from the porthole and pulled the little curtain across. 'I got over that. It was what came after I couldn't take. Or rather the nothingness. It was funny really I suppose, like Micawber waiting for something to turn up, anything. I'd hoped naively that someone would write and ask me to do some reviewing or an article of some kind but everything went on just like before. I knew two other people trying to do the same thing and one of them bought a tumbledown farm and went to live there, the other nearly killed himself, collapsed and was taken to hospital, trying to do two jobs. It was the isolation, never meeting anyone you could talk to and every day the little bit of money shrinking. And Anna hated it.' Sym paused, remembering how he'd lain awake at night sick with the endless round and round of what they should do. 'I hung on as long as I could until we'd begun to hate each other and when we were down to twenty quid I left, walked out and hitched to the Midlands. Got a job on the road. It was good pay. I sent them plenty home. They were better off than when I was there.'

'You didn't go back ever?'

'What was the use? Away from them I didn't hate them. I still wasn't writing. I'd gone dry, sterile, but at least I didn't have to face them everyday, to feel that if it wasn't for them I could live the way I wanted, like a pig if I had to, scrape along somehow without making other people suffer with me. She divorced me last year.'

'You made her decision for her.'

'You can't make other people suffer.'

'And yet you have to be yourself.'

'That's it.'

'That's Walden's problem too. But it's up to Joyce to decide.'

'And what about you?'

'I decided a long time ago.'

'What?'

'That's one of the things I'm teaching you not to ask.' She held out her arms to him.

January

. . . where boughs are bare
They clomben by cliffs where clengs the cold

ON New Year's Eve it snowed again, grittily at first from a sulphurous sky and then faster and faster in bigger and bigger flakes as if the Olympians were at some cosmic pillow fight, banging uproariously away at each other til the snow-plumes whirled and dizzied down on the ant figures scurrying ever uphill in the shaken paperweight of the city. As dark fell early under the weight of the clouds cars were abandoned, buses and trains crept behind schedule, late home-comers stamped and knocked their sodden shoes at the front door, turned the key in the lock and stepped inside thankfully, the old-man's-beard of eyebrows and forelock shrinking to drop-lets that shivered in the light before they were towelled away. While they stretched their bodies to the fire, and tottered to an early bed drugged with warmth and the mindless flitting of the night's programmes it fell in the empty streets and was still falling when the curtains were drawn in the morning. It was the end of the world. It would never stop until the city was blanketed twenty feet deep and only the grotesquely pointing aerials marked where the houses had been. All morning they watched it drift lazily, persistently past the office windows, a theme for speculation, an excuse to break the round by looking up and out, and then at lunchtime it stopped and the air was still and very, very cold so that the touch of metal seared the flesh like a branding iron.

Sym cleared the decks again and joined the trembling group at the local garage for paraffin. Oil heaters kept the boats very warm inside, almost too warm when the lamps were going as well. He wondered how Joyce was managing until he met

Walden dragging a sack of coal over the cat-walk on a trolley.

'You can't get enough at a time this way,' he said, 'and I'm always afraid of shooting the bloody lot into the river. I'll borrow Sassie's dinghy and fill that up at the coalyard below the bridge. You can come and give me a hand if you're not working. I've got plenty of wood but it burns away too bloody fast without a bit of coal. Can't have the kids freeze to death.' He seemed to grow larger against the background of snow waste and icy water. Clouds of steamy breath billowed away with every phrase. A great carthorse, Sym thought, that's what he's like. He expected him to stamp and snort but instead he put back his head and bellowed. 'You look like the bloody orphan of the storm standing there shivering. Do you good to move about a bit.' Sym looked at the glinting water where it slid over the weir below their feet.

'If you fell in there you'd freeze to death.'

'Then don't fall in. I'll see you in half an hour in Alec's.'

Standing at the bar, Sym wondered why he hadn't said no. It would have been quite easy. All he had to do was to refuse, make an excuse, say he was meeting Sassie. But Walden dominated him completely and he couldn't understand why. He's a crank, if not an absolute nut, and he's impotent, he told himself. Yet the physical presence of Walden, sweating and laughing and ducking his great head, the enormous undirected vitality, drew him along. He remembered a drawing of the castration of Chronos, the young gods hacking off his genitals with a stone sickle, and understood it at last. It was a legend he had never grasped before. Titans chained to rocks or breathing fire and brimstone clamped under volcanoes, green knights who swung their own decapitated heads and laughed from trunkless mouths daring you to fight them, he understood them all.

As he loaded the sacks with Walden he noticed that the bank here was edged with a film of ice. 'What about that then?'

Walden straightened his back. 'Something else for you to worry about. If the river freezes . . .'

'It couldn't could it? I mean it doesn't, hasn't done since the sixteen hundreds.'

'We'll see. That'll keep you on your toes. Have your bilges frozen yet?'

'I expect so. The tank's a solid block of ice.'

'Then if the river freezes it could nip the bottom of the boat off like a pair of scissors.' He laughed delightedly.

How does he know I'm frightened, Sym thought, and why isn't everyone else? Maybe they blow it up big to make it more interesting. Why am I so easily frightened? He thought about it as he pulled back towards the island, his thousand fears and apprehensions, of crashes, and sinking, of drowning although he knew he could swim, of inadequacy and responsibility that grew and weighed on him until he lived in a perpetual sick misery. It was a rationalisation of course and he wasn't alone in it. He was pretty sure of that. There were thousands of men all over the country who worried themselves into ulcers or thrombosis in the same way. That's why Bond and the spy cult was so popular. It's an age of anxiety, larded over with a rich cynicism and the only way people can get through day after day is to pretend that nothing matters, nothing else exists below the appearance level whereas if you look down into most men's eyes you see either the blankness of death or the dark maelstrom of a deep unease.

'Watch it,' Walden said. 'You're going into the bank.'

A thin sun had appeared by the time he had crunched his way across the island to *Mimosa*. Joyce had been glad to see the coal heaped beside the boat and Walden had kept the dinghy to return to Sassie later. Once Sym had been on the point of asking if Walden knew where it had come from but shut his mouth on the words. He remembered that Collins had told him that *Mimosa* had a dinghy. There had been no sign of it apart from the pair of oars he had found in the bows. Perhaps this was really his dinghy. Had been, he corrected himself. He couldn't imagine himself ever asking for it back.

Suki was lying out in the sun on a corner of the deck he had cleared. Sym was surprised to see her there, expecting her to be by the fire on the M.T.B. He put out his hand to the little cat. She moved her head and looked at him with eyes that seemed to have grown enormous since he had seen her last. That must be a couple of weeks ago now before the snow. Perhaps she had got herself shut out. He warmed some milk and took it up on deck hoping to entice her down. He put the saucer beside her and she stretched her head towards it without getting up. It was cooling rapidly in the cold air, its precious warmth streaming away in a cloud of steam. Still she didn't move. He put out a hand and scooped her up. There seemed to be nothing of her but light fur and when he set her down by the milk she lapped feebly and was hardly able to stand.

Sym picked her up again and stood undecided holding her against his coat. She didn't seem to have the strength to make it home. He would have to carry her. On the other hand he could take her down into *Mimosa*. He decided against this. Her owners might object. She ought to see a vet, had perhaps already seen one and was being treated. He had better take her home.

'No,' the man said when he opened the door. 'She doesn't seem too bright does she? Hasn't done for the last couple of weeks. The wife can take her along to the quack in the morning.'

'I'll pop in and see how she is tomorrow,' Sym said answering in kind.

'Yes, you do that. Thanks for bringing her.' And the door shut to.

He remembered Walden's comment on the bilges as dark fell and went up onto the deck with a hurricane lamp. Lifting the hatch he lowered the lamp as far as he could. Walden was right. There was very little water in there after his morning of baling but what there was was set as hard as black concrete. Now he had only to wait for the river to freeze. It was inevitable.

When he called next evening the man seemed a little apologetic. 'The quack said something she'd picked up from the rats. A little devil she was for that, fought like a tigress. Wasting her away. So the wife left her. There's the children to think of.

They might have caught it though the vet said not. They always say that. Want you to keep paying out of course. It would have meant taking her every day or getting the private chap to call and they charge a packet. So it seemed best. The kids are upset of course. But they'll get over it. She wasn't what you'd call an affectionate animal. Anyway it seemed for the best.

They had her son, the complacent neutered tom who would probably never tackle a rat in his life. Well they had got her in the end; the bite that had healed sealing the insidious poison in her thin body where it had burnt her down to big eyes and a handful of fur. He was sorry he hadn't followed his first impulse to keep her. He felt he had failed her. He should have fed her brandy and milk and paid for the vet to come. There might have been a chance. That night as he lay looking up at the skylight he heard the scrabble of ratclaws on the deck but no answering wail of defiance. Cold and hunger were making them bolder and there was no Suki anymore to keep them away.

From the deck in the morning he saw that the river was glazed with sheets of thin ice, a transparent patina that reached out from the banks towards the middle where the current still ran fast enough to stop the water stiffening and here the ducks swam and foraged, not only mallard but coots with white nasals fronting sooty heads and moorhen red-beaked, bobbing and twitching like nervous old women as they paddled. All these he was used to though there were more of them than usual. But there were others he had never seen before, dabchicks and small ducks in neat penguin suits with little tufts on their heads. Breaking the ice round the hull with the boathook was easy. It was brittle and clear, easy to smash and push away, the thin sheets sliding under those farther out to form a double layer but leaving the water round *Mimosa* open. The snow had been pounded hard by last night's frost-hammers and the weather forecast when he switched on promised freezing temperatures all day. The newscaster's voice was lowered to a respectful pitch as he catalogued the frost havoc throughout the country: frozen pipes, trains delayed, roads impassable, villages cut off, power cuts, civilisation crumpling under the impact of natural forces. Sym was surprised, tickled by a Walden-like amusement as he thought of them scurrying about with buckets of water or crouched over the watery orange glow of an electric fire. He held out his hands to the stove in satisfaction. The boatworld was so used to doing without mains services that it was hardly affected, almost self-supporting.

Since New Year Sassie had been elusive. He felt she was avoiding him. Perhaps she had committed herself, or thought she had, more than she had wanted. For a few moments he had thought he had seen possibility, some kind of future for their relationship and now she had shut the door against him again. Why wouldn't she trust him, chance it? But when he tried in his mind to move them from the river, to set them in the context of a flat together, of work, of food bought and cooked, of evenings reading or watching television, of the paraphernalia of modern living he couldn't do it. The images wouldn't come. Yet he knew he couldn't stay there forever. He had almost found what he had come for and then? He drew back. The *Yacht* distracted him.

'Have you seen Sassie?' Walden asked watching him closely.

'Not for a few days.'

'She's probably taking a cure.'

'A cure?'

'When she's had enough of us all she goes off for a week or two.' He seemed to sag a little, the trousers bagging as he leant lower on the bar. 'What do you do with people like us?' Then, 'Drink up, we're getting maudlin. It's this bloody weather.'

'Every day the ice is thicker, an inch now, opaque, milky but not quite reaching across from bank to bank. Today, coming back, I saw a strange bird far out heading into the stream, seemed motionless but must have been moving its webs to stay in the same place. Quite big and like the new ducks tufted but too far to see the markings. Must be the cold driving them here or perhaps it's the only bit of open water though how long before it's all frozen solid I don't know. Must look it up and see what it's called.' He paused listening intently but it was imagination and he went on: 'I have company. Decided to light the fire this afternoon. Sassie has been away a week now with no letter or any contact—not that I really expected her to write but I suppose you always hope. I thought a real blaze instead of the paraffin would be more cheerful. Opened the little cupboard by the stove where I kept the paper, sticks and firelighters and put my hand in for them. Out of half an eye noticed a strange shape—brown paper, shiny? As I reached in it moved. I snatched my hand back and slammed the door shut with my boot. But I'd seen it more clearly, bald flanks, a leathery hairless tail, a rat, a bloody big old one. I heard him scrabbling inside and picked up the poker, sweating, booted open the door and he was off somewhere through the back of the cupboard before I could take a smash at him. Then I thought of the store cupboard over the top and I opened that. Hadn't been eating at home for a few days so I hadn't looked in. It was a shambles. He'd been through everything, sampling and going on to the next: jam pots, flour, porridge, sugar, lard and worst of all a half-pound of bacon gone completely. The rest was all torn and spilt, boxes and wrappers gnawed, smears of jam powdered with flower. Made me sick to see it. I shut both doors and sat down to roll a fag and think about it. I'd been quiet about a minute when he was back, scrabbling about in there so I booted the door and the bugger went quiet. One thing was clear: he'd have to go. This boat isn't big enough for both of us. And the stink when I opened the food cupboard! Now I understand the term, "You stinking rat." There were traps and there was poison. It was almost as if he knew Suki had gone and had moved in on me. Then a metal safe to keep the food in. He was going to cost me money. I got up and took a bag and some extra money and as I was going out of the door I heard him. He was back again. "Just wait for me, mate," I said. "I'll be back and then we'll see."

Poison the man said was the best. He handed me a tin pointing out the description of what it did to them. "Paralyses their breathing nerves so they feel like they're choking and make a rush for the air. That way you don't have them dying on the premises. Better than traps. You don't have to get rid of them after. Smear it on a bit of kipper. They like that, nice and tasty. Carnivores you see really. We had a sweet shop once and it was alive. I made quite a study of them over the course of time. Blocked up their runs with wire netting; that foxed them. Cunning they are. A war of nerves."

"I've only seen one so far."

"Still where there's one . . ."

"How are they getting in?"

"The same way you do, up the gangplank. Come to me if you want my advice. Made a study of them I have."

"I'll do that. How much is the safe?"

"Forty-two and six. You want to get them out before February. That's when they start breeding. Nests under the floorboards. Still you'll know if you're sinking won't you?" he laughed at his own joke, "when they all make a dash for the shore."

I bought some kippers. I could have the rest for tea if I fancied them. Now then. There wasn't a flicker of pity in me because of Suki.

When I got back I booted the cupboard door just to let him know I was home. I didn't want him biting me, those rank teeth and the curdling poison of his drool; wasting away, burning up the blood. I baited the piece of kipper, opened the door and put it in. I sat down with the poker and waited. I could see the waft of that kipper drifting down to him like in the cartoons, his nose whiffling and following along the scent, into the cupboard, sniffing at it, taking a bite. I thought I heard a scratching, a rustling of the paper and then he flung himself at the door and I slammed it back and held it. The catch was only small and I could hear him going crazy in there fighting to get out. He must have bolted the lot and the stuff was working already. I hadn't expected it to happen so soon. I had thought of it as a delayed action thing, not that I should be holding the door against him while he choked and fought. Why didn't he go back the way he'd come or couldn't he find it in his terror? Suddenly it went quiet. Either he had died in there or he had found the way. I kept my foot against the door and the poker ready while I stood and smoked the fag I had been rolling. When I was through that I reckoned I could open up. He was gone. The bait was gone too.

A little while ago as I was writing this I heard a noise in the cupboard, crept to the door and when I opened it a rat whisked out of sight. So there are more of them. This one was quite different, smaller, slim, brown. A girl rat? I get to be able to discriminate. But she too will have to go. I shall lay the bait again tonight. Tomorrow I shall clean out the cupboards and from now on keep all foods in the safe. I can imagine them breaking their teeth trying to get in to that.'

The oil-stove flared a little in a sudden draught. He was tired, resigned now to a long battle. He had seen two, there were probably others and like tramps leaving their signs on the gatepost they had marked the way for others to follow just by the reek of their bodies. Even now they might be slipping in ones and twos up the gangplank, taking over. Glint of hot rat eyes in the dark, curl of leathery lip over yellow fang. He stacked his paper and put the folder away in the hold-all. The zip gave him a feeling of security. At least they wouldn't get in there. The thought of the white paper messed with rat droppings suggested an ultimate anarchy he couldn't face. He hadn't been able to face the kippers either. There was still one and a half left. He took the newspaper-wrapped packet from the safe and cut a piece of the dark hennaed flesh. His eye registered a building that had burnt to ash because of a frozen hydrant, flame against a dark sky, the slow drift of black flakes that soiled the snow where they fell; fire and ice. He smeared the yellow paste on the smoky meat, knocked on the cupboard door, waited and put it in.

As he lay awake in the dark with the torch beside him on a ledge he listened for sounds of activity but it was very still. No furry bodies scuffled and bumped overhead. No, he thought, too bloody cold for them out there. They're sitting in my cupboard munching on my food. But surely he would hear the rustle of paper. Could he? Suppose they ran across his face while he slept. He got up again and closed the cabin door. Then he thought of the fire still burning and opened it again. With the door shut no instinct would tell him if the stove flared, caught, licked at the wooden walls. He screwed down the valve. He would do without the fire. He shut the door again and got back quickly into the warm bunk. Already he could feel the temperature dropping, the water thickening round him, the heat zooming up into the cold bright sky, *Mimosa* like a frozen peashuck on a bed of ice. Huddled into himself he strained his ears; he lay there listening for a long time before he fell asleep.

In the morning the ceiling was iced thick with his congealed breath, the skylight double glazed, engraved with fern leaves and the goblin shapes of childhood, the blanket sprinkled with hard glass beads. Shivering he lit the stove and banged on the door to see if the bait had been taken. It was gone. Sym felt more cheerful in the white cold light though he still couldn't bring himself to eat the other kipper. He wondered if he would ever fancy kipper again. He ate two eggs for breakfast and began to clear out the cupboard, brushing the lot into a carrier bag, splashing disinfectant, piney and soothing, to obliterate the rodent stink. He would take it over to the dump and then do a bit of icebreaking and then? The rest of the day lay flat, grey and featureless as the wastes of snow in front of him.

Tom with the wall eye was hovering by the dump when he reached it with his bag of broken food. He had scraped away the coating of snow and was scattering paraffin to give the fire a chance. Sym added his contribution and stood back to watch, nodding a good morning to the hunched figure that touched his forehead to him. Of the two he preferred the gypsy. There was something obsequious, almost menial, about Tom. Not his fault of course but too much under Clack's thumb. He moved closer to Sym obviously in search of some kind of communication.

'We have to light it even in this weather. Keep the rats off. They're bad this year. Found a big old 'un this morning along the bank. Half bald he was. Stiff as a board. He's in there.' He jerked his head towards the flickering pyre. 'Poisoned I 'spect.

He were a big 'un though. I slung him in there so the others didn't get at him. Cannibals they are, you know.' Sym thought he was rather like a rat himself. He noticed the neck where the scarf fell back was pitted with blackheads. So old baldy had found his way out to the bank and died there. 'You seen the grebe?' the old man broke in on his thoughts.

'The big crested birds? So that's what they are. I was wondering.'

'Great crested grebe. You don't usually see them here. Shows what a winter it is. Must be frozen everywhere else. Not that there's much open water here still. They say they're sending the *Whale* up today as an icebreaker.'

'I've got some of my own to do,' Sym said. He would do his own and then go and look for the tug. It should be worth seeing.

'You're wise to keep it as free as you can. Reckon you're not so bad off here. All our pipes are frozen at home, all down the street. We have to fetch it, every drop in the kettle, from out in the road. What'll happen when it thaws and they find all the cracked pipes? Anyone who can mend a pipe'll make a fortune. And the current's so low there's no warmth to it. Took us all morning to cook the Sunday dinner but there you must have hot food inside of you to keep out the cold.'

Sym nodded away from the catalogue of miseries. Every day the ice thickened. He had to smash harder, push farther to clear a space. Many of the boat owners didn't bother he noticed. But he kept Sassie's clear as well and he would find an occasional duck paddling frantically, glad of the chance. Even the rarer tufted ones had become quite tame. Warmed by his stint with the boathook he set out for the lock. Passing the other boats he noticed that some of them had continued to empty elsans and garbage over the side even though it no longer sank out of sight but lay like a mediaeval midden staining the ice sheet. At night the rats would pick it over with their twitching snouts.

In the distance children slid and shouted far out over the river, their voices thin and high like birds' cries. They were Lowry pin figures, black against the dazzle. The sun shone cold and hard. The water was set quite fast, locked except for one narrow channel where the weir fell and raced for a hundred yards or so before the ice closed its fingers round it. Now there were a dozen of the grebe, facing against the current, ducking their long necks like crested snakes. Inshore an ungainly assortment of ducks and swans waddled and slithered on the ice, falling about like drunken portly old men. At the lock they were busy clearing the gates of ice, heaving and straining at the frozen wheel to set the mechanism going. Under the middle arch of the bridge *Whale* steamed and plunged, butting blunt-nosed through the barrier, leaving a churning debris of broken floes behind. Two men stood on the bow with long ironshod poles helping to smash and prod and the tough little engine snorted and coughed. The lower gates were opened and she crunched her way in, sending huge flaws pistolling through the panes of ice. The gates closed, champing and grinding on the frozen masses while the lock-keeper swore and shouted. It needed two men on the wheel and another couple to push the floating islands away.

Now they opened the upper gates, the weight of water helping to break the ice cascades and force the gates open. While the level rose the men sucked at mugs of tea, blowing and snorting, laughing in a cloud of steam and banging their gloved hands together. The engineer leant out of his donkeyhouse and quipped the lock-keeper on his easy shore-life. Then they were off again. The engine which had been hiccoughing contentedly to itself as it idled, belched and stuttered and they moved against the pack, upstream towards Richmond, scattering the skaters and the boys who were daring each other to cycle across.

And now again the wastes stretched in front of him. The gang had disintegrated under the persistent hand of cold. There was no longer even the distraction of work, the illusion of contact. He had enough to live on for a couple of months and then he would have to find something else. Even Walden was elusive these days. He seldom came into the *Yacht* and when he did showed no inclination to linger. He was off on business of his own. Without them both there was no fun in drinking though he still found his way there for a chat with Alec when the silence of *Mimosa* became unbearable. His life had shrunk to the merest physical pulsation so that the days seemed hardly to revolve at all. He slept or read away long hours, cooked and ate, fetched water or paraffin, set bait for his visitors. He was alone with the rats. Sometimes he thought that they too had left him. But they would be back. He slept with the door shut and a small heater burning in the cabin. Even so the frost iglooed round him. Beyond the neat radius of the little fire the roof was glassed with his breath. It would never stop. The world had tilted half a point on its axis and the Thames had become a glacier, London huddled in the centre of a snow plain. The sea froze along the coast. Only the almost imperceptible lengthening of the days showed that time moved on at all.

He woke in a sweat. There it was again. They had broken through at last. The unmistakable rasping of, chiselling of sharp fangs on wood and skitter of claws behind the panelling opposite the bunk. He sat up in bed, reached for his torch and switched it on. It was a new one, ex-army, that Walden had got for him. Its hard thick beam cut into the darkness. 'Go away,' he shouted, 'sod you. Go away!'

There was silence. He looked at his watch. It was four o'clock. He lay down again, straining his ears and eyes into the dark but there was no more movement and at last he fell asleep. And now a curious ritual began that was repeated every morning. As he lay half conscious part of his mind would be listening so that he was aware of the slightest sound. He slept like a cat waiting. And it came. No longer the gnawing, only the dried whisper of feet as it scampered through the tunnel from saloon to cabin and he would leap up in the dark, blaze out his torch and swear in a loud voice, and there would be silence again. Always it was four o'clock.

After a week he was exhausted. He laid bait for it but it was ignored. He bought an evil trap, a backbreaker that nearly took his hand off when he tried to set it, but it was always empty though he tempted it with better food than he ate himself. The seventh night he was so weary he sank down into sleep like a man drowning and could have cried when he was dragged up from the bottom, his stomach churning, his mouth rank with bile. 'Go away,' he cried it now almost hysterically even in his own ears. The sound stopped. He listened and waited although he knew the pattern by now. It wouldn't come again that night. There was no need to look at his watch.

Suddenly he began to laugh to himself in the dark. It was grotesque but it made a kind of loony sense. He had begun to ask himself why it came, what was it after and now he saw. It would make a good story: *The Rat Who Saw God*. He could tell it in the rat's own words. How once when it was out looking for food a great light suddenly shone on it and a voice called to it in a strange tongue. Surely it was God. And so every night he came again and the vision was renewed and he went away silent and happy.

Wire netting, the man in the shop had said. Why hadn't he remembered before? Tomorrow he would cover the holes and block the way through the panelling. There would be no more visions. 'And when I came again the way was closed against me. God withdrew himself and since then I wander seeking what I have lost and restless all my days. No one believes me anymore but I remember that once when I was young I saw God.'

Did we all see him when we were young? he wondered. He felt a kind of sympathy with the rat now he was omniscient, seeing what would happen tomorrow when he bought the wire. Is it something we apprehend so far and then have to do without in case we come to depend on it? At college he too had aspired to visions. He laughed now when he thought of his impudence. He had prayed and masturbated and agonised over his fidgeting hand. He had knelt in the dark emptying his mind until he had felt it lift up away from him as he retreated down away from the upper layers of consciousness and then he was poised, held among the stars with the earth slowly turning beneath him and he understood for an eternity of seconds. Then it had stopped. He had sweated and wrestled but there was nothing. A wall had grown up, sometimes it seemed almost a physical barrier just above his eyes inside his head, and he couldn't get past it, couldn't get past himself anymore. He concentrated until his head swam and his body was withered with numbness. He climbed into bed despairing. This was the dark night of the soul. Oh he had read all about it, he recognised it alright.

One man might help him if he had the guts to ask. Sym had heard him lecture, and seen him work miracles of comprehension in unleavened student minds, making them laugh and weep inside, and cheer him like a latter-day Abelard as he taught them love in a post-Christian society. The interview was given. Stumbling he explained, all of it. He had listened patiently and then he had answered. Perhaps Sym had mistaken his vocation. When he was married many of these problems would disappear. Many young men had them. He went away broken but accepting and got himself a girl-friend as quickly as possible. It was too lonely without. He stopped going to communion because she didn't go and it seemed to divide them. But he missed it, missed the feeling of power and identity, identification that flowed along his body to his fingertips. There was never anything like it again. Sex was quite different.

It had never occurred to him to doubt the rightness of the decision. He had been rejected and rightly. He wasn't the stuff saints are made of. He must find another way. He had turned to writing. He had become like everyone else, sceptical, finding hope only in a joyless humanism that was a continual intellectual grind, that had to be tempered and beaten in the belief that it gave a basis for living. Maybe science would find the answer even yet. At least in its principles it had to deal with the questions that had vexed philosophers. Perhaps we had to learn to be empirical about living, that you have to be and make up the rules as you go along, tossing them out of the window when more evidence turns up. But there ought to be a substitute for the power, the strength. We shouldn't be asked to do without it completely before we could grow up. He felt himself drifting, the ideas carrying him far out to sea. Tomorrow he would buy the wire.

The next night he listened as its teeth grated on the metal. He didn't speak or shine the light. It never came again. He took his wire barricades further, trying to stop them from getting in at all until *Mimosa* was like Nomansland and they retreated to the bank again. He threw away the baited remnants and hid the tin and the trap, cached against another attack. January would soon be over. Surely the snow would go sometime. And then Sassie was back.

She came walking along the bank to meet him as if she had known he would be there at just that moment and it was as if she had never been away. He knew better now than to ask where but he couldn't hide his delight. The cold seemed less strong and as they trudged across the slippery catwalk with its gleaming jet incrustations of polished ice, holding on to the metal handrail for safety although it seemed to flay the skin from his palm, he saw far out, riding the broken water, the flock of crested birds.

'Look!' He touched her arm. They stopped at the passing place. 'There are twenty-two now.'

Sassie nodded and smiled. 'They're quite rare near civilisation like this. You might never see as many again unless you went to live on an estuary.' They moved on across the river towards the *Yacht*. It almost seemed as though Walden had been waiting for them.

'There you are and just in time to buy a round. It's time we had a night out.' Alec set up the glasses.

After a couple of pints Sym found himself swung between the two like a thrown ball, caught for a moment and tossed again. He wanted to go home to bed more than anything but the weeks of abstinence had wound him tighter and tighter so that he swung back to the warmth and light, the ease, and Walden's voice booming above it all through a deepening cloud of drink. There had been days when he had sworn and kicked the door in his frustration unable to concentrate on reading or writing until he had deliberately, coldly, silenced his flesh, jeering at himself as he came and muttering fierce obscenities into the emptiness. Now he was hung up, strangled by his own tight noose. He would probably be impotent anyway. He lifted his mug for a long pull.

'Let's visit the big city, the unholy smoke,' Walden was saying. 'I haven't been there for weeks. Let's see how they're getting along with their daily dying.'

They were out in the cold again, Walden leading the way towards the little station that swarmed with tourists in the summer but was almost deserted now though there was a good fire in the waiting room. They bought single tickets. 'Who knows whether we shall ever come back,' Walden said. They took over a compartment in the little green electric train, wiped the steam from the windows and stared out into the grey barren afternoon as it trundled towards the city centre. 'Thousands of people do this every day of their lives. They are carried in the lighted, upholstered belly of this robot reptile to slave in glasshouses where they are forbidden to throw stones in case the whole thing should shatter into senseless fragments.' Walden was in full flight now.

Sym peered out at the suburban gardens under their pall of snow. Most of the houses had their lights on already. They were thinking about tea. Kettles were put on to boil. The children would come home, unwrapping their warm bodies, putting scuffed shoes and Wellingtons to dry for the next morning and behind their entrance the door would close, sealing off the world outside, making tight cocoons against the cold and dark. The incomprehensibility of other people's lives seized him. Perhaps he had been out in the snow too long and was dazzled by it.

Occasionally they drew up at an unidentified station. Doors slammed, a whistle blew. There were other travellers then. The pace quickened as if the train was in a hurry to be there. It fled between Wimbledon and Clapham Junction, the city thickening around it, the houses clotting into streets, lights going on everywhere now, the concentration stretching away from the windows, ageing as if they were rushing back in time as well as space through the depressive thirties to the gothic squalor of the late Victorian, uncovering the vast tell like a kicked antheap. They drew into Waterloo where the ants were already on the homeward march, swirling towards their train in a tide that would wash him away if he didn't thrust himself against it. He took Sassie's arm and pressed it a little. Ahead Walden bucked his way through the current, waiting for them to catch up beyond the barrier. Voices, sounds beat on their heads but Sym had the feeling of having come to a foreign country where he didn't speak the language. Perhaps in time he would learn to pick out a word here and there, to make himself understood.

'Look at them,' Walden roared. 'The fools, the mindless bloody herd. Come on.'

They followed him across the breaking waves of people and through the great portal that has the maniacal grandeur of fascist architecture, the wind reaching out to them, and down the steps to the street. It was almost dark now. The road seethed with home-going traffic. 'We'll never get across this lot. Let's take the subway.' He guided Sassie towards the hole in the ground. They clattered along the stone corridor and came into a strange underground amphitheatre big as a football pitch, the walls rising up sheer with pierced openings where the ants darted in and out. It was open to the air and dirty snow was packed hard on its concrete floor. It was dimly lit and cavernously depressing.

'What is it?' Sym almost felt impelled to whisper.

'A temple to Mammon,' Walden answered. The traffic growled and roared above them. 'For sacrifice of course. Sometimes they seal off those openings; leave just one and let a few unsuspecting victims trickle in. Then that's sealed too and they're left. They watch them on closed-circuit telly. It's amazing what happens. In the end there's just one left and they take him away and give him a pension and a knighthood for services to industry.'

'Come on,' Sassie shivered. 'I'm cold.' As they entered the

opposite mouth Sym looked back at the shadowy arena. It could have been.

The tunnel brought them to the foot of the bridge. They climbed the steps to the windy span and crossed the river, flowing here but littered with rafts of packice. Up and down stream the city lowered blackly above the banks, some sections in darkness from the power cuts. The air cut like steel wire. 'It reminds you of the blackout,' Sassie said. Only the passing buses were bright behind steamy windows. 'I'm hungry,' she said.

'Food first and then drink,' Walden agreed. They turned into a grill bar lit by candles and ate chicken and chips and apfel strudel to jukebox accompaniment, hanging out their coffee til opening time and then along the Strand towards Charing Cross. And all the way Sym felt this strange detachment as if he was seeing these people and places for the first time or in a dream; as if at any given signal they might all rise into the air or exhibit tongues of flame so alien were they. He remembered a poem of Graves about bringing the dead to life and wondered if that was what he was doing that all these untouchables, untouchable because they seemed to move on a different plane from his, should be walking about within his grasp but not of it since his mind was unable to grasp them, to understand what mechanical process kept them in motion, in being.

'How do they keep on going?' he asked when they had reached a warm refuge and the glasses were lined up in front of them. 'All this,' he waved his hand at the walls covered with Victorian handbills, relics of hansom cab days, a fritillary of bric-à-brac prettying the walls, 'all this lot, what is it supposed to evoke?' He was aware of Walden's glitter above his drink as he watched him fumbling for concepts. 'Did it ever add up to anything?'

'At the time do you mean? You can answer that better than anyone else here.'

Sym was startled, seeing himself in a new role, teacher, leader, the one who knows.

'Isn't that what they taught you?' Walden asked and this time it wasn't a sneer: it was a genuine wanting to know.

'At university you mean? No that wasn't what they taught you. That was something you had to find out in spite of them.' He considered carefully, 'It's something I'm finding out all the time. But aren't we all?' He turned to Sassie.

'We should be,' she swilled the pale drink in her glass. 'What do you think?' She turned to Walden, throwing him the problem lightly but unavoidably. 'Should we be learning?'

It was as though she had broken the rules of the game and he was free to throw down his hand, to toss it off, and Sym was aware of a kind of breathlessness as though they were waiting for him to show his cards but he only laughed loud and short into the waiting and said, 'Your turn to buy a round, Sassie,' and she pushed her bag obediently towards Sym and said:

'You get them.'

There was an almost sexual pleasure in opening the soft liquorice bag, burrowing his hand in the scented contents, so intimate that the bar faded round him. It was like being alone with her in the dark, the scent of her body beside him. I shall be in trouble if I go on like this, he thought. He took out the purse and snapped the catch to. Only a few seconds had passed but the three of them seemed poised like a tableau. Why had she given it to him? Why not bought her own? She always did at home. Suddenly he realised that it was the first time they had been out together apart from the night they had rowed up the river and that seemed worlds ago. As he ordered the drinks he looked round. Was this where she came on her nights off? He checked himself. 'Nights off' implied a permanency he couldn't rely on. But then she had said something about always going where the landlord knows you. She hadn't seemed to know anyone here or she wouldn't have asked him to get the round. He had come full circle. He picked up his glass.

'You haven't answered my question.' She smiled up at Walden, raising her glass in her left hand, the other making patterns in the spilt beer on the table-top so that the seal ring burned for a moment a dull ember against the dark wood.

'You know what I think about learning and its limitations.'

'People change. You might have.'

'Do they?' Sym heard the eagerness in his own voice.

'We are what we are,' Walden couldn't resist the challenge. 'And we become ourselves.'

'But which self?' she was tormenting him and he tossed his head, a buffalo flicking away a fly.

'There's only one self.'

'But we're not all as lucky as you. Sometimes there seem to be two or three and then how do you know which one to pick?'

'Psychology,' Walden took his mouth from the glass for a moment and again Sym was reminded of an animal feeding. 'Bullshit!' and put it to sup again.

'So there's no hope?' Sassie was determined to push him further.

'Hope. Kids' stuff. Lollypops under the bedclothes and a warm hand down your pyjama leg. There's only what is and that's yourself.'

'And this lot?' Sym waved an arm to include the other drinkers.

'They don't exist. Shadows, and I'm sick of them. Come on, drink up. Let's find somewhere else.'

Outside the drink gave them protection against the cold. They crossed to Trafalgar Square. The fountain basins were empty; lions, dolphins, nymphs bowed under dirty snow. Walden tilted his head.

'Is it cold up there?'

Two policemen strolling in long dark cloaks turned their heads as he bayed, decided he was harmless and continued their plod, their breath coming and going regularly like twin exhausts.

'See the benefits of moral conviction,' Walden said. 'They don't even feel the cold like the rest of us. Those were the days,' he waved towards the remote admiral sailing the rough sky above them. 'He was an individualist. Twisted things and people the way he wanted them and got away with it.'

'It wasn't much good to her.'

'I've often thought,' Sym craned his neck back, 'that there's something very symbolic about the way they put him right up there. As if they wanted to point out to the herd that he was so far above them that the ordinary rules didn't apply to him. He was the nation's darling. He must have been a great embarrassment to them all with his disregard for conventional morality.'

'Sticking him up there was a form of castration you mean?' Walden said. 'I reckon it would be too, on a cold night like this. And what about the famous last words? True or false?'

'I don't think it matters. What matters is that everyone wanted to think they were true. They liked the idea of him being so alive that he wanted human contact even when he was dying. Wanted to know he was loved.' Sym turned towards St. Martin's white steps. They were clear of snow. A newsboy's placard caught in the wind and crashed down, burying its meaningless headlines, the daily scream of disaster and chaos. The shadows under the portico were carved in black ice. A courting couple clung together for warmth, his hands seeking comfort under the folds of her coat as they pressed into each other. For a moment Sym envied them their absorption. The drink was wearing off. He and Sassie could have been at home now.

'It doesn't last long in this weather. Let's get in and stoke up or we shall be sober as judges. Sym's already getting his sermon look.' Walden pushed open a door into warmth and light. 'This is more like it.'

When they stepped out into the street again the lights were going out behind them. Sym felt himself awash. They had drunk and argued all evening, Walden paying two rounds to every one of theirs. Sym no longer knew what it had all been about. Once he had even thought he had seen the tall elderly man they had met at the Spanish hotel; Lance, he fumbled for the name. Once Walden had offered him a watch for three pounds. He had bought it from him and put it on, promising to pay later. Walden had laughed and told him not to take it into a repair shop for a little while if it went wrong. Sym decided not to ask why. He couldn't refuse it now without running into Walden's mockery but it felt like lead on his wrist.

Now they were out in the street with the other revellers, faced with the long journey home. Did they feel as bad as he did? Walden gave no sign apart from a narrowing of the eyes. Sassie didn't seem affected either but then she had been drinking shorts to their pints. He tried to do sums in his fuddled head. If one short equalled half a pint how much had she had in pints? He felt the walls of his mouth contract and run with saliva, and spat fiercely in the gutter to keep his gorge down. All along the street the pubs were emptying, anonymous figures stumbled onto the pavement blinking in the eye-watering wind.

'Just have a slash,' he muttered and made for the nearest dark alley.

'Mind it doesn't drop off,' Walden called. 'We'll wait for you.'

He spat hard again and again as he searched for a private corner. There was an unlit phone-box but he couldn't bring himself to use it. Besides, someone had probably beaten him to it already and the urinal stench might make him throw up. Maybe it would be better to ditch the lot at that. But he hated the anguished retching of drunkenness as if you were being torn inside out, the lacerated throat and trembling body. He would hang on as long as possible. He splashed tidily against a wall and thought how it would be frozen to a glacier in half an hour. Carefully he zipped up. Mustn't run the risk of breaking it, must adjust person before leaving. Then he walked very straight up the tunnel of the alley towards the light. Mustn't let Walden see.

At first he couldn't see Sassie. Walden's huge duffle seemed monolithic. Perhaps she had left him, or them, to totter home together. 'Where's Sassie?' he articulated carefully.

Walden pointed across the road and down. It was a minute before he could find her. A group of men had gathered in a circle, bound in menacing, drunken aggression. They had caught a victim, a shabby youngster, drunk too, swaying in time with his clenched fists. Sym moved closer. Sassie stood between the boy and the foremost of the group. Their faces and postures in the half shadow were Breughelesque, distorted.

'Leave him alone. He's only a kid,' Sym heard her say. Then as they muttered and shifted, 'I don't care what he's done. Leave him alone.'

'Is she alright?' Sym asked.

'Best not to interfere. We'd make things worse. End in a punch-up and then somebody might get hurt. Yes, she's alright. Watch.'

The boy had squared up to them. 'I'll fight them all. I'm not afraid of them.'

'And you don't be so silly,' she turned on him. 'Go home quietly or you'll get yourself hurt. Let him through now and go home all of you. Grown men on to one boy.' She gave him a little shove towards them and they fell away on either side as she followed him through. Suddenly they were aware of the cold, grumbled and pulled their collars up, began to drift away down the street. The boy lingered. 'Go on now, go home.' He turned away. Sym found himself standing sober with clenched fists.

'That was a crazy thing to do. They might have turned on you.'

'But they didn't. When you see something like that you don't think, don't stop I mean.' They walked slowly towards Charing Cross. 'I can't stand violence.'

'Suppose we'd had to come and help you out?' He was angry with her.

'But you didn't.'

'Walden seemed to think you could manage. They might have turned nasty.'

She didn't answer. He wanted to go on, could hear the rough words mounting in his head but he was saved by a busy road to cross, the station yard with its black devils of taxis and the problem of finding a train that would take them home.

‘Come back with me,’ he said when Walden had left them. ‘I’ve missed you.’

‘Have you? I thought you were angry with me.’

‘That was only because,’ Sym shrugged helplessly. ‘Sometimes I’ve wanted you so much I haven’t known what to do with myself.’

She touched his coat briefly, ‘Let’s sleep now. Suddenly I’m tired.’

‘Alright. But you’ll come back with me?’ He knew he was pushing her and he was afraid. But he knew too that he had to. He had been alone too long. There had been long tracts of the evening when he had looked at the people round him with a frightening detachment as though they belonged to another lifeform under his microscope. Later as they drank their coffee he noticed that the lines in her face at the corners of the eyes had deepened, and in her neck too.

‘You’re not looking at me are you?’ she bent her head.

‘I was thinking. Don’t go away again yet.’ He had to say it.

‘No, not yet.’

February

. . . clouds upliften,
Schire sheds the rain in showers full warm

'FEBRUARY. It is still very cold. I write my notes like a child. The class nature table with the daily weather recording, the little pictures of clouds and rain and sun. It's difficult to draw a picture of cold, iron frost that clenches the earth tighter and tighter, squeezing out every last drop of warmth and life. If it were the arctic we should be used to it; it would have a congealed beauty of its own but here it is bitter and featureless, the monotony of half-tones, a dingy grey. The snow is trampled and soiled, gritted and ashen, stripped from the branches by the wind, crusted with a black rind. Only if you go right into the heart of the island or far along the tow-path is it better. They have been feeding the sheep and deer in the park with fodder and mangels for weeks. The other day we went to see how they were doing. They looked wretched, long dismal sheepfaces, their fleece filthy against the snow, matted and trailing, bodies heavy with young, clumsy. Plunging into drifts, trying to shelter behind bunches of leafless sticks that used to be bushes. And the high antlers of the stags branchy as they lifted their heads and looked at us nervously. The old one on guard chivvying the does and youngsters away. Not to be trusted. They have stripped bark from the trees in places. Do the trees feel cold, naked, the white flesh showing, bone and flesh together, rigid. Soon it must break. Everyone says so but all days are the same. You walk huddled into yourself as if expecting a blow.

Loving is hard in the cold. We cling together as if we couldn't get enough of each other because of the clothes between. She has been back three weeks.

"I wonder by my troth, what thou and I
Did, till we lov'd?"

I never understood that before when we had to read it in our first year at St. Giles. We don't eat anymore or sleep much either. We live on air, talk, loving. We've both lost seven pounds in weight; even there we keep pace.

Today it snowed again, another heavy fall, but the crystals themselves are of a lighter, finer design than before. I thought I noticed an almost imperceptible rise in temperature, half a point perhaps, though it may be just wishful thinking. Everything much cleaner again. How did we ever live any other way except locked in by frost and snow? We hardly see Walden now and when we do he gives us a nod from the other side of the bar. Winter must be a hard time for pirates and smugglers.'

Sym eased his pencil and looked into the fire. A log fire-eaten on its underside crashed into the glowing bed of the stove and began to consume fiercely, the delicate lacework of ash breaking apart in the draught and roaring up the chimney.

'What are you smiling at?' Sassie lay watching him from the bunk.

'Was I? I was thinking how difficult the cold must make it for my smugglers.'

'I expect they find other ways. Walden's wrong,' she added.

'What do you mean?'

'He said, says, people don't change. But they do. You were quite shocked and a bit frightened when you first heard them.'

Sym remembered, 'So I was.'

'So you've changed.'

'That's your fault.'

'Is it?'

'Don't you know?'

'Then he's wrong again.' He looked at her questioning. 'He says everyone is responsible for themselves but if we can affect people, change them, then aren't we a bit responsible for them too?'

'I thought you agreed with Walden.'

'Perhaps I've changed too.'

'Don't change too much.'

A little later he said, 'Shall we stay in or shall we go out?'

She pulled the blanket around her up to the chin, hugging herself close. 'I'd rather stay in but I think we ought to go out. I took a few things to Joyce the other day. I thought they wouldn't be doing too well in the cold. She seemed jumpy, more worried than usual. We haven't really seen Walden for weeks. Perhaps we should go and make sure everything's alright.'

'Suppose we can't find him or he won't talk to us?'

'At least we'll have tried.'

They found him at once. After, Sym wondered if Sassie had known he would be there. He was leaning across the counter as if his head and shoulders were too heavy to support themselves and had to be propped.

'So you've run me down. Buy me a drink someone.' Sassie ordered. Sym was running low but she never seemed to be short of money. 'No need to ask how you pass these cold days and nights. Well you have my blessing.' He raised two fingers in a gesture that could have been ecclesiastical. 'It's always best to be self-supporting, generate your own heat and light.'

'How's Joyce?' Sym asked.

'She finds it a little chilly I think,' Walden looked back at him levelly. 'Both the kids have the snivels. But it won't last. Rumour has it the thaw is on the way.'

'When it comes it'll sweep us all away,' Sassie turned the glass in her hand, catching the light on the surface of the oily liquid. 'How's business, Alec?'

'Not so bad now, Mrs. Parks. Picking up a bit. At first people didn't want to come out much but it's gone on so long they've got bored with sitting at home so they come and burn my electricity and watch my fire instead.'

'It's a handsome fire, a real pub fire,' Sassie said.

'Excuse me,' Walden put his glass down suddenly. 'I have to see a man about a dog.' He made for the door. A small dark man had just come in but at a nod from Walden he went towards the gents. He was sparsely dressed for the weather, without any top coat and his grey suit thin with wear. A dirty white silk scarf under the turned up collar was his only concession to the cold. Dimly he reminded Sym of someone.

'What about the old man then?' Alec asked, twirling a white cloth round a clean glass.

'What old man?' Sym turned back to the bar.

'The old boy who was found dead, died of the cold like a bird.'

'Did he live on the island?'

'Oh yes. You know him,' Alec turned to Sassie, 'lived in a beached pontoon. Always drunk, used to talk to himself. I wouldn't have him in here; he stank and the customers didn't like it. He must have got it somewhere though. Meths maybe. Anyway he's gone. Been dead a few days they reckoned. Nosy old Tom had a look through the window and give himself a shock. Serve him right. Still I suppose it was a good thing. Might never have found him. They say the rats was getting in. They had to break the door down. I wonder you didn't notice the police all over the place.'

Sym remembered the bundle of rags he had stepped aside for in the fog. There was a kind of dignity in a solitude as intense as that but to be gnawed by rats was another thing. Sassie looked a bit pale too. He wondered where Walden had got to. The police had been to the island. He imagined the fragile human bundle stirred by a large boot. How did they feel about it? Used to it probably. Thinking, he missed Walden's return.

'Seeing a man about a dog used to mean something different,' Sym said to change the conversation.

'Did it?' Walden pulled deep on his glass.

'That little man reminds me of someone but I can't quite place it.'

'He came to give me a weather report. What have you been talking about behind my back?'

'The old man,' Alec put in. 'The one they found dead.'

'Ah yes. Well he had privacy for it which is more than he'd have got in a public ward.'

'Will there be an inquest?' Sassie asked.

'Bound to be. The place has been swarming with police. I wonder they haven't been to see you. Though perhaps it's only our side. I suppose you've been too busy to notice.' Alec moved away to serve a customer. 'I've something I'd like you to look after for me if you would. Just for a week or so.' He dropped his voice so that Sym had to listen carefully.

'I don't ask what it is,' Sym said. He noticed that Sassie was watching him too, gauging his reaction perhaps.

'A suitcase. Put it away somewhere. Come back with me later and I'll let you have it.' Walden smiled round at them, 'Now let's have another drink.' Sassie paid again.

'Wait here,' Walden paused at the edge of the gangplank. 'Keep an eye open but I think they're all home in their little beds.'

It was a bright clear night. For once Sym could have wished it darker. Soon Walden's huge shadow appeared again. There had been no sign of a light on *Grey Gull*. He had obviously known just where to put his hand on the case he held out to Sym. A pulse throbbed sickeningly in his throat as he took Sassie's hand and they set off for *Mimosa*. He waited for the hand on his shoulder, for the solid shadow that suddenly moved dissolving into a human shape but the island was deserted, silent.

Down in the safety of *Mimosa* they stood in the dark listening. 'Don't light a light, I want to look out.' As he had done when he first heard the bumping on the hull he stood on a stool and raised the skylight. Nothing moved along the banks or out on the ice gleaming under the luminous sky. 'Right, light up.' The lamp dazzled them. 'Make a bit of noise. Poke out the fire. I'm going into the bilges.'

Taking the torch he removed the companionway and opened the little door behind which led through into the bowel of the boat. It smelled damp and cold. He wedged the case on the low shelf behind the lengths of pig-iron that served as ballast and covered it with a bit of sacking. It was the best he could do. As the light fell on the bottom of the boat he saw that the ice was covered with a thin film of sweat. Perhaps it was a little warmer. He backed out and pulled the door to behind him, replacing the steps. Then he went back into the light. 'So I've joined the smugglers.'

Sassie handed him a mug of coffee. 'I shouldn't ask.'

'Oh I shan't. It's my own reactions I'm amused by. It's like being a kid and playing hookey from school.'

'Supposing it were gold bars?'

'But it isn't and even if it were what good would it do to lock him up? What good would it do Joyce and the children? But I shan't look and then if anyone asks I just don't know. I don't think I'd make much of a liar but then I wouldn't make a policeman either. Now let's go to bed and forget about it.'

Two days later she said, 'I'm going to see Joyce. God knows how she's coping with all this and the children in bed with colds.'

'Alright, I'll come with you. Maybe she needs coal or something that you couldn't manage by yourself.'

Crossing the island they were aware of a subtle difference in the morning. 'Listen,' Sym took her arm.

'What is it?'

'A bird. I hadn't realised before how silent they've been.' Somewhere hidden a bird was singing, unlocking the stillness of the river with a spiralling scale of notes. Another chirruped hesitantly at first like a morning cough, a clearing of the tiny larynx, and then stronger. 'How do they know? I thought the frost had got them all.'

'Look,' Sassie pointed to a low branch where the snow clung thick. A slow drip had formed at the tip and fell with a miniature thud. Soon the smooth white skin below would be punctured with little holes like buckshot wounds. 'Oh they know.'

He felt a great lightness. 'That's over then.'

'Yes, that's over.'

'It might freeze again.'

'No, not this time.'

As they reached *Grey Gull* they saw children sliding far out on the ice. 'If it really is the thaw,' Sym said, 'the ice will start to melt. Those kids had better be careful.' He led the way across the gangplank and pushed open the hatch door, knocking but not waiting for an answer in usual boat custom. It reminded him of the homes of his childhood where the back-door was never shut. Sassie followed him in and it was too late to back out when they saw the strangers there. One of them moved his blue bulk in the shadows, turning the deep Prussian helmet slowly in his hands as if examining some strange piece of evidence.

They had walked into a tableau: Walden sitting relaxed in the armchair, rolling himself a cigarette, Joyce with Sophy on her lap on an upright chair, Jane standing by her mother and a small sharp man in a grey raincoat perched on the edge of the table.

'Sorry,' Sym said. 'We'll come back later.'

'They were just going,' Walden looked at the man in the raincoat. 'Weren't you?'

The room was very cold and starkly bare, a minimum of furniture and no trace of any small comfort. Sym wondered if the new transistor was sitting chillily in his bilges. The watch on his wrist ticked sonorously into his pocket.

The man in the raincoat sighed. 'You're not helping,' he said.

'You've looked. I let you look although you'd no warrant, and you've found nothing of course.'

'You were seen together. It's only a matter of time before we find him and then he'll tell us and that's that.'

'Everyone's been seen with him,' Walden said. 'What does that mean? That we're some vast network? You've bought him a drink before now.' He looked at Sym. The man in the raincoat looked at him too.

'Who's that then?' Sym held his voice steady. The old fear was rising in him, set going by the dark blue shadow, the sharp questions. He had been caught scrumping, knocking on doors. He had seen the shape of authority pacing as irrevocable as a tank towards his front door while he watched from the corner. The rules were made to be kept and you had chosen to break them. There's only one crime and that's getting caught. Surely they could hear his heart thudding out time with the watch.

'Gypsy Dick,' Walden pulled at his lighted roll and blew the sweet smoke through his nostrils.

'Who, Clack's boy?'

'Dick Hynes,' the man in the raincoat said.

'We only know him as Dick,' Sassie said, moving towards the dead fireplace and taking her cigarette case and lighter from her bag. 'I suppose we've all bought him a drink in our time. I don't imagine Mr. Clack pays them very well.'

'Them?' He pounced on the inoffensive pronoun.

'Clack's got two boys. Well, we call them the boys. Tom's in his fifties; got a wall eye.'

'Yes. We've seen him of course.'

'What's he been up to?' Sym asked.

'Pinching timber from Keeley's yard,' Walden answered. 'They seem to think I've been helping him.'

Sym looked at the empty stove. 'You could certainly do with some.' He heard his accent rising up the social scale as the conversation progressed. He was almost beginning to enjoy it. Careful, he thought, that's when you start to make mistakes.

'Keeley's don't find it funny. They lose hundreds of pounds every year.'

'And Dick's responsible for all that?'

'Some of it. He happens to be the one we know about.'

'How does he get it away? By lorry I suppose. I can't see him carrying hundreds of pounds worth away under his coat.'

'They float it away on the river like a raft. This island is ideally placed.'

'I see. So they've had a rather thin time of it recently.'

The plainclothes man looked puzzled. 'What do you mean?'

'Well, with the river frozen and all.' Sym hoped he wasn't overdoing it.

'Maybe they've found other things to do. What's your profession, sir, if I may ask?'

Before Sym could think Sassie answered for him, 'He's a writer.'

'I see. Published anything?'

'A couple of books,' Sym said truthfully.

'So this is all material to you?'

'Oh nothing's ever wasted if that's what you mean. That's my job.'

The man got off the table, easing his cramped buttocks with a slight wince. 'That's all for the moment I think until we catch up with Hynes but if you take my advice you'll be careful what you get mixed up in.' He faced Walden. 'There's no glamour in petty crime. It's just petty and nothing more. I don't know why intelligent, educated people choose to live like this but that's your affair. My wife wouldn't put up with it for a holiday.' He nodded to them all, the blue shadow put on its helmet and they went up the stairs. Boots scraped over the deck above and then *Grey Gull* rocked as they stepped onto the gangplank.

'You bloody fool!' Joyce spat the words at Walden who had sunk down in his chair. 'What happens when they catch him?'

'They won't. That was bluff.'

'What about his family?' Sassie said. 'Won't he have to come back for them? If they try to leave they'll be followed.'

'The birds have flown, all gone.' Walden got up and stretched. 'As soon as Tom said he'd found the old man dead, Dick took off. He knew they'd be knocking on all the doors asking questions.'

'If he'd stayed put they might have passed him by,' Sassie said.

'No, he said once they'd been reminded of his existence they'd find something to pin on him. It looks as if he was right too.'

'But why bring you in on it?' Sym asked.

'I expect old Tom had too much to say. You noticed how that plainclothes boy pretended at first he didn't know him. Anyway they don't like me. My face doesn't fit and they can't think how I keep going without any visible means of support. It's moral to gamble in stocks and shares even though you ruin people, businesses, even whole countries in the process but not to live as I do.'

'Talk,' Joyce said, 'words. And what happens to them,' she indicated the children, absorbed now in the corner with the little terrier, 'if you get put away?'

'You'd manage. I don't underestimate you.'

'Joyce,' Sassie broke in, 'we came to see if you wanted some coal.'

'Coal?' For a moment Sym thought she was going to cry. 'Yes, we do need some. It's so cold for the children.'

'We'll get you some now. I'll take the trolley.'

Suddenly Walden seemed to rouse himself. He heaved his body out of the chair. 'Come on, kids. We'll go wooding. Our share for the war effort. War on want. The refugees need your help.' They ran to him at once leaving their silent game in the corner and he took their scarves and coats from a hook behind the door and began to button them in and arrange the lengths of wool across their thin chests.

'Can we take Trudy?' Sophy begged and the terrier sat to attention, one white forepaw lifted.

'Come on then,' Walden bellowed at it and Jane climbed on a chair to reach the lead hanging behind the coats. In a few minutes the little procession was scraping its way across the deck.

Joyce looked at the other two. 'I'd take them away, go back home, but they'd miss him so much. You see, don't you?'

'He'd miss them too. Don't worry. It'll be alright and now we'll get that coal. A fire will make everything seem better.'

'The trolley's up on deck.'

'Come on then,' Sym took Sassie's arm. 'If we bring it back right away Joyce can have it all warm by the time they get back.'

It was difficult keeping it on an even track across the catwalk, even more difficult bringing it back with a hundredweight sack to balance. 'I don't know if it's the moral glow of the do-gooder I feel or whether it really is warmer,' he shouted back over his shoulder as he sweated over the load. Sassie had bought buns to toast and a half-pound of butter as well. Walden seemed rejuvenated by the walk and proud of the sackful of wood they had found. The children had patches of fresh colour on their cheeks and the ends of their noses though the warmth from the new fire made them snivel and cough as they sat in front of the open stove on the floor taking turns to roast the buns. Walden showed them how to poke the prongs of the fork neatly into the soft white flesh so that the bun didn't fall off into the flames.

'What I still don't understand,' Sym said daringly as he bit into a sooty bun, 'is how he got away. They must have taken something with them. Why didn't the lock-keeper wonder at all that little tribe trooping away with their bundles into the cold?'

'He didn't see them. That's why. Too risky. They might have had someone watching.'

'How then?'

'Over the ice.' Walden prodded the fire for the next bun-half.

'It's my turn, Daddy, isn't it?' Sophy said.

'Yes, my sweetheart. It's your turn. Give her the fork, Jane. It was the only way to go. Nature was on our side for once.' He was there, Sym thought.

'Little pitchers . . .' Joyce said warningly.

'What's our family motto, Jane?'

She turned her reddening face from the fire and said gravely, 'Receive information and give none.'

'That's my girl.'

'It was a bit risky wasn't it?' Sym asked.

'I suppose so. But it was the only way and the ice was firm enough then. I warned the children this afternoon,' he turned to Joyce as if offering her, hesitantly, some kind of truce, 'not to go out on the ice anymore and to keep Trudy off too. When it goes it'll go quickly and we don't want them drowned trying to rescue her. You hear that, kids? Remember now. If Trudy falls in she'll get herself out or you must come for one of us. Don't go after her, you hear?'

'Trudy won't go in. She's too intelligent,' said Jane, taking the last piece of bun from the fork.

'I feel we've averted a crisis,' Sym said as they sat together in Alec's later. They had agreed it would look better if they made no alteration in their usual routine.

'Several.'

'I couldn't pinpoint them all, or break them down into words but I could feel them all the time.'

'You did very well.'

'We're an unbeatable combination. We should go into partnership,' he joked, and regretted it as he sensed the slight withdrawal that deepened the lines on her face, making it an abstraction, gone beyond time, beyond the moment. 'Which one do you think is the fuzz?' he changed the subject quickly.

'That one over there,' she nodded towards a stranger in a dark blue donkey jacket, reading an evening paper. They played that game til it was time to go. That night, as she sometimes did, she preferred to sleep alone on her own little boat. Seeing the tiredness in her face he couldn't argue as he occasionally did now, not out of weakness as it would have been once, a clinging, but out of strength, to make things easier for her in spite of herself. In the morning she was gone.

He stood on the bank undecided. With night and the falling temperature the thaw had ceased. Now it was cold and grey with low cloud. The day seemed poised, waiting for the sun. He was stunned, numb without her. He hadn't expected it so suddenly. It must have been what he had said last night. Well he would go on as if she was there. He would go and see Walden, make sure they had enough wood even if he couldn't buy them coal. He laughed at himself. It was sympathetic magic and he knew it. If I can get to the end of the road before a car comes round the corner I'll get all my sums right. Still he had nothing else to do. He moved towards *Grey Gull*.

Walden met him halfway. 'Ah, I was just coming to find you. I thought we might make a little expedition.'

'How are the gentlemen in blue?'

'Very quiet. They won't come back unless they find him and they won't find him.'

'You're sure of that?'

'I'm sure.'

They turned towards the heart of the island. 'Where are we going?'

'You'll see.' They didn't seem to be following any path but Walden led the way confidently between the almost identical tree trunks, their feet leaving tell-tale tracks in the thin snow.

'Anyone could follow us quite easily,' Sym said in a carrying whisper.

The figure ahead turned. Sym pointed back to the path of prints. 'But not for long,' Walden waved his hand at the low sky. 'It'll rain soon.'

'Or snow,' Sym suggested.

'Not this time,' Walden marched on. Ahead, as if they were coming to a 'T' junction, was a track. They turned along it. It was somehow familiar. He remembered his afternoon collecting wood and smiled to himself. He knew now where they were going.

The pontoon was exactly as he had seen it last except for the finger of smoke. Even more deserted now, fallen asleep as though in time a high hedge might grow up round it and it be completely forgotten. 'Dick's place,' he said.

Walden nodded and fished in the pocket of his sandjeans. Looking down Sym saw that the ground was flurried with tracks, some leading back along the path, mingling with their own, others going away along the side of the house out of sight. Walden was at the front door fitting a key in the lock. Sym followed him inside. 'Do the police know about this?' he asked.

'Oh they'll have been here by now. They didn't find anything though.'

The place had been stripped of all but a few sticks of furniture and the stove. Sym wondered how much they'd been able to carry away or if the pieces he could see represented all they had had. The swing of an open door took his attention into the other room. It was mostly taken up with two double beds. Walden kicked at a galvanised bath left on the floor and it clanged protestingly into the silence. How had they managed, more especially the wisp of a wife Sym had glimpsed once or twice, still in her early twenties with five small children? There was no tap, not even cold, and no lavatory. Had she cooked on that stove or had there been a calor gas cooker that they had taken with them? How did you decide what to leave?

Walden poked among the remains like a professional. 'Not much worth taking here. We could chop up these bits for firewood. The beds might be buggy. Joyce wouldn't like that. Best to burn them.'

'What about that chest of drawers?' Sym suggested.

Walden tugged at the warped top drawer. 'Tidy lot. They always put things back the way they found them. They must have been all through this place with a toothcomb.' The drawer gave suddenly. It was empty. He worked his way through from top to bottom. 'Here's something they missed. Or perhaps they didn't think they were worth worrying with.' He drew out a clean picked bone, and held it up for Sym's inspection. It was reminiscent of a chicken's leg but much larger.

'What is it?'

'Swan's bones.' He threw it to join a pile of rusting tins in the corner.

Sym imagined the illicit banquet, the children gathered round the table like Bob Cratchitt's brood. Swan's broth for the youngest, dark gamey meat for those old enough to chew. The rats watching hopefully through the chinks, Gypsy Dick laughing in the oil-light, his greasy black curls shining as he carved and hacked at the carcase. Swansdown for pillows, swansfat for ointment and balm. Nothing wasted but the bones. Why had they kept them? Perhaps the children played with them or Dick had some idea of carving them, knife handles; nothing wasted. Walden pushed the drawer back into place.

Closing the door behind them they stepped out into a slow

mizzle. 'Here it comes,' Walden lifted his head at the sky.

'How is it you and Sassie always know about the weather?'

'Instant forecasts,' Walden laughed. 'We are in communion with Mother Nature.'

'She's gone,' he hadn't meant to say it.

Walden paused. 'Now that I didn't know. The Spring perhaps, restless. She'll be back.' He walked on into a rain that was like falling dusk. 'Come back and have a drink with us.'

'I was going to bring you some more wood.'

'We can pick it up as we go,' Walden stooped to gather a dead branch, dragging it out of the melting snow and sog of blackened leaves. They followed the path all the way back. Sym was surprised to see it led to the slipway and the boatsheds.

Two figures stepped out of the dark oblong of the sheds, pierced on one side by a square of yellow light, two small figures, one stout, one thin, the features almost indistinguishable against the monochrome. Rain fell heavily now, more sharply cold than snow, penetrating to shivering depths, plopping noisily on the stiff snow-crust, worm-eating it away, undermining until it crumpled and sank into slush. The stout one stepped directly into their path. The other hovered scrawnily, becoming recognisable as they approached as Tom.

'Mr. Walden! A word with you.'

'Yes?' Walden's head was up, a foot over the other man's trim navy cap.

'I want you out, off my mooring.'

'Oh?' The sound was quizzical.

'That's it. You encouraged him, you and your anarchist ideas. He wouldn't have done it by himself.'

'Don't underestimate him,' Walden said. 'People are often more than you think.'

'I'm not here to listen to that. You're out. Keeley's a friend of mine and an employee of mine steals from him. But you put him up to it. Everyone knows you did and God knows what else beside that they haven't dug out yet. Well you're finished. Move that damn hulk of yours off the island.'

Walden held out a hand to the rain. 'It's raining. You know what'll happen now. The floods. We shan't be able to move as long as the river's high.'

Sym found himself speculating at what point the little man would explode. 'As soon as the river's navigable I want you gone. I'm giving you notice now.' He turned to Sym, 'I've no quarrel with you but I advise you not to get mixed up with this man. River rats that's all they are. Poison's too good for them.' He began to stump away towards the sheds but swivelled on his heel for a last shot. 'Off my mooring. Off!'

Soaked through they were glad to see *Grey Gull* and Sassie's coal burning steadily in the stove. 'So that's Clack himself,' Sym shook the water drops from his hair into the stove where they hissed and spat as they evaporated. Walden draped the two coats over a couple of kitchen chairs to dry. Like that they seemed weary, reaching out to the fire like thin old men. 'Old clothes upon a stick to scare a bird,' Sym thought.

'That's the boyo,' Walden said, 'a little inflated puff-ball of a man.'

Joyce appeared from the door leading to the galley. She smiled briefly at Sym. 'I sent the kids to school. They seemed so much better this morning. Jane's cough's nearly gone.'

'What about some tea? We're perished.' She went to put the kettle on.

'Did he mean it?' Sym asked, rubbing his wet red hands together to dry them.

'Oh yes, he meant it.'

'Meant what?' Joyce had come back with three mugs and a bottle half full of milk in time to catch the last words.

'We met that little bastard Clack. He's given us the push.'

'Told us to go?' She bent to arrange the things on the table but Sym thought he saw a shade of something, perhaps relief, cross her face though she was careful to keep it out of her voice.

'I pointed out that it was impossible for the moment. He couldn't get round that of course. Accused me of leading Dick astray. I liked that. That was a good touch.'

'Where will we go?' The kettle began to scream from the galley. While she was gone Walden stared into the fire.

As the brown tea spouted into the mugs he said, 'We'll take her up to the public moorings. Live rent free while we look about.'

She handed him a mug and held the sugar basin while he helped himself to two heaping spoonsful. Sym felt he was watching a ritual where every commonplace gesture had meaning and the words spoken were only a surface layer covering stratified depths of intimations.

'Supposing there isn't room?'

'We can lie where the barges come in. When we know one's due we can drop back a bit and lie outside it as long as it's there.'

'How will you get there?' Sym accepted a steaming mug.

'How do you think? I can do a bit of work on the engines while we're waiting for the river to go down in the next few weeks. I'm sick of this island anyway. We've been here four years. That's a hell of a long time.' Joyce sat quietly stirring her tea. Walden seemed to have taken a new lease of life at the thought of moving.

'He doesn't seem worried at all,' Sym said when he had gone outside for a moment.

'It gives him an excuse to tinker with the boat,' Joyce spoke as if of a child. 'That's when he's happiest really, down in the engine room with an oilrag.'

'And you?'

She shook her head and got up. He sensed she was almost holding her breath, giving nothing away. 'More tea?'

He held out the mug and she took it with head bent, not looking at him. He felt the temperature begin to rise. 'Sassie's gone away.'

'She'll be back soon.' She gave him back the filled mug and momentarily their fingers met on the handle. 'You and I shouldn't be alone together.'

'No.' As he said it he thought that there are situations it is best not to touch. He didn't love her but she attracted him and he knew that at any moment he might find himself making love to her and then involved, up to the neck, with nothing but misery all round to follow. It was a shock to his inbred puritanism that he could want another woman while he was in love with one. But he couldn't delude himself it was because Sassie was away. He wondered if it was the situation, the idea, that involved him rather than the person. Then it was best to be a voyeur of life. He stirred his sugarless tea and avoided Joyce's face.

When Walden came back he was full of delight. 'It's breaking up fast. There'll be some trouble now. When it starts to flood and brings down the chunks of ice that haven't melted: that's when you've got to look out. You'll have to let the ropes out a bit so she can rise with the water. Do Sassie's too if she's not back.'

Sym took his steaming coat from the chair. It smelt wetly of wool, a remembered childhood smell. He would go home and defend his little cockleshell against the weight and power of the river. Under the rain there was a new feeling abroad as he stepped outside. The air was alive. He imagined plants unfolding, slow-motioned, like a film, seeds stretching their sides in the dark until the brown skin split and a fleshy feeler unfurled for its probe up into the light. Animals stirred in their winter sleep, fur frowsty with dust and the scarcely perceptible to and fro of the breath. The ice still lay from bank to bank but there were long cracks in it, opaque patches and brown holes where the water boiled and frothed eating into the glassy rind.

In the next two days he saw it crumble and shatter, long stretches of open water free themselves. What had seemed so permanent was a trick of season and temperature. Water had become solid and now was liquid again. He poled great punts of ice, six inches thick and several feet across, away from *Mimosa*'s sides until his arms cracked with the agony after all these weeks of idleness. The glittering masses bore down on them like galleons as he thrust and fended until the tide caught them and bobbed them away. When *Mimosa* was safe he fought for Sassie's little boat, easier because it was moored among others, a converted lifeboat on the outside protecting it; the ice pack banging against its round metal hull and bounding away again. Reports of sinkings came from all around, some holed below the water line, some supported by the ice that had sprung undetected leaks and now began to wallow and stagger as the river seeped in. Men baled and pumped. Clack could be heard shouting himself hoarse with instructions to the shambling Tom as moorings were slackened and strengthened to take the rising race of the waters. Two more sluices were opened on the weir as the ice fleets poured down from the upper reaches of the river on their way to the sea. Anxiously Sym watched over his two charges but they behaved impeccably, *Mimosa* jogging on her ropes like a plastic duck in the bath.

At night he forced himself against weariness to put it all down, though his eyes were glazed with staring into the water and his head swirled and tugged against thought. The island itself was melting into the river, the snow washed away, and the mud streaming down the banks like cocoa where men slipped and skidded; more treacherous than the ice. Even the water tank on deck unfroze. The ice cascades on the lock gates shattered and fell in sculptured fragments as the gates were opened and *Whale* chunted her way up river. When Sym went for his first walk beyond the lock in three days the lock-keepers were oiling and painting, busy as rooks in their dark uniforms. As he crossed the catwalk, washed clean of cinders by the rain, he stood for a moment staring out against the splintering drops that drove into his face and eyes. Far out he peered where the river ran fastest. The grebe had all gone. Not one tufted snake head lifted over the twisting water. Only the mallard were left, caught in a mating frenzy as if they had time to catch up on.

By the end of the week the river rolled swollen brown and sinuous. No, not brown, he decided as he leant on the hand rail, ochrous was more like it: yellow ochre spumed with flake white. But sinuous yes, as if it were a beast flexing its muscles in leap after tireless leap. The pace and suck drew you down, drowned, hurried along with your body tumbling helplessly engulfed. The level crept up the bank until the grass grew waving under water. He hoped *Mimosa*'s gangplank would be long enough. The ropes were nearly out to their fullest extent. He relied most on a heavy chain he had found in the chain locker in the bows. It must have been used for the anchor in her navy days. There were two big anchors up on the top deck, either of which he imagined would have held a battleship. Well they might have to be used again if she ever broke loose. He would probably throw himself in with them if he had to drop them over the side. He saw himself sinking down clinging to the anchor, a stream of bubbles from his nostrils, his hair on end like the grass, shrunk to dwarf dream-size and laughed. She would come back soon. He pushed open the door of the *Yacht*.

She was standing with her back to him talking to Alec. As he walked across the bar towards her the room seemed to be holding its breath but perhaps it was only himself. 'You've missed a lot,' he said as he took his place beside her.

'You'll have to tell me all the news.'

'It's hard to know where to begin.'

Sassie looked at him critically. 'You look half starved, the orphan child.'

'Thanks, that makes me feel a lot better.'

'It was a clumsy way of suggesting a proper meal. Let's take a bus. There's a good Chinese place I want to show you.' They were edgy, circling each other. She had never been like this before when she had come back. He had always been the one to show strain.

'Alright then. One for the road first.' Sym jingled his last few coins in his pocket. Either he would have to get a job now the worst of the weather was over or he would have to go on assistance.

'I'll get it,' she opened the familiar bag and took a note from her purse. For the first time it occurred to him to wonder where it came from but he shoved the thought fiercely away. Not today, not now.

After drinks and food, they found a coffee bar where they sat out the afternoon in the warm, downing cup after cup of pale Italian froth and playing the juke-box like teenagers who had nowhere to go. In the restaurant she had said to him, 'You must be short of money by now,' and made him take a five-pound note, on loan to salve his pride.

'How long before the river goes down?' he asked.

'This is the end of February. March we'll get the high winds that'll help keep it up and make it difficult to move *Grey Gull* even as far as the public mooring. They'll probably go about the middle of the month.'

'And I'll have to get a job of some sort. "The old order changeth," the voice of the turtle and all that.'

'Come on,' Sassie said. 'They must be open by now. Coffee makes you sad. We need another drink.'

'And then home?'

'You mustn't be so impatient,' but she was smiling. 'It takes a woman longer to re-adjust.'

'Don't let's go back to Alec's. Let's find somewhere here.' He wanted her to himself for this evening.

'Alright. We'll go to the *Dragon*. It'll be quiet there.'

The cold air hit him a bit coming out but he had been careful not to drink too much and the reaction soon passed so that by the time they got off the bus he was quite sober and took her arm for the walk from the bridge out of a need for human warmth, to know she was really back.

A black police saloon was drawn up before the entrance to the lock, signifying more trouble, and that late at night. Sym led the way across the catwalk. Ahead of them lights flashed on the island, powerful torch beams slicing the dark. They came from a little to the left, the direction of *Grey Gull*. 'What's up now?' Sym swore to himself softly. But she was already moving ahead in their direction.

Figures were grouped on the bank in front of the gangplank: Walden and Joyce and a couple of uniformed policemen with torches. Joyce moved towards them as they stepped into the light. 'Have you seen them?' They knew at once she meant the children.

'How long have they been gone?' Sassie asked.

'They didn't come home from school.' Joyce was on the edge of tears.

'We don't know if they went to school,' Walden said.

'We can find that out in the morning,' one of the policemen spoke for the first time.

'Morning! That means all night. I can't go all night, not knowing.'

'I'm sorry, madam, there's not much we can do in the dark, They might be anywhere. Where could we begin?'

'You could bring dogs, tracker dogs,' Walden said. 'You could do something.'

'All the officers on duty will be told to keep a special look-out of course but in the dark there are dozens of places a child might be. One thing, wherever they are they're together. You can take a bit of comfort from that.'

'Comfort!' Joyce said disbelievingly.

'Two children together argues that they've run away. One child, it could be anything, fallen in the river, enticed away, run over. But not two at once. They're hiding somewhere and they'll probably come home when they're hungry. Anyway that's how I read it. I should persuade your wife to get some sleep. Things'll look different in the morning. They'll probably be back for breakfast.'

'And supposing they aren't?'

'Then we'll be back tomorrow. But you'll be on the phone first to tell us not to bother.' He ducked his head in a farewell and the lights of the torches diminished into the night.

'Bastard coppers,' Walden swore and spat into the mud.

'Well, what the hell did you expect!' Joyce swung on him angrily. 'They won't play your game because you wouldn't play theirs and between the both of you my children are lost.'

'Come on now,' Sassie put out a hand and touched her arm, 'let's go in and have some tea and see what we can do.'

'Every minute, every minute they're out there,' she choked

on the rest and let herself be led into the boat.

Walden stood undecided, opening and closing his fists as if he would have liked to tighten them around something solid.

'What about ringing the hospital?' Sym said. 'I didn't like to suggest it in front of Joyce but it could be that one of them got into some kind of trouble and the other one's frightened to come home.'

Walden seized the idea hopefully. 'If Sophy was hurt Jane would feel it was her fault for not looking after her. Yes, that could be it.'

Sym dragged a handful of small change from his pocket. 'Take this and ring all the ones round about. They wouldn't have gone up to London would they?'

'You can't be sure of course but I don't think so. They would have thought about the fare. Besides why should they?'

'Why do children run away?'

'We don't know they have.'

'Well let's hope so. I'll go and see how they're getting on in there.'

'Right then,' Walden moved away along the bank, became part of the shadows.

Joyce was staring into the fire with the fixity of the blind. Sassie clattered cups cheerfully in the galley.

'Do you think he's right?' Joyce spoke without altering her gaze.

'The copper? I think so. They must get a lot of this sort of thing, kids running off. They know what the signs are.' He began to roll himself a cigarette as Sassie brought in a loaded tray. Taking a fresh packet from her bag she offered one to Joyce and took one herself, flicking a neat oval flame from her lighter.

Joyce drew down the smoke gratefully. 'But why, why should they?'

'I don't know. Most kids want to at some point in their tiny lives. I know I did, didn't you?' He glanced at Sassie for support.

'Did you?' Joyce asked harshly.

'I was too scared,' he tried a laugh. 'What have they been reading lately? *Huckleberry Finn.* That's a terribly subversive book, should never be allowed in children's hands.' He wished Sassie would say something, make some little joke. He heard the inanity of his comments like laughter at a funeral.

'Where's Walden?' Joyce noticed his absence for the first time.

'Gone to make a few phone calls.' He looked across at Sassie, anticipating Joyce's reaction. She put her hand quickly to her mouth like a child caught up in a Punch and Judy show. Sassie moved forward holding out her hand with a cup of tea.

'When they didn't come in I wasn't bothered at first. I thought they were playing out til it was dark. Then I called them for their teas and they didn't come. They're usually in bed by eight. Half past seven he went along the bank calling them. The water's so high I was frightened . . .' The trickle of words dried. Boots thudded on the deck. They turned towards the door. Sym had never seen a man so shaken. Joyce stood up.

'They've got a child in Tollington Hospital. They want us to go over.'

'Is she . . .?'

He nodded. 'Someone pulled her out of the river.'

'How will you get there?' Sym looked at his watch. 'There aren't any more buses tonight.'

'Taxi,' Sassie opened her bag. 'You can get one from the station yard or ring for one. Take this.'

Joyce looked round the circle of faces. Action had made her stronger. 'One of us ought to stay here. They'll only need one at the hospital. If Jane comes back there must be somebody here. She'll be frightened.' Already, Sym thought, she's decided, braced herself with the worst. Or was it the worst? Suppose it was Jane?

'We don't know . . .' Walden began and stopped. 'You go. I'll stay here.'

'I'll come with you.' Sassie pulled her coat together. 'I don't suppose we'll be long.'

'It'll give us a chance to look around,' Sym said.

When the two women had gone he turned to Walden. His great body was heaped broken in a chair as if someone had thrown it away. 'I'll never forgive myself.'

'We don't know . . .' Sym heard his voice echo. 'Have you tried Dick's old place? They could be there.' Walden roused himself and picked up a hurricane lamp from the table.

'We'll leave the lights on and the door open in case.' Sym followed him, the rays of the lamp striking against the bare trunks as they crossed the island. The pontoon was a deep black mass against the lighter sky. Walden opened the door with the key and they went inside. There was a scamper and clatter from the pile of tins in the corner but no sign of human inhabitants. 'Rats,' Walden swung the lamp so that the shadows ran up the walls and down again. 'They don't waste much time in moving in.'

'What about the other one where the old man was?'

'I think they'd be too frightened but we can only try.'

There was no key this time so they could only peer through the dusty windows into the inner darkness. 'Jane!' Walden called quietly. There was no answer. The place was desolate, uninviting.

'Not a place I'd choose myself,' Sym looked back the way they'd come. The old man had lived farthest of all from the rest of his kind, set back from the bank, among branches that must have lashed at the windows on windy nights.

'I've taught them not to be afraid of the dark, of being alone. Perhaps I've taught them all the wrong things.'

They searched the high vault of the boatshed and the office, where the letters and calor gas were stored, though Walden had already been there that afternoon but there wasn't even a sweet paper to suggest that two children might be hiding there. Then they went back to sit on *Grey Gull*, passing the odd word like a shared butt between them and listening for returning feet on the deck.

'It wasn't her,' Joyce said, laughing as she stood in the doorway and then she cried, a noisy sobbing that broke uncontrolled from her throat. Walden put his arm round her and led her to a chair. 'It wasn't her.'

'The doctor gave her a sedative but she has to have one of these and go to bed. There's one for you too. Then lock up the bottle.' Sassie handed him a small square bottle in brown glass. 'Now I think we should all try to sleep. We'll be round in the morning.'

'I'll keep a light burning all night,' Walden said. Joyce was calmer, her eyes glazing under the impact of the drug.

'What happened?' Sym asked when they were back on *Mimosa.*

She leaned back wearily. 'As soon as they took the sheet away we saw it wasn't Sophy, or Jane. It could have been Sophy, same age, same colouring, but it wasn't. There was another woman coming in as we went out, crying. Maybe it was hers. She has to be somebody's. Someone has to lose.'

'Come on,' he eased her shoes off, 'you're tired out. In the morning we'll be able to think better. You should have had one of those little bombs the doctor gave Joyce. Have you got something else you can take?'

She stretched out a hand for her bag. 'I've got some phenobarb. here. I'll take a couple of those. What about you?'

He shook his head, 'I don't think I'll need any rocking tonight.' He wanted to be up early to investigate an idea that had come to him. If he was right it could wait til the morning and he didn't want anyone else around in case he was wrong. It was a fifty-fifty chance and not worth rousing the Waldens' hopes with.

He woke almost as soon as it was light by a childhood trick of the will. Sassie was still deeply asleep, restless, holding her breath and letting it out in little cries and moans. If he woke in the night he would shush her and she would smile a bit in sleep and murmur but a few minutes later would return to her old restlessness. She could never remember what she dreamed, couldn't or wouldn't, never relax the grip she held herself in waking, and all night she fought to hold it against the loosening of sleep. It was easy for him to slip out without disturbing her; he slept on the outside of the bunk always.

The air was calm with a taste of Spring again. There was still no sign of buds breaking but he thought the grass looked greener as if life was flowing in it as he crossed the island and took the little path beside Dick's place and on into the thicker brush where it faded. Would he be able to find it again? He pushed on against the twining brambles and whippy branches. He must be near. Then he broke through into the clearing.

Someone was there before him and at first his pulse bounded with excitement and then steadied as he realised the significance of it. The little terrier sat beside the heap of brush that covered the hideout. When she saw him she whimpered and dug at the base of the heap sending a shower of twigs, leaves and earth flying out behind. He called her and she stopped her useless digging and ran towards him. 'So they left you behind and you came to find them,' he muttered as he rubbed her cat-soft ears. They weren't there but he would make sure. He crossed the clearing and pulled the camouflage away. It was empty. He was glad he hadn't mentioned it to anyone. He tried another tack. 'Find them, Trudy. Where are they? Find them!' he called excitedly, siccing her on. She ran round in confused circles for a moment and then began barking frustratedly at him. Ah well, it wasn't her fault she wasn't a bloodhound. He retraced his steps through the woods and when he came to the fork in the path pointed along the way to *Grey Gull*. 'Home, good girl! Home!' She turned her pointed face up to him and then set off in the right direction, trotting neatly, the back legs slightly to one side of the front, the small paws as precise as a ballerina's.

Sassie was just stirring when he got back. He made tea and told her of his abortive idea. 'They obviously didn't trust me not to split so they found somewhere else. Funny thing, it would have been quite an effort to tell anyone. I was hoping I wouldn't have to, that I could persuade them to give up.' As he said it he realised the overtones of the phrase. 'Give in or I'll break your arm,' they had said as children, cruelly twisting an arm behind a thin back til the victim squirmed and cried for mercy.

She sipped the hot tea. 'It sounds more like hunting criminals than looking for children. The trouble is, though it may have begun as a joke, by now it might be serious. The river's very dangerous when it's as high and fast as this, apart from all the other things one daren't even mention.'

'Maybe they're back home having breakfast by now like the copper said.' But there was no conviction in his voice and they were neither of them surprised to be met by drawn, blank faces that had closed against feeling.

Sym and Walden set out to search every square and bush on the island while Joyce went to the school to check with the class teacher. The children had eaten their dinner as usual and then not answered the afternoon register. No one had thought it strange: their comings and goings at school had always been erratic. The police had no more help to offer. No one had reported seeing them getting on a bus or train. There had been no suspicious men in raincoats with bags of sweets for small girls. They would all keep looking. Soon the public would have to be asked to help.

The search of the island brought nothing new. Again Walden rang the hospitals. This time there was an unconscious child, run over by a lorry.

'Your turn,' Joyce said grimly. They hardly spoke to each other now except to convey the simplest facts. Walden came back from the hospital even more sunk in upon himself, his skin dirty with fatigue and misery. But it wasn't Jane or Sophy.

'And they only show us the girls,' her voice was bitter. Sym noticed how her slight accent had grown stronger under stress as if she was drawing strength from her own childhood. 'You begin to think all the kids in the world are suffering, lost. And every time I'm glad because it's not mine.'

'You can't think like that,' Walden said.

'How else can I think when I see the other mothers and know how they feel?'

As it grew dark for the second time both of them moved into

a desolation so complete no words could rouse them. The other two left them sitting in silence staring into the fire which Walden had moved to bank up when he lit the lamps before sinking into apathy again.

'I could do with a drink.'

'Me too.'

But the silence had eaten into their thoughts so deeply that they too stared into the slowly revolving pools of liquid in their hands while they tracked and re-tracked the same ground, seeking, turning over the possibilities with blind fingers.

'Why do they hate each other?' Sym asked suddenly. 'I thought this sort of thing was supposed to bring you together.'

'Joyce blames Walden, and Walden blames himself so they end up hating each other.'

'If the children turned up now what would happen?'

'I don't know. They might come through.'

'Everything's gone wrong since Christmas.' He was drinking too much and he knew it but he wanted to sleep, to forget it all for a few hours. Perhaps it was the ring, unlucky after all. Sometimes he thought it was like a malevolent yellow eye. Should he tell her? He half formed the words and then rejected them. It might increase its power to have the words spoken. The magic formula that unlocked the door like taking a stopper out of a bottle.

'Come on,' Sassie was on her feet looking down at him. 'You're nearly asleep.'

It was late before he moved in the morning and when he did he was aware that he was alone and turned over on to her pillow to sleep again, his face on the cool linen that still held the scent of her; the valley where her head had been. When he woke again it was to the rattle of the poker in the fire and a shrill complaint from the kettle.

'I thought you were going to sleep all day.'

'My tongue's like a parrot cage.' She brought him a fizzing glass and he drank it down gratefully. Then he looked at her closely. 'They're back, aren't they?' She nodded. 'You found them?' She nodded again. 'Make that tea and tell me what happened.' He lay back waiting for the drink and the news to work on him as she went into the galley.

She had got up early and gone out to test her idea without waking him. 'In case it didn't come off,' she said.

'I know.'

'It was your idea really, at least you started me thinking along those lines when you told me how you went to their hideout. I thought to myself, "Where would I go if I were a child?" Jane's very shrewd. It would have to be somewhere well thought out, where she knew they would be dry and could eat. She's very much the big sister. I couldn't see her not looking after Sophy. And then they didn't take Trudy so it might be somewhere Trudy would give them away. It had to be somewhere they knew too, very well. Somewhere near, that they'd often been. Somewhere too that would make running away an adventure. Boys run away to sea. They get on trains to Portsmouth or Southampton. What would a girl like?'

'You tell me.'

'The palace. To sleep in a big double bed where the kings and queens slept.'

As she talked he saw it all happening before him as if he were a boy again sitting on the rug in front of the fire turning the thick cardboardy pages with the large print, his face scorching under the heat of the flames, his eyes dazzled with fantasy so that when he was called to the table he looked up and round as if he had expected quite different places and faces to be there. Two small figures slipped in through the gate in the wall, across the courtyard where he had carried the wood and up the vaulted stair, lost themselves with a party touring the royal apartments, hung back, vanished under a dusty bed, lay there with the dust tickling their nostrils while the light faded from the mullions and the ghosts and shadows glided through the rooms. Hand in hand they walked while the portraits looked down at them, dodging the keepers, light as ghosts themselves. Tried beds and chairs, sat at the dressing tables and fell asleep under a silk canopy. They were hungry in the morning until they found a basket dangling from a window high up on a long rope, miraculously full of food: a loaf, half a pound of butter, jam and some other things they didn't bother with.

Sym looked at her questioningly, unwilling to interrupt the story. 'The grace and favour residents,' Sassie explained. 'That's how they have their shopping delivered. I wonder what the old dear said when she found her basket was half empty.'

'How did you find them?'

'I bought a ticket and went round with a party. Then I lost myself too.' She had gone from room to room calling quietly until she had heard Sophy giggle. 'I think by that time they were rather glad to be found. They were pretty dusty, hair uncombed and Sophy had spilt jam down her front. I said they didn't look much like princesses to me. Princesses always washed and wore pretty clothes'

'Not always. Why did she do it?'

'Jane? It was Jane's idea of course. She'd overheard Joyce and Walden discussing the move and had got it wrong. Thought they were going up to Joyce's mother again like they do in the summer and Walden was staying behind. She decided she didn't want to go. The rest she made up to get Sophy to hide away with her.'

'I wish I'd been there to see you coming along the bank with them.'

Her face shadowed. 'Walden was prodding in the shallows with a boathook. Joyce just standing watching him. From their faces they'd given up hope.' Sophy had run forward to her mother, Jane hung back til Walden called her. 'I think she suddenly realised it was wrong and wondered what he would say, if she would be punished.' Joyce had cooked them eggs and bacon and while they ate Sassie had explained, her voice low, hoping the children couldn't hear. 'They hear too much.'

'And now?'

'I don't know. We shall have to wait and see.'

March

Birds busken to build and bremlich singen
For solace of the soft summer . . .

THEY lay awake side by side and listened to the wind, felt the pull and knock of *Mimosa* as she strained bucking against her ropes. Sym had unstepped the mast to decrease the resistance but she still rocked and swung, nose up to the current, as if she was pawing the water.

'Sometimes it feels as if she wants to get away, be off down river to the sea. It must be dull for her always tied up here after all she's seen and done.'

'Do you remember when you were ashamed of her?'

'That was a long time ago. It's unkind to remind me of it.'

She laughed and traced a boat shape on his shoulder with a finger. 'We ought to get up.'

He watched the smoke unwind from the end of his cigarette like a drawn thread. 'What's going to happen?'

'Something soon. You'll see. It's best not to ask. Wait.' He put his arms round her again and moved his mouth gently up her neck to her hair. He felt her hands stroking his shoulders.

'We never have seconds do we? And we never talk about it?'

'Do you want to?'

'Sometimes.'

'It's never occurred to me. Once seems so right.'

'But over so soon.' He wondered if it was because she was a woman or older. He could never imagine how an experience could be so deep it would be superfluous to repeat it. Or could he? With Anna there had always been a straining after climax, as if they couldn't wait, but now he found there was no need to fret or to hold back. It was as natural as breathing and after they slept like children, deeply and refreshingly. She had no tricks, no arts as he might have expected; she simply was and that was enough. They came together easily but it hadn't become mere habit. Was that how she felt too?

'Listen!' Someone was knocking on the hatch. 'I said we ought to get up.'

'Anybody in?' Walden's voice called, echoing through the wooden hull.

'We'll be out in a minute,' Sym called back, grabbing his jeans and swinging his legs over the side of the bunk.

'We're going for a drink,' Walden said. 'I have some news to rejoice the hearts of all right-minded citizens.' The stock phrases were there but the edge was a little blunted, Sym thought as they waited for Sassie to join them. Alec set up their usual round without asking. 'I have decided to become an honest man.' Walden raised his glass. 'Here's to capitulation.'

'Perhaps it's only an armed truce,' Sassie suggested.

'I haven't your facility for compromise or should it be faculty? I'm already forgetting how to talk. Come and see me in a year's time and I shan't be able to string two phrases together like all the rest of the morons.'

'What are you going to do?' It was Sassie who asked the question. Walden was obviously getting a certain lugubrious kick out of keeping the mystery as long as he could.

'I have taken my place on the treadmill. I have joined the world's workers. I am old and responsible.'

'Where?' she asked.

'A little boatyard on the Swale.'

'To do what?'

'Design, run the office, general dogsbody.'

Sassie nodded her head.

Sym tried to gauge her real reaction to this, whether she was glad or sorry so that he could have some clue to his own probable feelings. He wanted to ask why, what Walden's motives were.

'I shall need your help,' Walden was saying. 'As soon as that wind drops.' They listened to it for a moment prowling outside, shaking the doors and windows and hurling itself through the gap whenever a new customer entered. Through the glass they could see the river bounding along, licked and cuffed into whitecaps, smashed against the piers of the bridge, over-flowing into lush water meadows on either side. 'We couldn't get under the bridge at the moment and the weather reports say it's pretty rough in the channel. But as soon as it's calmer I've promised Joyce we'll go. She wants the kids settled in a new school as soon as possible so Jane can make up before the eleven plus.' He looked away over their heads, not meeting their eyes and Sym realised it was because he was afraid. Afraid of me, he thought, and what I might say. To reassure him he nodded Alec up for another round.

'Does that mean the open sea at one point?' he asked as the full mugs were set down on the bar.

'Yep. But not for long. An hour or so should see us round.'

'Can she do it?'

'By the time I've done with her she will.'

'Will you need us both?'

'Sassie can take the wheel while you and I do the donkey work. She's used to it.'

'Are you?' Sym looked at her surprised.

She smiled back at him. 'You can see me in my nautical rig.'

'Why don't you both come too? Get *Mimosa* towed down if the engine can't be put right. No trouble finding a mooring down there. Cheap too.' For a moment he was carried along on the flood of a new idea and then it subsided. Was he afraid to be alone? Sym had never heard him ask anything from anyone before and now he was admitting a need. For a dream's length Sym imagined them all there together. It would solve everything. And then it faded. It would solve nothing.

'When do you think it'll be?' he asked instead.

'About the middle of the month. If the seasons aren't too cock-eyed. Before Easter so the kids can start a new term in a new place.'

'How did she do it?' Sym asked Sassie later.

'I don't think she had much difficulty. I think he realised himself when the children were lost.'

'Will it work do you think?'

'As long as they have the children.'

'And after?'

'By then he'll be too old to change.'

'I don't know what to think, whether to be glad or sorry.'

'Is it ever any good being either?'

'I still like to try and get my attitudes sorted out.'

He sat alone by the stove with the stack of paper in front of him. He noticed he had passed the halfway mark some time back without realising. Now he was three-quarters down the unused pile while the sheets marred with his writing rose thick and heavy, higher for being scrawled on as if the words themselves were tangible and added their own density to the thickness of the paper. A superstitious fear took hold of him. What would happen when he had finished them all? He began to write, consuming another blank page as if he had set a match to it and it was charring, curling, dropping into ash in front of him by his own will, his own act. Why hadn't he said yes when Walden had suggested that they should all go? She had wanted to sleep alone tonight. Was she possessed by the same feeling of the end of things? He pushed the paper away again and leant back. Old man Tennyson, he mocked himself but the words went on, round and round in his head until he got up and climbed the ladder to the deck and stood against the wind watching the cloud scud through the pale reaches of sky. The river itself seemed quieter, a hairline of mud along the bank showing that it had dropped a little. The wind too, he realised, no longer gusted and buffeted but drove strongly with a bridled force. He went down into the cabin, kicked the iron doors of the stove shut. The mallard grumbled drowsily. There were no more pirates to listen for.

He had been knocking some time before he heard her calling. The voice came from the river and the dinghy had gone from the back of the little boat.

'What are you doing out there?'

She waved back. 'I'm just coming in. Catch the rope for me.' She pulled towards him, fending her way between the other boats. The race had slackened even more while he slept though it still ran fast enough to tug the boat strongly as if it was trying to wrench the rope from his hands. He took a couple of turns round a convenient cleat and helped her on board. 'Take this first,' she pushed a bundle of soaking feathers that struggled feebly into his hands.

'Now what have you got?' But he knew from the brown and buff mottling that it was a female mallard.

'I spotted it this morning. Just about got it in time I think. It wouldn't have lasted much longer.'

'What's the matter with it?'

'It's waterlogged.'

'What about water off a duck's back?'

'It's the males. When it's a bad year there aren't enough females to go round.'

'So they all try to have it away with the same one?'

'That's it.' She put the duck into a big cardboard box and closed the lid.

'What will you do with it?'

'Keep it in there a couple of days until its feathers have got their oiliness back. Then I'll let it go.'

'And they'll start on it again?'

'What else can you do except try, and then it has to take its chance?'

'Does that apply to humans too?' He regretted it as soon as said. 'Never mind, don't answer that one. How soon do you think the river will drop?'

'Give it another fortnight.'

He looked round the little cabin. 'I'll have to get a job. I'm all spent up.'

Sassie smoothed the thick pile of his sweater, the ring tawny against the dark wool. 'Not just yet. Wait a bit till they've gone. It looks bad to start with a day off and we can't manage it alone. *Grey Gull*'s too big to go that far with just the two of us.'

'Can you swim?'

'No.'

'That settles it then, I'm coming.'

The morning wept over them as they struggled with the mooring ropes, the knots swollen tight, the cables themselves heavy and cold with the rain. It fell relentlessly like a detached grief and the branches above added the force of their tears making the decks slippery, the bank a skidpan where they slithered and stumbled in their rubber boots. To Sym's surprise the engine ran smoothly. The heavy gangplank was taken in, the springers cast off. Now she was held only by the stern and bow ropes. The children stood back by the wheelhouse, Joyce beside them with a boathook to fend off if they should swing back in towards the bank. The stern rope was slackened off, passed once round the post and on board to Walden.

'You'd better do the same with the bow rope and then get up here or you'll be left behind,' he grinned down at Sym. 'Sassie, take it from him when he passes it up.'

Sym untied the rope and threw it up to her. It seemed a long way to the deck, and the boat, freed of the restraining springers, had drifted out until now there was a sizable gap. He hoped he wouldn't fall back into the river between the bank and the side of the hull to be crushed like a nut between them. He swung himself up, scrambled, fought for handhold and then Walden reached down an arm and yanked him onto the deck. 'Now hang on to this while I get to the wheel.' He gave Sym the heavy stern rope, spoke some instruction to Sassie who nodded, and then Sym saw his head over the top of the open wheelhouse. The engine throbbed and shuddered under his feet with added power. 'Right,' Walden roared, 'let the bow go slowly.'

Sassie payed the rope out gently and the nose of the boat began to swing out into midstream as the current caught it. The stream still ran fast though the level had dropped a good eighteen inches. Sym was aware, as Sassie's rope end fell leaden into the water and the boat turned in a great arc, that he was now the only link with the land. The whole weight of the boat and the drag of the tons of swirling water hung on the stern rope.

'Hold on!' Walden shouted, 'hold her steady. Take another turn round the cleat.'

He wrapped the free end round in a great loop and the fibres creaked as they took the strain. *Grey Gull* was still swinging, in now towards the bank. Sym braced himself for the crash. 'Fend off,' Walden called and Joyce stepped forward with the boat-hook. Sassie joined her with an oar and they leant over the side together levering their poles against the bank to check the momentum. 'Right,' Walden said, 'that's got it.' They had turned *Grey Gull* so that she was pointing downstream. 'Now, Sym, let her go easy as I get her under way. You two be ready in case she swings back. Here we go. Let her out.'

Sym took the double loop from the cleat as the engine pulled against him. Little by little he let it pass through his hands until the end fell with a slap into the water. 'Haul in quickly,' Walden called and he heaved on the dripping cable realising it was dangling close to the turning screw. He bent the intransigent stuff into as neat a coil as he could manage as he had seen others do. Sassie's already lay like a bedded serpent on the deck. He was a novice at this game. Everyone knew more than he did and he didn't want to look a fool. He thought he was doing alright so far. Mentally he ticked off the jobs accomplished while the rain fell ceaselessly and the boat headed towards the lock. He looked at his watch. It was twenty past eight. The rest of the world would be getting up and going to work while they worked their way down to the sea. Behind them bobbed the dinghy. They had taken it out of the water last night and carried it across to *Grey Gull*. Sassie was giving it to them. Where they were going they would be moored some way out on the edge of a mud bank. They would need a dinghy to get ashore. Joyce would spend a lot of her time being ferry-man unless they could rig up some other system. She didn't seem to mind. Perhaps it was a concession she was willing to make in return for other things. Now she was down below getting breakfast. The three of them could manage the lock quite easily. Once they were through they could eat in relays. Glancing at Jane he speculated on the thoughts behind the calm face as she watched the island slip away. Trudy began to bark loudly. They were halted while the lock filled up and she had spotted the boatman's dog, an old enemy challenging her from the bank. 'Be quiet, Trudy,' Sophy said and slapped the white coat.

Sym looked back at the island. It almost seemed as if he was leaving too and turning suddenly he surprised the same expression on Sassie's face though she smiled at him quickly to hide it. As the lock gates opened and they passed through the keeper waved to them and they waved back. 'I feel as if I'm on the *Queen Mary*,' she said. They took the centre stream and followed the current under the middle arch of the bridge.

'Lucky we remembered to get the mast in,' Walden called. 'We'd never have made it otherwise.'

Or before the river went down, Sym thought. He could see the damp levels where it had crept up the brickwork still green with plant life that was gradually drying to a dull sage. The chimneys and towers of the palace drifted past and he wondered if the children saw it as a kind of dream and would remember it like that, something to be locked away and almost forgotten, a secret knowledge. The children at the new school would never believe them. 'We slept in a palace, in the queen's bed.' Joyce called them below to eat. By the time they came up on deck again the familiar would have slipped away. He looked at Sassie. She was soaked through. He must be too.

All morning they chugged through the city, a long trance-like meandering under bridges, past towers of glass and concrete, spires, lattice of cranes above the docks through the dark ooze of the river under its iridescent oilskin. Sometimes a great sea-going vessel overtook them, hailed them from its towering superstructure, the huge anchors dangling above, toys big enough to hole and sink them if they should suddenly drop. The giant ship ploughed on, leaving them bouncing on its wash. 'Now I know what Gulliver felt like on his second trip,' Sym said looking up at the black cliff that was the *Ophelia* looming past.

At the Houses of Parliament Joyce had called them for mugs of hot coffee. Sym took one for himself and another for Walden up to the wheelhouse. Watching his calm face as he sipped, the hand so confident on the wheel, he said, 'Were you ever in the navy?'

'That's right. During the war.'

'I'd have thought you might have been a pacifist. But then, thinking again, it wouldn't really fit would it.'

Walden laughed shortly like a bark, 'Not with my views. Besides I wanted the experience of it. The trouble is you're never the same again one way or the other.'

'Events shape people then?'

'You're not always strong enough to stop them or you don't realise what's happening to you til too late. It's always the same during a war. You think it can never go back to being the same again and then as soon as peace comes everyone chickens out on all the things they've agreed on and fought for, and falls for comfort and materialism, and you're back to where you started. I suppose you'd call it human nature, just human nature to want the things you've never had when they're offered on a plate but it sickened me. They spend six years fighting for freedom and justice, and then they trade it in for a telly and a tin box on wheels and never have another thought in their lives. They made me so angry I opted right out of the whole stinking show.'

Sym saw him like a bear raging on the end of a chain, a blind bear flailing great paws ineffectually at the hounds who would pull him down. 'And now?'

'I'm caught like all the rest. When you have children you can't opt out.'

Sym wanted to say, 'Don't give in. It'll be alright,' but the words seemed insulting, childish. Instead he pointed ahead to the cardboard towers and turrets of the Tower. A customs boat flashed across their path, hailing them but letting them pass.

Walden looked at his watch. 'We're carrying the tide. By the time we get to the mouth of the Medway it'll be low water. We'll have to lie up there for a few hours until we can make it up The Swale.'

'How fast are we going?' It seemed fast but the big ships overhauled them quickly.

'About seven knots.'

Sym nodded, trying to remember what that meant in miles per hour, about a third he thought. That didn't sound enough.

'A knot equals a bit over a mile an hour.'

'Thanks. It had me worried.'

Once they had passed the docks the ships were even bigger, the expanse of water on either side of them receded below Woolwich Ferry as it wound among the flat lands of Erith and Dagenham, and the banks were encrusted with low grey industrial buildings, desolate under the rain. It could have been a journey without destination Sym thought, as they gradually lost sight of the land. This was what sailors must feel every trip out, this falling away until you were floating without ties, a complex cell turning in upon itself as the days passed and there was only the grey sea and sky hardly distinguishable from each other. The wind blew harder, carrying away the rain and whipping the sea into tumbling, running crests. How did you steer a little boat like this without instruments, radio? Walden showed him the charts and pointed to the tiny marker buoys, scarcely discernible dots plotting the channel they must follow

'See that one.' Walden pointed to a green bell buoy rising and dropping out of sight with the swell. 'That's a wreck. You have to watch out for them.'

' "Full fathom five thy father lies . . ." '

'That's it. You have a trick while I go below for a bit. Have to take a pill. Like Nelson I get seasick. Just keep her heading up so that we pass about the middle of those two. Then look for the next and make for them.'

'Is this the sea?'

'Difficult to say where the sea ends and the estuary begins but you could say it was the sea.'

He was steering a boat alone at sea. Walden had gone. It was cold in the wind and his clothes were still soaked but an occasional gleam of sun flushed the thick grey water, highlighting the whitecaps. How rough could it get before it became dangerous? Soon Sassie joined him and they watched the waters together. Joyce was cooking below, hot soup and sausage rolls.

'How's Walden feeling?'

'Not too bad. He'll be up in a minute so we can eat. It always hits him like this.'

The soup and warmth of the cabin made him drowsy. He wanted to sleep. They had been up late the night before, working by hurricane lamp to make everything ready and the alarum had gone at half past six that morning. There was a clatter on the companionway. Walden's head ducked through the door.

'We've lost the dinghy. I need some more eyes.' They followed him up into the wind. Sassie took the wheel while they peered back the way they had come. It seemed hopeless. The horizon was empty. How would they ever spot a tiny boat against the waves? Walden trained a pair of binoculars, carefully sweeping the sea from left to right. When his eyes grew tired he passed them to Sym. Anxiously he raked the leaden waters hoping to be the one to see it and feeling that he had hardly justified his food so far. Then he gave them back to Walden.

'That's it. I'm bloody sure that's it.' He gripped Sym's arm willing his gaze to a patch of sea far behind. 'If you look hard you can see what looks like a wave, a line that isn't going up and down like the rest.' He gave Sym the glasses and he stared through them until he could see nothing but a series of dark lines, dashes on a grey ground but nothing he could identify as a dinghy, not even a line that was thicker than the others. 'We'll go back and see but I'm sure that's it.' He went up to the wheelhouse and took over from Sassie. *Grey Gull* swung about in an arc and headed back the long way they had come.

It was the dinghy. As they drew nearer the line thickened, steadied to the naked eye, became a shape, a drifting boat. The tow rope had slipped. Walden swore. He had tied it himself. 'Now we have to get hold of the damn thing.' They were high above it and it rose and fell to a different rhythm.

Sassie took the wheel again. 'Keep her as steady as you can.' Leaning over they managed to hook it with the boathook but they were no closer to securing it. It was too dangerous to risk jumping down. The rope still dangled from the ring in the bow. 'If I could get that . . .'

Now that they were idling the waves seemed rougher, the whole world in motion, up and down. Joyce coming up from below to help was caught by a sudden lift and thrown to the deck. Only a rickety barrier of struts and wire, broken in places, hedged the flat upper deck. 'Get back,' Walden waved at her angrily. He called to Sym, the words blown away at once by the wind. 'Hang on to my legs. I'm going to try and get hold of the rope.' Both men lay flat on the heaving planks, Walden hanging head down over the side, Sym his arms cracking as he pinned the dead weight to the deck. If he should let him go it would be a kind of murder by default. How long could he hold on? He dug his fingers, twining in Walden's trousers, scrabbling at the cloth and praying it would hold.

'I've got it!' Walden began to wriggle backwards as Sym clawed him on board again. They sat on the deck, collapsed, panting with the effort. Sym noticed the ache in his arms, the torn nails. Was it worth it? Walden held up the dripping rope end. 'This time I'll tie it tighter.' He laughed and Sym tried to smile but the thought came again: if I had let him go? The responsibility of it made him feel sick. Perhaps there was something wrong with him that he always saw things in these terms. Already the others had brushed it aside. Sassie had swung the boat back on course. Joyce and Walden were laughing together as he re-tied the rope, making it really fast this time. Soon they were passing the point where they had first noticed the dinghy's loss. Sym looked at his watch. The whole thing had taken half an hour. He felt he had died and risen again. All the shine had gone from the trip for him. He supposed no one would guess how he felt. He must be what used to be called a coward. He joined them all in the wheelhouse and made a pretence at laughter as they went through it all again as if it had been a game. To them it was an isolated event, to Sym all events were part of a chain of cause and effect and he could never see them divorced from each other.

'Another hour,' Walden's blunt forefinger tapped their position on the chart, 'and we'll tie up at Queenborough. Just make it before dark.'

'The Isle of Grain?'

'We're running alongside it now only we can't see it. Next thing we'll see will be the lighthouse at Sheerness. That tells us when to turn for the mouth of the Medway. The wind's dropping. Once we get past here we're sheltered by the land and it won't be so rough.'

It was comforting to be between banks again, off the route of the great metal dinosaurs, in calm water. The children came up on deck and watched the light fade. Walden brought *Grey Gull* gently into Queenborough and Sym slipped the mooring rope through the ring on the top of the big iron buoy. The lights of the little town beckoned in the distance but they were all too tired to row ashore. Though it was only six o'cock they all slept while the boat swayed on her mooring as the tide ran in lifting her for her journey inland.

Joyce woke them with tea. It was half past ten and cold on deck after the warmth of sleep. The banks were black under the moon while the surface of the water shone faintly. The engine was kicked into life again, the mooring slipped and they moved forward under the white face of the moon gleaming moistly on the mud shoals. 'Did you pick tonight purposely?' Sym asked Walden as *Grey Gull* nosed her way up the silent river.

'The moon you mean? We couldn't have done it on a dark night. This stretch is a bit tricky, pretty narrow and all sorts of obstacles, mud and shingle banks, wreckage. You have to look out for your marks and keep pretty close to them.' His voice was subdued. Tiredness perhaps or the situation itself. It was a kind of surrender.

'You seem to know this way quite well.' To Sym it all looked the same in the strange opaque light. He followed their slow progress wonderingly with his eye like a tracking camera exploring the degrees of darkness, of definition: lines and textures rather than recognisable objects.

'I was born here. I sailed it as a kid.' It was a homecoming then, a return. 'Look, that's Kingsferry Bridge. They'll have to raise it for us. I'll give them a shout.' He pressed a button and the mournful call of the siren went out over the water. There was no reply from the bridge though Sym wasn't sure quite what sort of answer Walden expected: a rumbling of cog wheels and the span lifting, tilting into the sky, a lantern waving, and answering wail?

They waited, calling intermittently like a night bird for ten minutes which seemed like twenty. 'Perhaps they're all asleep.'

'Or dead.'

' "Though three men dwell on Flannan Isle . . ." '

'What do we do? We can't stop here all night.'

'If we lose the tide it'll be too shallow for us further on. We'll have to go and wake him up,' Walden decided.

'I'll go.'

'Good. You'll find a patch of fairly firm landing at the foot of the bridge. Don't forget to make the dinghy fast to something. If it drifts away you won't be able to get back on board.'

The dinghy was untied, brought alongside and Sym lowered himself gingerly in. He had no fancy for a cold bath by moonlight. Walden passed him down rowlocks and oars and shoved him off with the boathook. He looked back over his shoulder at the patch of inkblack shadow that lay at the foot of the piers and began to pull towards it. He was grateful for the half-light and hoped no one would see if his rowing was a bit erratic. His tired muscles protested but he forced them on. Fortunately there was little current to pull against him. It was long and lonely drawing towards the shore. From time to time he looked back to see the distance narrow. Ahead was the dark shape of *Grey Gull*, her sides pierced with light and the green starboard light a cat's eye glinting back at him. The firm patch was a mud bank where he slithered and sank ankle deep. He dragged the dinghy up a couple of yards and began to scramble up towards harder ground. The only way up to the bridge seemed to be to climb the steep embankment onto the railway line. Up there the wind blew coldly. He ran along the track hoping nothing would bear down on him with a shriek and scatter him in little pieces along the bridge. An iron ladder led up to the lighted box where he supposed the keeper was quietly snoring. He peered in and tapped on the glass. The door opened.

'I wondered how long before somebody'd be up.'

'We wondered if you'd seen us.'

'Couldn't miss you. Look.' He guided Sym to the window and they looked down on *Grey Gull.* At that moment she called sadly. 'I showed my light. Why does she keep on hooting?'

'I don't think they can see it from down there.'

'Ah.' The keeper seemed glad of the company. 'I'm waiting for a train. That's why I can't lift. Shouldn't be long now. Then you'll be alright. Might as well stay up here in the warm, then you can see the train go past and the bridge go up and your friends pass through.' They looked down on the track below. 'Here she comes.' There was a shriek, a rush of light and wind and the train threw itself out of the dark and was gone. The keeper explained the working of the bridge to Sym, proud of its push-button efficiency that could raise a length of track like a piece of meccano. He admired the gleaming oiled machinery. The keeper seemed quite sorry to let him go. First he had to watch as *Grey Gull* passed slowly beneath them and the bridge was lowered again.

It was even colder outside after the warm box. He made his way back to the dinghy, squelching through the ooze and set off after the others, avoiding the centre spans where the tide ran fast. Knives turned in his shoulder blades as the cold air burrowed down his neck. His muddy boots skidded against the side as they hauled him on board again. He went down into the saloon where Joyce had made hot coffee. It was good to be there with them both listening as he told his small adventure.

'Walden says we'll be there in another couple of hours. Then we can sleep.' It was only eleven o'clock but Sym felt as if they had been going again for hours and it must be at least two.

Steadily *Grey Gull* moved between the narrowing banks lit now by a powerful spotlight as well as the moon. Below Elmley Ferry the water broadened again into a deceptively wide strip shoaled with mud banks. Ahead was a small island. Walden swung the beam of light towards it. 'That's Fowley Island. The entrance we want is behind there but the water's very shallow from this side so I'll take her on past and come in from the other, South Deep, where the channel's deeper.' He nursed the boat along. Sym was stationed on the bow with the boathook to sound the bottom and push them off if they should go aground. Walden brought *Grey Gull* round in a wide sweep and they crept between the island and the shore past the sea wall towards the entrance to the tiny creek. A series of stakes jutting out of the water marked the channel and Walden manœuvred between them delicately. They passed what looked like a small factory and then there were other boats, a little colony. *Grey Gull* nosed her way, the engines almost stopped, towards a vacant strip of water. There was some anxious poling as she drifted over the mud and began to ground. The anchor dropped with a splash. This time Walden got into the dinghy and put a line ashore.

'Just in time,' he said as Sym hauled him onto the deck. 'It's turning now. Soon it'll be running out fast and then we couldn't have made it until the next high water. We can see to the ropes in the morning when everyone gets up. This'll do for now.'

Anxiously they waited while the water left her in case she should tilt but she settled gradually like a tired bird tucking up its legs to rest, evenly on the soft mud. 'That's that then. Now we can sleep.'

Late in the morning when they looked out the water had gone. Along with the others they rested on a soft shoal that bubbled and gleamed like porridge and was flecked with colour, rust and weed green, the full spectrum of an oil patch, every tone of dun and black. Walden was already busy putting out more lines. In the distance Sym picked out three small figures, one a dog, scavenging along the foreshore while gulls wheeled and called, disturbed from their own beachcombing along the waterline. For a time they talked hazily of the trip while the tide flowed in again and then Walden rowed them ashore for the last time and put them on a bus that would take them to the London train. There was nothing and everything to be said. Alone in a compartment while they racketed towards the city they both leant back against the headrest with closed eyes. Once he reached for her hand and held it without pressure and she let it lie unmoving, lifeless almost in his.

He told himself it was just fatigue. They would be better with sleep. They felt flat after the journey. They would think what to do later. 'I'll see you tomorrow then.'

She smiled gently. 'Tomorrow.' And she was gone into the little boat. He made his way along to *Mimosa*, busied himself lighting the fire, cooking beans and eggs and then he slept as if he had been keeping watch for hours and had at last been relieved. Dreams jumbled and chased each other through his sleep. Once he nearly started awake but sank again, deeper, like *Grey Gull* settling into the mud.

The cry that finally hauled him awake set him dragging on his boots and coat, shivering with fright and sudden cold; up the steps across the gangplank in a couple of strides and pounding along the bank. Afterwards he was never sure if he had heard it, could have heard it from that distance. It was very dark and his eye sought for the hands of his watch as he ran; just after midnight. He was aware of a noise ahead, other people running, shouts, and the sinister glow out on the river; the terror of all ships great and small, fire. His breath came hard and he quickened his pace, passing others. Instinct, fear told him it was the little boat burning. A high flame shot up against the dark. He reached the gangway, leapt across so that the deck rocked and plunged under his feet and tore at the hatch cover. Swearing and crying he wrenched it open and ducked through the billow of smoke that poured out, down into the little cabin. Flame had run up the wall and caught the roof, spreading fast. Sassie seemed to be still asleep on the bunk. He picked her up roughly, shook her and slapped her face but she only stirred a little without opening her eyes. The smoke choked and blinded him, at any second the roof might fall. He picked her up again and forced her limp body through the hatch, following clumsily to carry her across to land. It had taken only a few seconds.

'How is she?' someone asked. It was the owner of the M.T.B., carrying a fire extinguisher.

'Alright I think. It's the roof.'

'We'll see to that.' The high flames lit up their faces. 'Any more extinguishers? If they don't do the trick we'll need buckets.' He seemed to have taken charge. Men darted away for containers while those with the long red cylinders followed him over the gangway. Women stood in groups still in their night clothes with coats pulled round them. They murmured together and one stepped forward.

'You want to bring her into my place? It's close by.'

'It's alright thanks.' He held her so that shadow fell on her face and it seemed as if she was resting against him. 'Thanks for the offer. I think she'll be better soon.' He caught a whisper of hospital from the group. Lifting her again he carried her away from them. Once, as he walked, he turned to look back. Black figures moved against the glow but the leaping flames had fallen to the jets of rushing foam. It was further than he had thought. His arms and legs ached as if they would burst but he went on, climbed unsteadily down into the cabin and laid her on the bunk. Her face was smudged with smoke and ash, her hair tangled but she breathed steadily. Why didn't she wake? 'Sassie, Sassie. Come on now. Wake up.' She murmured and smiled as she did when he moved her at nights but her eyes didn't open.

Suppose she needed medical care, a doctor? He thought of concussion, shock but her sleep seemed so natural. He would watch her; let her sleep. Was the fire under control yet? He couldn't leave her to find out. They would enjoy playing firemen in the dark. He pulled himself up at the thought. They had all been very good, quick and efficient. He had no right to laugh at them. He looked down at her again. Suppose she were really ill? If she died? Horrified he watched himself play with the idea, though part of him tried to push it away. It would be all over. He saw himself alone and pitied the desolate figure. He watched his emptiness, his attempts to begin again. Did he love her at all if he could think like this or could he only love himself and not even that very well? As the hours passed and she slept on he tormented himself, moving through scene after scene, guilt and loss and pity. Sometimes he tried to block his thoughts, turn them aside but they drifted back again. Once he moved his mouth across the hollows of her throat and over the unresisting face. He imagined making love to her as she slept, parting her thighs and riding her again and again so that she might wake in the middle and cry out, push at him with weak fingers. His mind reeled and whirled as it fled from image to image pursued by his own disgust. Alone, with her there and yet not there, he learnt himself, dredged among his desires and found nothing he could honestly label loving or even compassionate.

When dawn came grey through the skylight he left her briefly and went along the bank to the burnt-out hull. It was a mess of charred wood and black slime. He remembered the prints, bright curtains and incense. The roof had gone completely but he thought it could be repaired and there didn't seem to be any water coming in. He stepped down into the mess and looked about though he wasn't sure what he was looking for. A broken glass had rolled onto the floor. He turned over the heap of sodden bedclothes, the pillow and took out the small brown bottle from underneath. He put it in his pocket thinking he knew now why she had slept on. The police might come to enquire. He didn't know what they did about these things, if anything. Probably nothing as long as no one was hurt and it didn't spread to other boats. He took a last look round but there was nothing else he felt he should move until he spotted the strap of her handbag poking out from under a blanket and took that too. Hardly thinking he opened it and then shut it again. The wallet-shaped purse she always used was full of notes. Anyone could have found it lying there. He noticed the top of the oilstove was black with soot. Perhaps that had been it, a sudden draught, a flare. He lashed out at it with his boot and went up the steps and back to *Mimosa*. Now he was tired. He wanted to lie down beside her warmth and draw strength from it but he had put her in the saloon bunk and covered her with blankets and there wasn't room for both of them. For a moment he thought of moving her. Then he lay down coldly by himself in the cabin and huddled into sleep.

Hunger woke him next. He made himself breakfast and then took up his watch again. Sometimes he grew frightened of this strange sleep that wouldn't let go and he would roll and light a thick quick cigarette, drawing on it fiercely til it was gone. Watching her breathing closely for signs of change he saw her face still in the full daylight, the lines un-noticed in motion or artificial light, the patches of dry skin flaky, the larger pores at the base of each nostril. He had never known Anna in such detail. It was a different kind of love. Once or twice she clenched her face as if in pain and then relaxed again. He wanted to see what had been done about the boat but he didn't dare to leave her in case she woke and he came back to find her gone.

Late in the afternoon when he had begun to wonder if he had always lived waiting and watching like this she began to stir and toss. The signs were a preliminary to waking; he knew them well. He put on a kettle to boil and sat down again beside her. The eyelids flickered and opened, she half sat up and looked frightened round the dusky cabin. 'The fire?'

Leaning forward Sym took her arms and pushed her gently back against the pillow. 'It's alright, you're alright.'

She turned her head sideways away from him and he saw the tears form between the meshed lashes and gather in the fold at the corner of each eye. 'I'll make some tea.'

Holding and sipping at the steaming mug calmed her. 'How do you feel?'

She smiled at him. 'Better. You look as if you've been up all night.'

He ran a hand over the burred surface of his chin. 'I think I have, most of it. How much do you remember?'

'Not much. I took some tablets to get to sleep but they didn't seem to work so I got up and took some more. I got back into bed and I half knew something was wrong but by then they were working too well. I couldn't get up again.'

'Do you do that often?' He saw her face change. He hadn't meant to say it then, but to leave it til she was stronger. 'I'm sorry but you frightened me.' It sounded querulous. 'We won't talk about it now. You ought to eat something.'

She shook her head. 'Tell me what happened.' He told it as simply and as briefly as he could. It was a relief to him to talk about it and she listened without comment, sipping at the tea.

'It's a complete write-off. I suppose it could be repaired.'

'I want to see it.'

'Now?'

'Yes. Can you lend me some of your clothes?'

He brought out a pair of jeans and a sweater which she pulled on over her pyjamas, fumblingly, her movements still furred with sleep. Then he helped her up on to the bank and followed her along to where the charred boat still pulled at its moorings. Sassie stood for a long time staring at it as if fixing it in her mind. Turning she put out a hand to him. 'Take me back.'

As she washed and tidied herself so that they could go out and eat he made up his mind not to ask. She would have to tell him. 'I found your bag,' he called into the little washroom.

'Good, now we can eat properly.'

Watching her across the table he grew frightened again. She was too calm, too untouched by it all. Afterwards they had a couple of quiet drinks at a place they didn't usually go to and came back early to the safety of *Mimosa.* They made love more fiercely than they had ever done and as they smoked after, the two lighted ends glowing in the lamplight, he said, seeing the slow upward drift of their smoke, 'Will you promise me something?'

'Yes.'

'No games. The truth now.'

'Yes.'

'Will you promise me you'll still be here in the morning when I wake up?'

'I promise.' For the first time they made love again.

But the next morning it couldn't be put off any longer. The questions grew up like an invisible, inexorable hedge around her. There were things he had to know. 'What will you do now?'

She looked up at the March turbulence of sky and cloud beyond the skylight. 'Let's go for a walk. Let's go to the park.'

Walden's face looked out at him as they went through the iron gate into the park. Once again he felt time suspended as if they were walking through a tapestry land, only now it was Spring. The ground was stitched with new green between the old brown threads, small birds darted busily in looping flight, the sheep were accompanied by their compact woolly young like the metal farm animals he remembered from childhood, buds broke from their smooth brown skins. Sassie lifted her face to sniff the air. She was very calm, smiling a little, while he felt as if he would fly apart and be whirled away by the wind, hurled about the sky in fragments. 'You can ask me anything,' she said.

Some words ran quickly through his head, an echo. 'The Spring wherein everything renews save only the lover.' 'You're going aren't you?'

'Yes.'

'And never coming back this time. But why, why can't we go on as we are?'

'Nothing ever does.'

'Then we'll go away and start something different.'

She shook her head. 'It wouldn't work. You have to get on

with your life and I wouldn't be any use to you there. This is better.'

'But you can't just stop like this. It isn't a game. Or is it?' He wanted to hurt her now. 'Is it just something you and Walden amused yourselves with and now he's gone you can't be bothered any more?'

'You're making it very hard.'

'Hard! I want it to be hard, bloody hard. I love you. Or aren't I supposed to say that according to the rules? Is it too simple? What am I supposed to do while you walk off? Ask, you said. But there aren't any answers are there. Alright then I'll ask you something you can answer. Where does the money come from?'

'From Lance.'

The words exploded in his head as if someone had put a pistol to it and pulled the trigger while he had thought it was all a joke and still had the laughter on his face. 'My Christ.'

'He keeps me.' She was very pale.

'Did you?' He had to ask. The withered stalk of the old man sickened him.

'No. He can't and anyway he'd just as soon it was you as me. He likes to watch that's all, a sort of emotional voyeur.'

He took her roughly by the arms and shook her. 'Is this the truth? Tell me.'

She looked back at him steadily. 'Walden was right. You are intolerant.'

'I'm fighting for my life and you call it intolerant. Where did you go when you went away? To get more money?'

'Sometimes. Sometimes I didn't go at all.'

He stared at her not understanding. 'The other night I found this empty.' He took the brown bottle out of his pocket.

'Sometimes when I'm tired I just want to sleep. I sleep for about a day and a half.'

'Tired?'

'Alright then, depressed, miserable. Call it what you like.'

He considered this. She had been miserable with him. 'Supposing you overdid it? You could kill yourself like that. Look at the other night. Don't ever do that again. There might not be anyone around next time.' He turned away from her, feeling a great lump of misery rising in him, sticking in his chest like a bunched fist so that he could hardly breathe. 'What does it mean to love somebody?' he kicked at a hassock of turf. 'Anything, does it mean anything?'

'Sometimes it means doing without them.'

'Have you ever really loved me?' He had to know.

'I've never loved anyone else. Why do you think I was miserable? We had our own little world here and then you came along like a catalyst suddenly dropped in and I saw it all happen and I knew it was all over. We should have to come to terms with what other people call reality and in the end I'd have nothing. Just as it is.'

'But why? Why can't we try?'

'On Lance's money? Could you see us? You've told me how it was with Anna. Imagine it.'

He had and he knew she was right. 'What will you do?'

'I'm going away. I've got some friends who live in Cornwall. I've known them for years. A family. I know they're always there when I need them. I want you to do something for me. Burn the boat, all of it, so I know I can't ever come back. Now I want you to take me to the station.' They turned and walked back the way they had come, out through the gate, along the towpath and over the bridge to the little station where she bought a ticket. The train was already standing there.

'Please,' he said, 'send me a card. Let me know you get there and you're alright. If you don't I shall come and find you.'

She nodded and touched him lightly. He reached out and held her against him. After a moment she pushed him away. 'I mustn't cry, makes me look old.' As she turned the handle and got up into the train he saw the tears staining her face. It was an empty compartment. She took the far corner and bent her head away from him, staring blindly out of the window. The whistle blew, the guard called and she drew away from him. He turned and walked out of the station into the sunlight.

She had left an envelope he found: money to keep him for a couple of weeks and instructions about the boat. It was just as well. The next day he found Clack and Tom on the bank staring at the charred hulk.

'What's to be done about this?' the little man demanded.

'Taken out of the water and burnt.'

'I'll need something in writing before I can agree to that.'

'It's alright, I've got it here.'

'That's that then.' Clack handed him back the piece of paper. 'Just as well. I couldn't have been responsible for it. Course she still owes me a month's rent in lieu of notice.'

'You'll get it.'

'Yes, yes. I'm sure I shall. You'll need a block and tackle and someone to help you. The sooner the better. I like the mooring to look ship-shape. Tom'll give you a hand and the new chap.' He had found a replacement for Gypsy Dick then.

Sym would have preferred to do it himself. There seemed an element of desecration in Tom's hands hauling and clawing at the poor remains as it swung up, ungainly as a stranded whale, the blackened contents rolling into the stern. Someone had been and helped themselves to anything of value, saucepans, crockery but there hadn't been much. Sym wondered if she had kept things somewhere else. He would never know now. There were so many questions he hadn't asked when the time came. He picked out the Chinese print from the mess. Someone had put a boot on it and the glass was broken but inside the picture still glowed, apple blossom and small brown birds. He flicked away the fragments of glass, rolled it and put it in his jacket.

They lowered the boat onto rollers and dragged it into the trees. He threw a couple of cans of paraffin over it, lit a twist of paper and tossed it into the middle. It took a long time to burn. The old man stood back from the stinging smoke enjoying the heat and the spectacle. Sym thought that it should have been a floating pyre and remembered the great fire on the cliff top and the warriors who rode round it seven days and nights. It was still burning in the dusk, the smouldering heap suddenly finding a piece that was unconsumed and leaping into flame again. It was too long. He crossed the catwalk to the *Yacht*. He had dreaded questions about the fire but only Alec knew him well enough to ask and he was tactfully silent. Tom came in with the new hand, a cheerful big-built lad, and he stood them both a drink which they took to the chimney piece where he had first seen Clack's boys and he heard Walden's voice booming in his head. The bar was full of echoes, ghosts. Last night he had tried to ease his ache by putting it all down but nothing would come. He would have a couple of pints and try again.

After two Alec bought him another and then he bought Alec one back. He remembered he hadn't eaten and bought a bag of crisps and suddenly he was back six months, his first time in there and Walden joking about communion in both kinds. Well it had all come round again, the merry circle had taken a full whirl and he was alone with himself as if the interim had never been, only he was sore all over, bruised and tender like after Anna. He laughed at himself. That was an old wound, quite healed now he had a new fresh one to dwell on like the bloody hole where a tooth had been. He bought one more for the road going nowhere. It was still early. He would go back to *Mimosa* and try. Outside the night was very still, the stars high and faint. None of them had changed since he had first looked up at them through the skylight. The whole affair was nothing but the flicker of an eyelid. 'Time is relative. What do we know about time?' Walden said at his elbow. He would go and see them. They would understand. But they had changed, compromised, perhaps they wouldn't want to see him, be embarrassed. 'Come in, come in', and all the time waiting for him to go. They had all moved on and left him standing there. He walked fast and straight across the catwalk with his hands in his pockets, disdaining the handrail. At the passing point he stopped and looked down-stream towards the bridge. The water flowed smooth, an easy glide that you could slip into and rest. He tried to focus on the lights but they blurred and winked back at him. If he fell he would make no effort to resist, that would be the end. He was too tired to start again, to pick up and go on. Twice was too often. A third time would make a mockery of it all.

Cutting through the middle of the island he avoided the place where her boat had been, now filled by the metal lifeboat conversion, and the heap of embers that must be still sinking redly into ash like the contents of a giant crucible, and came out above *Mimosa*. It had been light when he left and no lights burned. On board it struck damp and desolate, reproachful. He lit up and laid out his paper and pencils meticulously. Then he sat back. He was feeling a bit sick. A sandwich and coffee and he would try again.

The sickness passed leaving a blank. There was nothing he could say that hadn't been said too often before, nothing unique in his misery. Human feelings were trivial and repetitious, art the fruitless turning of exhausted ground. He put that down with a kind of barren satisfaction. 'In the end there is no end and nothing worth recording. I have been here before as someone said and it's a desert where nothing moves and time is marked simply by the alternations of pitiless light and the smothering dark.'

One of the lamps had burned down to a charred fringe and he could hardly see. He filled it carefully, his hand steady, his eye exact. He felt remote and controlled. As he hung it back on its nail the light fell on the buff spine banded with red, the gilt lettering blackened by the damp. If he read a bit he might sleep. Packing his paper and pencils carefully away he made himself more coffee and began to read, dipping here and there, bending his will to the characters that tried to dance away from him off the page, cutting short and moving on when the long dead grew tedious with their dusty whispering. Suddenly he clapped the book shut and sat trembling. He had forgotten the trap of words, the clawing pain that could spring up and tear him as he fought to get away. They were there, had led him on with a harmless first verse and then closed on him so that he was caught and must go back to them again and again. He found the page. He should have known it would be there.

'Thancked be fortune, it hath ben othrewise
Twenty times better; but ons in speciall,
In thyn arraye after a pleasunt gyse,
When her lose gowne from her shoulders did fall,
And she me caught in her armes long and small;
Therewithall swetely did me kysse,
And softely saide, *dere hert, howe like you this?*

It was no dreme: I lay brode waking.
But all is torned thorough my gentilnes
Into a straunge fasshion of forsaking;
And I have leave to goo of her goodenes,
And she also to use new fangilnes.
But syns that I so kyndely ame served,
I would fain knowe what she hath deserved.'

The second time he read them aloud, and then a third, over and over until the pain stopped and they were balm to soothe him, and he was brought up against his own limitation and his strength that nothing had meaning for him until it was translated into words. Had she known that? She had never said but that proved nothing. She knew, he was sure she knew and that was why she had gone. They had all moved on and he couldn't go back to the withdrawn isolation that had brought him to the island. He would sleep now and in the morning he would know what to do.

The two letters came together, Anna's forwarded by his bank to tell him she was marrying again and that her new husband wanted to adopt the child. He was a dentist with a lucrative practice so she would be well taken care of. The other was the promised card. It made him realise how little he had seen of her handwriting, a looped running hand like drapes, and took away any lingering hope. 'Arrived safely. All is well. S.' It was postmarked Charlesford, a tiny town by the sea with a couple of thousand people. She had trusted him not to follow her. It was better than nothing. He could visualise her now walking along the shore. He would put *Mimosa* up for sale. It took a fortnight for the advert to come out so he could spend that time getting her ready.

The evenings were the worst as he had known they would be. All day he painted and cleaned. The bilges were baled out and coated with bitumen, rotten flooring replaced, and everywhere there were signs of his winter habitation: a rat's nest of shredded paper and rags under the planks, stinking of decayed bacon; a pencil he had lost and never found; a lipstick in a gilt case smeared with engine oil. At night after he had eaten he went over the weir to Alec's, once even up to the city where he wandered into pubs he had known years ago looking for any familiar face. He forced himself one day to sit down and write to his old publisher. He was invited to meet the new young editor, given drinks and welcome and asked when his new book would be ready. He felt very old and wise as he listened and watched but it was good to have the illusion that all the world had been waiting for was a word from him.

In the middle of the second week he fell in. He had been adjusting the blue polythene cover at the stern when suddenly his feet slipped and he was falling, surprised at first and then very calm. He saw the water green and full of drifting motes as it closed over his head and the dark curve of *Mimosa*'s hull as she slid past him. He seemed to be going down and down, the river must shelve steeply here. Kicking out he stopped the downward drift and felt himself rising again, his head breaking surface. He blinked and spat and paddled while he got his breath back. The taste of the river water and the knowledge of what went into it was flat and vile. He had drifted off some way from *Mimosa* already and she was high above him. He doubted whether he would be able to pull himself up in his waterlogged clothes and with the wind knocked out of him by the shock. Swinging on the stern rope for a moment's rest he considered what to do. Further along there were steps in the parapet. If he could make those he could drag himself out. As a boy he had been a strong swimmer but he was out of practice and softened by drinking and smoking. Still there was nothing else for it. If he exhausted himself trying to climb up he might fall back, crack his head on some projection and drown. He didn't want to drown he decided very calmly, and launched himself away from *Mimosa* into the stream. The main thing was to keep your head and swim slowly, not thresh about like a stranded fish. As he swam his clothes grew heavier. It was about twenty-five or thirty yards to the steps. The sweater Sassie had given him for Christmas seemed to have a life of its own; it bagged and swirled around him always one movement behind so that as he swam one way it flowed away from him another. Should he try to cast it off? Perhaps it would drag him down. But he was so near now he would keep it. He heaved himself onto the steps like a seal and lay there, the water streaming away from him, until he had strength enough to sit up and begin to wring out his clothing. Looking up and down the river he saw that there was no one about. He could have slipped away and no one would have known that it was an accident, that he hadn't intended it. His body would have turned up somewhere down-stream and she would have thought. . . . The water he had swallowed made him retch. He clambered to his feet and walked slowly back to *Mimosa* leaving a trail of damp patches behind him.

Inside he peeled off his wet things, wrung them out and stretched them to dry. His own lack of feeling about the whole thing was what surprised him most, and then he began to retch and shiver. Would he ever be warm and dry again? He towelled his naked body hard, punishing the mottled flesh back into life, put on the kettle and made tea. Then he dressed in fresh clothes and crept close to the fire. The shivering and retching was like sobbing. It had hit him harder than he had thought. Perhaps if he took some aspirins and slept he would get warm. Drifting into sleep he felt as if he was drowning and woke to the taste of the river still in his throat.

They were, of course, the last people he had expected to take her. All day they had come in cars, by bus and scooter or just walking along the towpath, poking and questioning until he had wanted them all to go away and leave him and *Mimosa* in peace. They had asked her age, commented on her shape and appearance, the facilities and gone away muttering judiciously. He was sick of them. They had no understanding, no respect. The thought that they would have to go through this, possibly for weeks, made him want to give up and keep her himself. The last two were middle-aged, diffident. They wanted something for weekends. They had come to the end of the resources of home and garden. They liked the fact that she looked like a real boat not a child's toy of marine ply and fibre glass. The husband saw his wife's face as she described how they would spend summer weekends afloat. Sym tried to dissuade them. It wasn't easy cooking and washing on board. He didn't want them to be disappointed. The husband wrote the cheque and they drove away.

That night he drank too much saying goodbye to Alec. In the morning he ate up what was left in the cupboard and packed his few things. Most of the things he had bought he was leaving with *Mimosa*. They belonged there and he wouldn't need them any more. Firmly he kept his mind to practical details, looking at the double bunk, the chair by the fire, the two blue-ringed mugs with eyes that saw only the outward appearance. At last he was ready. The calor turned off, the oil stove screwed down, the blue flame guttering with a little plopping noise. Picking up the duffle bag and the new hold-all he closed the saloon door behind him, went up the steps, lowered and padlocked the hatch and went over the gangplank. Halfway along the bank he stopped and looked back. She was riding alone as he had first seen her, smarter now for his months of work, rocking gently with the current, a flurry of mallard muttering and dipping their bright heads under the bow chain. Once more he looked back as he crossed the catwalk but he couldn't see her anymore, only the sun-dance on the river that dazzled his eyes, blurring his sight like rain on a window. The holdall with its weight of words hung heavy in his hand.